SEPTEMBER
CANVAS

Visit us at www.boldstrokesbooks.com

What Reviewers Say About Gun Brooke's Books

Sheridan's Fate

"Sheridan's fire and Lark's warm embers are enough to make this book sizzle. Brooke, however, has gone beyond the wonderful emotional explorations of these characters to tell the story of those who, for various reasons, become differently-abled. Whether it is a bullet, an illness, or a problem at birth, many women and men find themselves in Sheridan's situation. Her courage and Lark's gentleness and determination send this romance into a 'must read.'"—*Just About Write*

Coffee Sonata

"In *Coffee Sonata*, the lives of these four women become intertwined. In forming friendships and love, closets and disabilities are discussed, along with differences in age and backgrounds. Love and friendship are areas filled with complexity and nuances. Brooke takes her time to savor the complexities while her main characters savor their excellent cups of coffee. If you enjoy a good love story, a great setting, and wonderful characters, look for *Coffee Sonata* at your favorite gay and lesbian bookstore."—*Family & Friends* magazine

Protector of the Realm

"Brooke is an amazing author, and has written in other genres. Never have I read a book where I started at the top of the page and don't know what will happen two paragraphs later…She keeps the excitement going, and the pages turning. In a century when marriage Is recognized between two adults and gender is not an issue, Brooke shows that love and romance and passion can grow. Likewise, she reveals to us the soft vulnerable side of these two strong, battle-hearty women. Let's just say, I can't wait for the second in the trilogy to see what happens next."—*MegaScene*

Course of Action

"Brooke's words capture the intensity of their growing relationship. Her prose throughout the book is breathtaking and heart-stopping. Where have you been hiding, Gun Brooke? I, for one, would like to see more romances from this author."—*Independent Gay Writer*

By the Author

September Canvas

by
Gun Brooke

2009

SEPTEMBER CANVAS

© 2009 BY GUN BROOKE. ALL RIGHTS RESERVED.

ISBN 10: 1-60282-080-5
ISBN 13: 978-1-60282-080-7

THIS TRADE PAPERBACK ORIGINAL IS PUBLISHED BY
BOLD STROKES BOOKS, INC.
P.O. BOX 249
VALLEY FALLS, NY 12185

FIRST EDITION: JUNE 2009

CREDITS
EDITORS: SHELLEY THRASHER AND STACIA SEAMAN
PRODUCTION DESIGN: STACIA SEAMAN
COVER ART BY: GUN BROOKE
COVER DESIGN BY SHERI (GRAPHICARTIST2020@HOTMAIL.COM)

Acknowledgments

I still can't quite fathom that this is my seventh published novel. It never gets old to hold your author copies tightly squeezed to your chest and then peruse the cover, the layout, and read a snippet here and there. More than four years ago, Radclyffe took a chance on a writer from Sweden whose English was good, but whose learning curve was steep. Still is, sometimes, since writers are never fully trained. Radclyffe put me and my stories in Shelley Thrasher's tender hands, and Shelley has been my editor ever since, something I'm very grateful for. The cover layout is done by Sheri, who makes beautiful covers. When Sheri thought I was getting good enough at my 3D artwork to make my own cover images, she let Rad know, and thus, this is my second cover. I want to thank my friend Pol for helping me with scenery research and for "beta reading" the image for me. I also want to acknowledge Cindy, Julia, Connie, Lori, Paula, Lee, and all the others at BSB who give of themselves and their time for us writers to shine. The finished product wouldn't look half as professional if it weren't for your hard work.

On a personal note, my beta readers and first readers, Ruth, Wendy, Trish, and Maggie, did a terrific job of helping me not lose face when submitting the manuscript to BSB. *smile* I wouldn't be able to write the way I do without the strong support of my family. They never fail to say they're proud of me, happy for me, and then they present their wish lists of stuff they want if I ever become super-famous. *groan*

Dedication

For Lilian, my mom, with all my love,
and for Gunnar (1919–1986), my dad,
whom I love and miss so much.
Through ups and downs, I never doubt your love for your
children. My brother and I are very lucky.

PROLOGUE

S he ought to be locked up!"

Deanna Moore froze, her hand on the spine of a book. Obviously she wasn't alone in the small bookstore. The woman on the other side of the shelf must have thought the same thing, because she didn't bother to lower her voice.

"Legally she hasn't committed a crime," another female voice said.

"It doesn't matter. She's immoral and obviously doesn't hesitate to prey on innocent young people. If I had known how she'd betray our trust—"

"But you didn't, Gloria. None of us did."

Deanna squeezed her eyes shut and took a deep breath. She knew who Gloria was.

"And two years later, poor Savannah is still paying the price." Gloria sounded cold. "My angel's reputation is forever linked to *that woman*. I can't imagine how this will affect her. Long term, I mean."

"There now, Gloria," the other woman said. "Savannah's strong. She'll come to her senses and go to an Ivy League school before you know it. Meanwhile you just have to make sure she spends time with the right crowd. She might even get back together with Ned."

"Oh, don't get me started on poor Ned. He was totally humiliated, and I had to face his mother and try to explain how this monster dug her claws into my baby. You'll never know how terrible that felt. They're one of the Boston Fraziers."

"I can just imagine. But you don't have anything to worry about. You made sure that woman will never teach at this or any other Vermont school again. Everyone considers you a hero for standing up for your daughter like that."

"I tried to do the right thing, but everybody gossiped about my sweet angel."

Deanna grimaced at Gloria's holier-than-thou tone. If she could only slip out of the store without facing the women…but she couldn't show such weakness in front of Gloria Mueller, Grantville's self-proclaimed first lady. Deanna pulled a book from the shelf and strode up to the counter where the store owner was glancing nervously at Gloria and her friend.

"I'll take this one, please." Deanna was happy that her voice held.

"Oh. Right. That's…that'll be eighteen-eighty, please." The store owner cleared her throat and placed the book in a bag.

Deanna paid, and as she turned to leave Gloria and her friend, the new mayor's wife, stood only a few feet away. "Excuse me," Deanna murmured and stepped toward them.

Gloria's eyes were slits of disgust. "You have some nerve."

"I have no idea what you're talking about." Deanna made sure she sounded completely indifferent. "Remember, though, that your voice carries a long way. Discussing personal topics in a public place is a lawsuit waiting to happen. Slander can be expensive."

Gloria gasped and clutched her purse. "Slander! If I had my way, you'd be run out of town, you—"

Deanna moved closer, her anger rising like bile. "Careful, *Gloria.*"

The woman next to Gloria tugged her friend aside and Deanna passed them, keeping her eyes straight ahead.

"Did you hear her? Did you *hear* how she threatened me?" Gloria's voice followed Deanna out of the store.

She hurried to her car and slumped into the front seat, her knees buckling. It had taken all her strength not to show any sign of weakness. In the rearview mirror her dark blue eyes looked stormy. No wonder the two women had seemed almost afraid of her. *How long will this go on? And how long can I stand it?*

CHAPTER ONE

"I have to let you go now, Mom. I need to focus on the traffic and make sure I don't miss the sign to Grantville." Faythe Hamilton listened to her mother's concerns for what she called "Faythe's moment of insanity" half a minute longer before she interrupted again. "I hear you, Mom, and I'll think about it. Right now I need a vacation and I've made up my mind about taking this break."

"Honestly, child—"

"I'm not a child. Tell Bruno hello for me."

"Bruno? Oh, please, darling. Bruno left for Europe weeks ago. I'm seeing Chester again."

Faythe tried not to groan. "All right. I'll try to remember Chester. Ciao, Mom. End call." Faythe sighed. Chester. Bruno. Who could keep track of her mother's lovers? Two days after Faythe graduated from college, her mother had divorced Faythe's father, and since then entertained one young lover after another. Her father followed his ex-wife's example and traded one girlfriend for another at least once a year. *Like his cars.* Faythe frowned and accelerated past a dirty old Volvo.

Faythe loved to drive, and living in Manhattan didn't allow for much of that. She was her father's daughter in that she adored her car, a silver-gray Chrysler Crossfire, but unlike her father, she didn't trade for a newer model every year. She was happy with the one she had, which was far from worn out.

Faythe gripped the steering wheel and changed lanes. A sign farther up the road said Grantville, 5 miles, and she took in the beautiful scenery as she approached the exit to the local road. Maple trees on fire, from the brightest yellow to the darkest red, lined the road. Billowing fields of green, and quaint villages with houses dating back to the Civil War and earlier, created a unique atmosphere. She hadn't been to Vermont since she was a teenager, but had longed to go back ever since. The summer at her Aunt Nellie's lakeside cabin was one of the happiest in Faythe's life.

Nowadays, Nellie spent hardly any time in Vermont. Instead she lived in Florida all year and lent her Vermont cabin to Faythe for as long as she needed it. Usually, when Faythe took a rare few days off, she visited Nellie in Fort Lauderdale for a weekend, but this time, this long break when so much hung in the balance, Faythe needed to spend some time alone.

Her cell phone rang again, making her jump. She glanced at the display. *Mom.* "Ignore." Faythe knew she ought to feel guilty for screening her parents' calls, but she had explained to them why she needed this time by herself to figure things out. If they couldn't understand and respect her decision, she couldn't do much about it.

She approached a new sign. Grantville. Est. 1812. Population 8245. This number easily doubled in the summer. The lake was a popular place for water sports and fishing. Wealthy New Yorkers like Aunt Nellie kept houses here and employed one of the locals to care for them in the winter. Faythe intended to stay at least until Christmas, which would give her plenty of time to figure out her future and make plans. *I might just write something.*

Seeing the familiar shops along Main Street, she was transported ten years into the past. After graduating from high school, she'd stayed at Aunt Nellie's for three months before she went to college. So many things fell into place during that magical summer, and Faythe gave her aunt all the credit.

Whereas Faythe's parents were calculating and materialistic, Nellie was down-to-earth and caring. Faythe often wished Nellie had brought her up. Instead she had to face the fact that she'd been marinaded in her parent's shallowness since the day she was born. Her mother Cornelia's mantra was "possessions and position."

Faythe took a right and drove along the lake, spotting new houses where empty fields and trees used to be. When she reached the narrow gravel road that led down to her aunt's property, she slowed.

The cabin looked unchanged. Faythe stepped out of the car and stood still for a moment, taking it all in. But this was no cabin. The one-story house boasted six bedrooms, four and a half baths, a living room, an entertainment room, an open-plan kitchen, and a library. Slowly, Faythe circled the house and walked down to the water. The lake was like a mirror, and the wind seemed to hold its breath as Faythe leaned against a tree, absorbing the calmness. The setting sun's last rays made the water look transparent and poured gold on its surface before it dropped behind the treetops.

Most of the time she enjoyed everything the Big Apple had to offer, and she loved her neighborhood and her many friends, but this serenity, the fresh air...she couldn't find this in New York.

Looking to her left, Faythe noticed a light in the neighboring cabin. The dark shingled house resembled Nellie's, but was much smaller, maybe two or three bedrooms. A young family rented it when Faythe visited ten years ago. Were they still around?

She was about to walk back up to the house when her neighbor's porch door opened. Curious, Faythe remained half hidden behind the tree. A tall figure walked onto the porch and stood by the railing, gazing over the water. It was a woman, but her shoulder-length black hair hid her face. She held the railing with both hands and stood motionless for more than a minute. Faythe shivered in the evening air, which had become increasingly colder. She didn't want the other woman to catch her spying, so she tried to ignore the goose bumps on her arms.

The woman suddenly banged both fists on the railing and shouted. Faythe pressed closer against the tree, intrigued. The woman rubbed her face with both hands, then put her arms around herself in a tight squeeze. The gesture, which Faythe interpreted as loneliness, stirred an unwelcome memory of doing the same thing many times during her adolescence.

The slamming door made Faythe look up to find that the other woman had disappeared. Faythe eventually made her way up the path to her car, careful not to trip in the poor light.

She carried her two sport bags that doubled as suitcases to the deck. Nellie had arranged to have a set of keys mailed to Faythe's condo earlier in the week, and now she opened the door, expecting the house to smell musty. Instead it smelled fresh and polished, which was exactly what it was, she discovered as she switched the light on. Every surface was clean and so were the curtains, the kitchen towels on the rack, and everything else. The service Aunt Nellie employed had done a good job.

The rustic pieces in Nellie's cabin were both durable and attractive. As Faythe walked from room to room, every memory that surfaced soothed her. The tautly wound spring inside her slowly uncoiled, and she yawned as she returned to the car for her briefcase. She'd brought only her cell phone and her laptop, and purged every work document from both of them before she packed.

Faythe wasn't hungry but still looked longingly into the empty refrigerator. She would have to go into Grantville and stock up in the morning. Right now the instant decaffeinated coffee her aunt kept in the pantry would do. Faythe made herself a large mug of steaming brew and found some powdered creamer to mellow it. It was six months past its use-by date, but as long as it didn't look weird when she stirred it into the coffee, she'd be all right.

Faythe decided to use the main bedroom, where her aunt usually slept. It had the biggest, softest bed in the house, which was too tempting. Nellie kept the bed linen in the hallway, and the familiar scent of lavender filled Faythe's nostrils as she pulled out sheets, pillowcases, and blankets. After making the bed, she curled up under the covers, clutching the coffee mug, and merely sat there in the dark, watching distant lights on the other side of the lake. Faythe thought again about the woman next door, how she'd slammed her fists into the railing and cried out. Had that been fury in her voice, or despair? Maybe both, Faythe mused, and sipped her coffee. She had done her fair share of fist-slamming into desks lately, and only when that no longer alleviated the stress did she realize she had to do something radical.

Suzy, her agent, wasn't thrilled. In fact, she had blurted out, "God Almighty, are you stark raving mad?" raising her voice with every word. "Your contract is up for renewal, and you're in a position to ask for a substantial raise. And you quit?"

"I'm not quitting. I'm taking a break."

"Same thing in this business," Suzy said, then downed the last of her Scotch. The waiter showed up to take their orders, but backed off when Suzy glared at him and shook her head.

"I don't care." Faythe spoke slowly, knowing that Suzy was like a petulant child when she threw a temper tantrum like this. "I'm twenty-nine, and I've worked more or less nonstop since I was twenty-two. Seven years and zero vacation."

"Seven successful years *because* of that."

"And my life is passing me by. Don't complain, Suzy. I'm not ungrateful. You've been fantastic, but you've also made a lot of money as my agent. If I were to sign on for another season for the network, I'm sure you'd make an even bigger chunk, but...I can't let your commission determine my decision. I need a break. I need to figure out what I want to do next."

"Next?" Suzy looked at Faythe as if her prize possession was melting. "You always wanted to work in the media."

"I always wanted to be a good reporter. And someday, a *great* journalist. And I'm nothing but a glorified co-host of a morning show who introduces everything from earthquakes to dancing lima beans."

"You're so popular. A household name." Suzy gestured impatiently with a flick of her wrist. "The money's not bad either."

"There has to be more to a job than that." Frustrated with her agent, but not surprised, Faythe knew no matter how she tried to explain, her words wouldn't sink in. Like Faythe's mother, Suzy was very much about appearances, and on the surface Faythe's life was perfect. "I don't mind the hours, but the days are rushing by me. I have friends and live in a great area, but no time to enjoy it, no one to come home to. I sacrifice a lot for a job that doesn't seem worth it."

Suzy kept trying to convince Faythe to reconsider, but she didn't budge. The next day she called Nellie and arranged to stay at the lake.

Faythe settled against the pillows, her mind drifting back to the woman next door. She wondered what had annoyed or frustrated her enough to pound the railing. After her outburst she stood there in the fading light like an obsidian statue, black hair the only thing moving in the breeze.

Faythe padded over to the bathroom and brushed her teeth. She could hardly remember when she had thought so much about another woman. She wiped her mouth and made a wry face at her reflection. She was *not* going to count how many months had passed since she had been on a date, or even had time and energy to think about it. At least she could admit that it was far too long ago and that it was time for a change.

❖

Deanna moved the pencil in long sweeping strokes across the paper, annoyed that her mental image refused to translate to the sheet on the table before her. She tried to wrap her mind around the loose idea, knowing that she wouldn't be able to get it out of her head until she put it on paper. She had managed to outline a female figure, but the woman in her picture was faceless. When she squinted, Deanna could almost see the person she was trying to depict.

It wasn't hard to figure out what distracted her. Her dinner sat uneaten on the kitchen counter, and though she tried to ignore the voices of the women in the bookstore earlier that day, they pierced her thoughts. Deanna was well aware of Gloria Henderson's leading position in Grantville. She lived with her husband and daughter in a colonial mansion and chaired several charities with absolute power. Gloria's daughter, Savannah, had ruled Grantville High School much the same way. She'd held court with her peers in the hallways or the cafeteria, and was the undisputed queen bee among the girls.

Deanna jerked at a sharp sound and stared at the broken pencil that had perforated the sheet of paper before her. The shattered remainder had stabbed the sketchy woman in the heart.

Chapter Two

Faythe drew a deep breath, then several more as she stretched her calf muscles to warm up for her run. She pulled her short ponytail tight and took off along the path that led down to the water. She kept an even rhythm, paying attention to roots and rocks that might send her flying if she tripped on them. She smiled widely, suddenly feeling free.

What a difference it was to run on honest-to-God forest paths, rather than on a treadmill at the gym. There people always appeared to inspect and judge her, which was certainly one of the downsides of being a household name. And the paparazzi sometimes seemed to live on her doorstep, especially after her interview with the glamorous Hollywood starlet Isabella Talbert. Nobody, especially Faythe, had anticipated the little vixen would reveal such sordid details on an eight a.m. morning show.

What began as a common interview, designed to plug Isabella's debut movie, had turned into something entirely different when she broke down, sobbing and throwing herself into Faythe's arms. Isabella confessed to a romance with the director, who was married to a very rich and powerful Hollywood mogul's daughter. It hadn't been quite clear if Isabella was crying because he broke up with her, or because she feared his wife would kill Isabella's budding career. The director was at least thirty years older than Isabella, which the tabloids found titillating, and Isabella quickly developed a crush on a reluctant Faythe, which put her in the limelight too. Faythe kept her distance. She wasn't interested in having a fling before the telephoto lenses of the paparazzi.

Faythe jogged around a broken section of old wooden fencing and gulped the crisp September air. She should have done this long ago. Manhattan was not only expensive, but it was never quiet and didn't have fresh air. One of her colleagues tried to get Faythe to move to the suburbs, but the only thing worse than the noise and the city air was being stuck in traffic several hours a day. She already worked around the clock. No way was she going to spend the remaining hours among honking, cursing drivers.

Faythe returned to the Isabella mess. Even if she could laugh at it now, more than a year afterward, at the time she'd been ready to shoot the girl. But once the paparazzi found her scent, *all* potential relationships were suddenly in the public eye. Isabella wasn't her type. "I haven't been out with anyone in so long now, I may not have a type anymore. I probably wouldn't recognize my type even if I stumbled over her."

"Excuse me?"

Faythe stopped so quickly at the sound of the pleasant alto voice that she nearly toppled over. She waved her arms to regain her balance and looked up at a tall, black-haired woman propped against a tree by the water. It took her a few moments to recognize her neighbor, the woman she'd seen last evening.

"Oh. Hi." Faythe glanced around. "I'm not trespassing, am I?"

"Technically, yes."

"I'm so sorry." Faythe was confused. "I used to run here years ago when I visited my aunt. It was never a problem."

"I didn't say it was. You asked if you were trespassing."

"I see. So it's okay?" Faythe kept jogging in place, careful not to get cold.

"Yes."

"Thanks. I'm Faythe." She extended a hand.

The woman looked at it, then raised her gaze to meet Faythe's. Her eyes were dark blue with black rims, and her long black eyelashes cast shadows on her pale cheeks. Faythe had never seen anyone so pale with such blue-black hair.

"Deanna." The woman shook Faythe's hand and quickly let go.

"Nice to meet you, Deanna. Guess we'll be neighbors this fall." An unexpected butterfly took up residence just below Faythe's ribs at the brief touch. Taken aback, she smiled broadly to cover up her reaction.

"So it would seem." Deanna pushed away from the tree. She

sounded completely indifferent. She obviously wasn't the neighbor you popped over to for coffee or to borrow a cup of sugar. "Be careful running down by the Mahoney place. They're doing construction work on their dock."

Faythe had been ready to write Deanna off as being annoyingly aloof when her thoughtful words changed her mind. "Thanks. Which one is the Mahoney place?"

"Fourth house down. You can't miss it. They have two illuminated plastic flamingoes in their yard."

"Still?" Faythe laughed, remembering. "I never knew their name, but they had those when I was a kid." She shook her head and laughed again.

Deanna looked as if she meant to say something more, but instead she merely nodded. "Bye." She strode up the path to her cabin.

The abrupt departure intrigued Faythe. She was good at reading people; it was part of her job as an interviewer. Deanna had undoubtedly begun to relax and immediately regretted it. She hadn't allowed the hint of amusement to develop into a smile. Instead, Deanna, tall, dark, and mysterious, had slammed down a mask of politeness and made good use of those long denim-clad legs. Deanna's gray sweater hinted at a very slender body, which Faythe found thoroughly sexy. She looked down her own body, knowing she was far from voluptuous either. *Wonder if she appreciates a B-cup?* Faythe snorted at herself and resumed her jog. For all she knew, Deanna was as straight as they came and couldn't care less about Faythe's breasts.

Faythe completed her run in forty-five minutes, making sure she didn't fall over the construction workers at the Mahoneys' dock. The three men whistled appreciatively and she waved at them. She didn't think they recognized the sweaty jogger as Faythe Hamilton, so-called glamorous TV personality, which was refreshing. She glanced through the trees toward Deanna's cabin when she passed it, but caught no sign of her, then sprinted the last of the way once she reached Nellie's property.

❖

When Faythe jogged past Deanna's cabin a second time, she told herself she merely wanted to make sure her new neighbor was all right after she passed the construction workers. Faythe seemed to look her way, but she wasn't sure. She easily pictured Faythe tossing her head back and laughing at the thought of the stupid flamingoes. Her laughter, musical and slightly husky, had tugged at the corners of Deanna's mouth. She couldn't remember when she'd smiled last, or laughed so freely. Faythe was a stunningly beautiful woman, but the way her eyes sparkled lingered with Deanna more than her physical beauty. The mere fact that it did linger worried her. She had to ignore this response and focus on what mattered, like she normally did. The townspeople would soon tell Faythe what kind of person Deanna was.

Deanna's cell phone rang, and she jumped and checked the display. The words "Miranda's School" made her frown and she answered quickly. "Deanna Moore speaking."

"Deanna, this is Irene Costa."

"Irene! Is something wrong?"

"No, no. Miranda is doing fine. I just wanted to tell you that you can't visit her this evening."

Deanna knew what Irene would say. "My mother is visiting when she's not supposed to." Squeezing her eyes closed, Deanna tried to suppress the anger that rose inside her. "It's Saturday."

"And she normally comes on Sundays. She called the floor and told us she'd be here today instead."

"It will mess with Miranda's head. She doesn't do too well with last-minute changes. Mother *knows* that."

"We just have to work around it. Should I tell Miranda you'll see her tomorrow instead?"

"No, don't do that. Miranda knows I come on Mondays, Thursdays, and Saturdays. If I change days so soon after our mother, she'll be all screwed up." Over the last two years Miranda had become completely dependent on having set routines on certain weekdays. "Tell her that I will see her on Monday, since Mother is coming today. Perhaps she'll buy it."

"Good thinking. She just might. Miranda's doing so well. It would be a shame for her to have a setback because of this." Irene's voice softened. "Why don't you put your free Saturday evening to good use?"

Deanna bristled, but Irene meant well. The middle-aged woman had taken care of Miranda ever since their mother enrolled her at the

Tremayne Foundation and School nine years ago, when she was seven. Irene was in charge of the six students in the section of the boardinghouse where Miranda lived and had been very good to her.

"Has she spoken a lot today?" Deanna directed the subject away from her nonexistent private life.

"Actually, she has. She really loved your picnic in the garden the other day. She's talked about it a lot and seems to want to do it again."

Deanna had packed a picnic basket and invited Miranda to go outside. Miranda was usually nervous about being outdoors and thrived in a disturbance-free environment, but Irene had made sure they had the lawn to themselves for an hour. Of course, Miranda had acted as if she were seeing the garden for the first time, though, as usual, she rocked and murmured the same unintelligible sounds. She calmed down only when Deanna poured orange juice for them and unpacked the cinnamon buns and other treats, since they always seemed to reach her. Soon she was on her back pointing at the clouds, outlining their shapes with her fingers.

Deanna looked over at her desk. Pinned to the wall were four pencil studies of her sister that she'd done during that precious hour. In three of them, Miranda was seriously contemplating the clouds, the strands of grass beneath her fingers, and, in the distance, some ducks that had initially startled her with their quacking. In the fourth one, Deanna captured Miranda's rare, enigmatic smile—a tiny uplift at the corners of her mouth, which was faintly pursed. Deanna had spilt some orange juice on her white shirt, and her low curse had made Miranda's eyes widen. Then a slow, barely visible, smile appeared. It surfaced rarely, and Deanna had gripped her pencil again, eager to capture it. Although most people would pull out a camera, Deanna was happy that she was an illustrator, given Miranda's fear of mechanical devices. The only pictures of Miranda that showed her smiling were those their parents had taken when Miranda was a baby.

"Deanna?" Irene cleared her throat, pulling Deanna from her reverie.

"Yes, of course. Tell Miranda that we'll do it again next Saturday."

"All right. I work the late shift Monday, so I'll see you then."

"Right, Irene. Bye."

Deanna pocketed the cell phone and walked over to her desk,

where she studied the half-completed drawing she was working on. Something was blocking her inspiration. It had been so easy to draw Miranda; the pencil had moved practically on its own during their picnic. Now she sat down on her chair and reached for a new, freshly sharpened one. She had to capture that elusive inspiration. Her deadline for this first draft was in three days.

❖

"Can I get you anything else?" the woman manning the cash register asked politely. Her nametag said *Kitty*, and she had adorned the "i" with a little heart instead of a dot.

"No, that'll be all." Faythe opened her wallet and handed over her Visa card. "Here you go."

"Thanks." Kitty-with-a-heart charged the seventy-eight some dollars to Faythe's card and rapped her long fingernails on the conveyor belt while she waited for the transaction to go through. "Tourist?" she asked.

"What? No, not really. I'm going to stay a while." Faythe began to sack her groceries.

"Oh, really? Where are you staying? The inn?"

"In a relative's cabin. On the lake, just off Gordon Macy's Road."

Kitty-with-a-heart frowned. "In Nellie Hamilton's house?"

"Yes." Kitty had figured that out too easily.

"But…" She squinted, then donned a pair of glasses. "You're Faythe Hamilton!"

For the love of… Faythe nodded, fighting back an acerbic comment. "Yes."

"And you're here to stay a bit? Oh, this is fantastic. I love your show. I tape it every day."

"That's great." It seemed appropriate to show some enthusiasm, but Faythe wanted to gather up her groceries and run. "I really must—"

"Oh, you need to take care out there." Kitty-with-a-heart looked worried now.

"Why's that?" Faythe had expected requests for autographs for family members or friends, not a warning.

"You're living right next door to *that woman*." Kitty-with-a-heart leaned forward, lowering her voice. "You need to be very careful around her."

"Who?" Faythe had no idea what Kitty was talking about.

"Deanna Moore. She's terrible. Can be dangerous, even. Do you have someone living there with you? I mean, like a husband or something?"

Faythe wasn't about to announce to Kitty or anyone else that she lived alone in Nellie's cabin. "I'll be fine." She grabbed the grocery-filled bags and placed them in the shopping cart. "Have a good day." Faythe disappeared out of the store before Kitty could ask anything more.

What could Deanna have said or done to Kitty-with-a-heart that made such an impact? *Dangerous?* Faythe placed the grocery bags in the passenger seat. *People sure can exaggerate.*

CHAPTER THREE

Deanna studied the quick pencil sketches she'd made of a woman in motion. She had stood on her deck watching the morning mist leave the surface of the lake when Faythe Hamilton ran by. Grabbing her sketchbook, Deanna worked for as long as she could glimpse Faythe's lithe body between the trees. She hadn't bothered with details yet, wanting only to capture the essence of Faythe with long, sweeping movements.

Now Deanna let her fingertip follow the outline. "You were in such a hurry this morning. Running from something, eh?" Her old habit of talking to herself emerged and she tore out the pages, pinning them to her message board above her work area.

Her latest drawings were mostly of Miranda, and now she had these four sketches of a stranger. But several deadlines were coming up in rapid succession. She had to go outside today and take some pictures of the fiery maple trees, which she needed for a book cover.

After a quick shower, Deanna put on her usual jeans, T-shirt, and sweater, then pulled her hair back in a tight twist. She needed to cut her bangs, she thought absentmindedly as she passed the hallway mirror. They reached her eyelashes, which made her blink repeatedly at times so she wouldn't get hair in her eyes.

Deanna draped the camera strap around her neck and went outside. She locked the door and headed for the lake. Her camera had a good zoom, and the trees on the other side of the lake were beautiful. When she reached the water, she looked for a good place to stand. The old dock was not dependable; she had stepped right through it and nearly broken her left ankle last spring. Deanna pushed through some bushes and raised her camera.

The sun cast a fiery glow on the maples across the lake, and even the three-inch screen on Deanna's camera showed the magical scene clearly. After snapping about ten pictures, she thought she had what she needed. She had noticed some fallen logs farther to the right through the camera and wanted to make sure she had them. She was browsing through the shots when she spotted something she'd missed before. To the very left in the corner of her display was an object floating on the water and a...hand? Deanna snapped her head back and looked out over the lake.

A wooden rowing boat drifted about twenty-five yards from shore. Deanna blinked, not sure if she saw anyone in it. She raised the camera again and zoomed in, glimpsed golden brown hair, and her new neighbor popped into view.

"What the hell...?" The rowboat looked just like the old wreck that normally lay upside down at Nellie's. Surely Faythe hadn't been stupid enough to use it? Another glance through the display of her camera confirmed Deanna's fear.

"Hey! Can you quit taking pictures and get a hold of someone to help me get back to shore?" Faythe sounded more annoyed than afraid.

"I'm not taking pictures. I'm assessing your predicament," Deanna yelled back.

"Well, cut that out and do something. This damn strainer of a boat is taking in water like there's no tomorrow." Faythe was obviously trying to keep her feet away from the bottom of the boat, which rocked precariously, and she clutched the edge. One oar was already floating several feet from the boat, and now the other one slipped away with a soft splash. The current was more treacherous than the serene lake betrayed at first glance. The boat was already drifting away from Deanna, and without a second thought, she tore off her sweater and boots, risked running along the dock, and jumped into the water.

The water was cool enough to shock Deanna's system. Faythe's surprised cry echoed across the water as Deanna began to swim toward the boat with long strokes.

"Jesus, woman, I meant for you to call someone!"

"No time." Deanna wasn't sure Faythe heard her, but kept

swimming. The boat was half underwater now, and the hint of panic on Faythe's face confirmed that she realized she wouldn't make it to shore.

Deanna reached the boat just as its stern gurgled and disappeared. Faythe lost her balance and slid into the water with a yelp.

"Oh, sweet Jesus, it's cold." She clawed at the sinking boat, but Deanna jerked Faythe's hands off the rotting wood. "No, we need to swim back. Now." She tugged Faythe with her and to her relief Faythe didn't panic, but started to swim.

"Deanna…I…my jacket…" Faythe had swum only a few strokes when she stopped. "I can't move." She trod water while frantically pulling at her jacket, which was waterlogged and weighing her down. Deanna tried to help unzip it, but Faythe sank deeper as they fought the stubborn clasp, obviously having problems keeping her chin above water.

"Oh, damn, this isn't working." Faythe kicked so hard to stay afloat that she connected with Deanna's shin underwater.

Cupping Faythe's chin, Deanna helped her keep her head up, treading water furiously. "Listen to me, Faythe. Let me tow you. Just kick as I pull you in." She maneuvered Faythe over on her back and began to drag her. Faythe cooperated, but the heavy jacket and her boots were still pulling her under. Using all her remaining strength, Deanna swam with Faythe in tow until she felt the bottom of the lake. From there, it didn't take long to get them on shore, where Deanna helped a stumbling Faythe to her feet, both of them shivering.

"You all right?" Deanna scrutinized Faythe, who looked pale but seemed unscathed. "We better get warm right away."

"Thank you." Trembling now, Faythe clung to Deanna's arm. "It all happened so fast."

"Yes. I can't believe you pulled a stunt like this. That boat hasn't been in the water for years."

"I used to go out in it every summer…when I was a kid." Faythe blushed, two burning spots on her pale cheeks. "It looked okay to me."

"Hmm." Deanna shook her head. "Come on. We have to get you warm."

"I'll just run up to my house, and—"

"You're pale, bluish, and shivering. You could faint or something.

I'll have a fire going in no time. You need to get warm quickly and so do I." Deanna was reluctant to let Faythe into her cabin, but even more reluctant to send her off to fend for herself. Faythe was shivering and looked nauseous.

"All right. T-thanks." Faythe's teeth clattered.

Inside the cabin, Deanna showed Faythe to the bathroom where she ran the shower. A steamy cloud formed and Deanna nodded toward the stall. "Get warm and I'll find you some sweats."

Faythe raised her hands to her jacket zipper, but couldn't stop shaking enough to pull it down. Deanna groaned inwardly and pushed Faythe's hands away, unzipping the drenched garment. "There. Think you can manage now?"

"Sure. Thanks." Faythe's dazed look didn't escape Deanna and she hurried to her room, jerking off her wet clothes. She wrapped an old terry-cloth robe around herself before looking for something for Faythe to wear. Not comfortable sharing intimate items like underwear, Deanna also picked out a T-shirt. She walked back to the bathroom and detected a faint outline of Faythe behind the frosted glass.

"Better?" Deanna's voice was suddenly thicker.

"Tons. I'll be out in a minute so you can rinse off the lake water and get warm."

"Take your time." Deanna placed the clothes on the toilet lid and fled to the large living room, where she knelt in front of the fireplace, its focal point. Her hands trembled as she lit a fire. The flickering flames licked the wood, and soon the crackling drowned out the sound of her pounding heart.

"Oh, fab." Faythe sat next to Deanna on the floor, her hair hanging in wet tousled tresses around her shoulders. The clothes were at least four sizes too large for Faythe's small frame, but at least she was dry. "Thank you for hauling me back to the shore," Faythe said quietly. "If you hadn't showed up—"

"I did. That's all that matters." Deanna didn't dare look at Faythe, finding the moment awkward, especially since she couldn't think of anything helpful to say. "Last time I saw that old boat, it was covered with weeds. It should've told you something. You need to keep up the maintenance of boats every year. Then there's the thing about life vests—"

"I know that!" Faythe raised her voice, her face now flushed with anger. "You don't have to make me sound like a total moron."

"I never said you were a moron." Startled at Faythe's unexpected outburst, Deanna quickly scanned her memory of what she had said. "I merely pointed out that you should not be so careless when you're—"

"It was a stupid thing to do, okay? You don't have to lecture me as if I was a child."

Deanna hesitated. Faythe *had* acted carelessly, and without any safety measures, and now she was obviously blaming Deanna for pointing this out. "Well, you're from the city," Deanna began slowly, "and not used to thinking about such things. To use a boat is not like getting behind the wheel of a car and driving."

"Oh, for God's sakes, don't make it worse by being condescending on top of everything." Faythe quieted for a moment, her body rigid. "It says a lot about what you'd expect from an airhead from the city, right? A brainless maneuver like that."

Deanna had no idea what triggered the hostility she sensed in Faythe. "Don't worry. You're safe. I'm safe. The boat's not going to cause any problems ever again."

"It can't, can it? The damn thing sank."

"Yes, it did," Deanna said gravely.

Faythe stared into the fire and suddenly the corners of her mouth started to twitch. Soon she was wiping tears of laughter from her cheeks. "Oh, my. I'm sorry. It's really not very funny." She laughed even harder, the sound tinged with irony.

Deanna smiled carefully. "It's not funny at all," she said, agreeing in principle. "But yes, it's in your best interest that it sank."

"That's what I was thinking." Eventually Faythe pulled herself together. "I should be going home. I have an idea, though, since you did save my life. How about I make us dinner tonight, to celebrate my not sinking to the bottom of the lake?"

The thought of their struggle in the water, when it looked like the drenched jacket was going to pull Faythe under, made Deanna tremble. "You really don't have to go through the trouble—"

"It's no trouble. I bought enough food in town to—what?"

"You went grocery shopping. Ah." Deanna straightened her back and her rib cage tightened around her lungs, making it hard to breathe.

"Yes. Got the third degree from the woman at the cash register. As I was going to say, I bought enough food to feed a small army. Please, join me."

Scrubbed clean from the shower, Faythe looked so innocent and beautiful, even younger than before. That fact alone was a red flag. Deanna scanned Faythe's facial expression but saw no sign that she was about to join the special clique in town that heeded every word Gloria Henderson uttered. The local grocery store was one of the places where gossip festered and grew. The library was another and the gas station yet another.

"Deanna, I'd be so honored if I could repay you somehow. I mean, it's only dinner, and I'm a decent cook, nothing special. It's not a lot, really, to offer spaghetti Bolognese when someone just saved your life, but it's all I can think of right now."

"Okay," Deanna heard herself say. "If you insist, then I'd be happy to let you cook tonight." Deanna wanted to take everything back, but it was too late. She'd accepted an invitation to the home of an unattached woman, which in her case was highly suspicious, to quote the Mueller mob.

Faythe's soft, open smile scratched at Deanna's defenses. Standing, Faythe brushed off her borrowed sweats. "It's a deal, then. Do you have a bag to put my wet clothes in? I should have the key to Nellie's house tucked away in a jacket pocket. I hope."

"Of course." Deanna rose and fetched two empty grocery sacks from the kitchen. "Will these do?"

"Sure thing." Faythe went back into the bathroom and returned seconds later with her clothes jammed into the bags, wiggling the key in her other hand. "See you at seven thirty? I should go home and wash my clothes. Maybe I can save the jacket."

"All right. Should I bring anything?"

"If you have some red wine, that'd be great."

"I'll look. I may have something in the basement." She'd been so intent on turning Faythe's offer down, she was taken aback by her urge to follow through with the invitation. A small voice in the back of her mind kept saying that nothing good would come from this. Perhaps she could still devise a plausible excuse, one that didn't offend Faythe. Deanna looked straight into Faythe's green eyes and opened her mouth to verbalize her apology. "See you at seven thirty."

CHAPTER FOUR

Faythe tasted the meat sauce from the pot on the stove and frowned. It needed something. Black pepper? She ground some into the simmering sauce and left it for a few moments as she put a pot of water on another burner. Aunt Nellie had plenty of cooking appliances and utensils. Shaking her head, Faythe tried to remember ever actually seeing her aunt make anything more than toast with marmalade.

"Am I early?"

Faythe wheeled around. Deanna stood in the doorway, holding a bottle of wine in one hand and what looked like an envelope in the other. "I...um, well, I knocked."

"You did." Faythe took a deep breath and refused to press a hand against her chest like some damsel in distress. "You did? Obviously I didn't hear you."

"That's pretty clear." Deanna's dark eyes glittered with telltale mirth. "I hope this wine will do. It's a Pepperwood Grove."

"Ah, a domestic wine. Zinfandel grapes." The bottle looked worn, its label nearly rubbed off in places. "Goodness, it's a 2001!"

"It's been sitting in the basement since then. Hope it's still good."

"Guess we'll find out." Faythe grabbed a corkscrew and easily uncorked the bottle. "Some say a red wine should breathe, some say it doesn't matter. Let's not risk anything." She set the open bottle on the counter and checked on the pasta sauce. "I hope you're not allergic to garlic."

"No allergies." Deanna remained by the door, looking reluctant.

"Don't just stand over there. Come in and I'll pour us some wine in a minute. I have a fire going in the living room. At least I hope I do. It looked a bit weak when I left it."

"I'll check on it." Deanna seemed relieved to excuse herself, and Faythe in turn had a hard time reconciling the different images she now had of Deanna. At first she had mostly appeared aloof and shy, even annoyed at Faythe's presence. Deanna clearly wasn't the easygoing, open-natured type, but Faythe had spotted signs of humor and repressed laughter, if only briefly.

Deanna returned, brushing her hands off. "I added a log and some more kindling."

"Thanks. Need to wash up? Hand soap's over there." Faythe pointed at the sink.

"I better." Deanne brushed by Faythe and her lingering scent of soap mingled with faint musk. Faythe inhaled greedily and hoped Deanna hadn't heard her sharp intake of air. Faythe glanced at Deanna's back, admiring her slender frame. She was dressed in black jeans and a white cotton shirt, and her black hair hung loose around her shoulders, shiny, but a little unruly. Wondering what Deanna's story was, since she was so clearly on guard, Faythe dumped the spaghetti into a large pot of boiling water. She moved too fast, splashing the hot water onto her hand.

"Ow!" Faythe yanked her hand back, rubbing the stinging spot on her wrist.

"Did you burn yourself?" Deanna quickly turned the faucet to cold and pulled Faythe close to the sink. "This hand?"

"Yes. It's not bad—"

"Cold water." Deanne held Faythe's hand under the running faucet. "You don't want it to blister."

"No, you're right." The cold water took the sting out of the small burn. Faythe was more aware of standing in such close proximity to Deanna than any residual pain. "Jeez, you must think I'm a complete disaster," she murmured. "I'm usually cool and collected."

"I'll take your word for it."

"You have to, don't you?" Faythe wrinkled her nose and sighed. "I haven't actually given you any proof."

"You seem trustworthy." Deanna kept hold of Faythe's lower arm.

"Don't you think this is good enough? The water's *really* cold."

"You need a few more minutes to cool the skin cells properly. Trust me. My…sister burned her leg once and I had her in a cold shower for more than half an hour. The doctors said that was why she didn't even get a scar."

"Okay, I believe you."

"Good. Stand still."

Faythe's hand was completely numb by the time Deanna finally let her pull it back. Reaching for a clean kitchen towel, she dabbed it dry. "Let's check on the spaghetti and see if it's ruined or done." Feeling irritated with herself, Faythe avoided looking directly at Deanna and peered into the pot instead. "Looks like it's time to drain it."

"Let me do it." Deanna grabbed the pot and poured the contents into a large colander sitting in the sink. Faythe handed her some olive oil to dribble over the pasta.

"What? You don't trust me to do it? Do you think I'm so undependable I can't even drain my own spaghetti?" Deanna gave her a strange look that made Faythe realize she sounded like an idiot. "I hope you're hungry," she said, and eyed the amount of spaghetti and meat sauce.

"I am, actually." Deanna sounded surprised. "It smells wonderful."

"Thanks. It's a meat-sauce recipe from Aunt Nellie's cook. She put up with me in the kitchen when I was a kid."

"You enjoy cooking?"

"I do, but I rarely have—I mean, *make* the time. Guess that's part of being a workaholic. Want to grab those for me?" Pointing at the pasta bowls, Faythe took the salad from the refrigerator. "It's just lettuce and tomatoes." She filled the bowls and carried them over to the dining table by the window. "I love eating here. The view is amazing. But you have the same view so that's hardly news to you, is it?"

"I never get tired of it." Deanna followed with their wineglasses and the bottle. "Should I pour?"

"Yes, please."

The red wine reflected the soft light of the lamps in the room. Dusk was settling and soon it would be pitch black outside. Faythe raised her glass and gazed at Deanna over the rim. Her dark blue eyes were amazing, and her eyelashes were long and sooty black, without a trace of makeup. Nobody ever went without makeup at the network station on Manhattan, and many of her friends and coworkers had annual nips and tucks to stay young and attractive. Deanna had tiny crow's-feet at the outer corners of her eyes, and her eyebrows, black and unplucked, gave her features additional strength.

Faythe raised her glass. "Here's to the rowboat. May it rest in peace at the bottom of the lake. Rather it than me."

Deanna returned the smile with the smallest of angling of the corners of her mouth. "To the rowboat." She sipped the wine slowly and nodded. "Not bad."

Faythe followed suit. "Not bad at all. It's obviously been sitting well in your basement. Dig in, now." Faythe gestured toward the pasta and salad and twirled her fork in her spoon, fishing out a mouthful of the spaghetti. She chewed it carefully, relieved that her aunt's cook's recipe hadn't failed her this time either.

"Very tasty," Deanna said. "You did very well, despite the mishap with the water."

"Yeah." Embarrassed, Faythe kept eating, not wanting to dwell on the fact that she'd been nothing but a clumsy fool since she started talking to Deanna. Eager to change the subject, she focused on the yellow tomatoes in the salad. "So, what do you do for a living?"

The pause was longer than normal for such a safe question, and Faythe looked curiously at Deanna, who was twirling her spaghetti over and over in her spoon.

"I don't mean to pry," Faythe hurried to say. "I was just interested."

"I'm an illustrator. Book covers mostly. Some children's books and some avant-garde stuff." Deanna spoke quietly.

"You're an artist? That's amazing. Have I seen any of your work?"

"I don't know. Do you read fantasy or science fiction?"

"As a matter of fact, I'm a big sci-fi fan. I read, watch, and listen to it any chance I get."

Deanna lit up. "You do? I read, mainly, but I have quite a few audiobooks as well. Convenient when I can work and listen at the same time. Who's your favorite author?"

"Oh, I like a lot of them. Mercedes Lackey and Anne McCaffrey when it comes to fantasy. David Weber, when it comes to science fiction." Faythe gestured with her fork. "Then there's Celia Conroy." She looked carefully at Deanna, since Celia Conroy was famous for her erotic space saga.

"Have all of hers," Deanna said calmly. "The audiobooks sure give her stories an extra dimension."

Faythe giggled. "I bet. Some of those scenes would affect anyone."

"It's pretty obvious that the actress who performs all Conroy's books is very much a fan. And pretty affected, I'd say."

Faythe blinked at the unexpected openness. "Who performs them?"

"I think her name is Carolyn Black."

"Carolyn Black. I've met her." Faythe recalled the charismatic actress with the famous, throaty voice. "She's fantastic. Have you heard her read the Diana Maddox books?"

"No, I haven't. Are they sci-fi?"

Faythe was surprised at the question. "Eh, the Diana Maddox books are quite famous. The first one stars Black as Maddox, and they're filming the second book as we speak."

"Really. Well, I don't watch TV. I used to go to the movies a lot, but lately…I've worked. Mostly."

"And you've managed not to hear about some of the most famous books ever or the biggest scoop two years ago, when Carolyn Black got the part."

"Guess I'm not that interested in entertainment news." Deanna put her fork and spoon down, looking ill at ease.

Faythe didn't want Deanna to feel uncomfortable around her. "It's not important," she said reassuringly, using the inflection she knew calmed down nervous interview subjects. "I'm so thrilled you like Conroy's books. If you're not into crime stories, that's totally okay."

Deanna relaxed marginally. "You said you met her? Black, I mean?"

"Yes. I did a story on the gated communities down in Florida. You know, the Gold Coast?"

"A story? You're a reporter?" Deanna recoiled visibly, a deep frown marring her forehead under her thick bangs.

"Well, yeah—and no. I—" Faythe interrupted herself, looking at Deanna in disbelief and relief. "You don't recognize me, do you?"

"Should I?" Deanna's tone was decidedly frosty now and she was making a wrinkly mess of the linen napkin.

"Well, I've been on TV nearly every day for seven years."

"I said I don't watch TV."

Faythe laughed, trying to lighten the mood. "People say that a lot, but when you start mentioning programs, usually they watch all the soaps and *Deal or No Deal* every day."

"I don't."

"Well, I'm not sure what I said to upset you, but I certainly didn't mean to." Faythe tried to remain calm, but she was simultaneously angry and sorry she'd said anything. Deanna looked like she was ready to run out the door.

"You didn't upset me. I'm not comfortable around reporters, that's all. You may be a very good reporter, even an honorable one, but I've never met one like that."

"Not much chance of that happening if you bolt as soon as you're in the same room as one. I can set your mind at ease. I'm not an investigative reporter, alas, but a morning television talk-show host. And I'm not working right now. I'm on vacation."

"A good reporter never quite relaxes, does she?" Deanna's smirk was rigid, bordering on scornful.

"This one does. This reporter is trying to have a nice home-cooked meal with a neighbor who happened to pull her out of a lake and probably saved her life. And for all you know, I might be a really bad reporter who wouldn't know a scoop if it jumped up and bit my ass!" Faythe frowned and crossed her arms over her chest.

Deanna glowered back at her for several seconds, and then her mouth curved up and she snorted. "Your ass?" She leaned forward, placing her elbows on the table. "Really?"

Faythe drew a deep breath, then burst out giggling. "Really. And honestly, Deanna, I have no idea about my ability as a reporter, I mean a real, honest-to-God investigative reporter. I haven't worked as one for ten years. I've been doing morning entertainment."

"You sound like you resent it."

"I'm fed up. I meet a lot of celebrities, and some people claim I'm something of a celebrity myself, which I couldn't care less about. The woman in the grocery store recognized me on the spot, and that's why I figured you did too, but were too polite to say so."

"I didn't. I still can't piece your name together with anything I may have caught on TV when I've visited my sister. So far, I draw a blank."

"Good." Faythe meant it. She liked the fact that Deanna had no preconceived ideas about her. "Does your sister live around here?"

"Yes." Deanna spoke casually. "She goes to a boarding school just outside town."

"Great that you can be near her." Deanna's tone spiked Faythe's curiosity but she didn't pursue the subject. It really wasn't her business where Deanna's sister got her education.

They ate in silence for a few minutes. "I apologize for coming on so strong about the whole reporter thing," Deanna said suddenly.

"A sore toe?"

"Very."

"Gotcha." Faythe looked out the window but saw only Deanna's and her own reflection. "Want some coffee?"

"No. I should get back. It was a lovely meal, but I have a deadline two days from today, and I need to get some things done." Deanna rose and took her plate and utensils into the kitchen. "Oh, that's right. Here. It's just a small thank-you for dinner." She handed Faythe the envelope she'd brought.

"For me?" Giddy, on top of all her other turbulent feelings, Faythe opened the envelope and pulled out a pencil drawing of a woman jogging between some trees. She stared at the familiar haphazard ponytail and the equally familiar leggings and sweatshirt. "It's me." She knew very little about art, but knew enough to see beyond the mere likeness. This was an artist's rendition of her as she flew across roots and rocks on the forest path. Deanna had given her more than a fleeting glance, since the details were so accurate. *Even the way I tied my shoes!*

"Thank you," Faythe said quietly, looking up at Deanna. "I'm so flattered. Nobody has ever portrayed me like this. Just me running." Feeling a little foolish, Faythe blinked to relieve the burning sensation behind her eyelids. This drawing was miles away from the glossy pictures in the tabloid magazines.

"Glad you like it." Deanna studied her shoes briefly. "Well, I should go."

Faythe rose on her toes and kissed Deanna's cheek. "Thank you."

"Oh." Deanna gasped. "You're welcome." She lifted her hand

halfway to her cheek, then murmured a barely audible good night before she stepped out into the darkness. Faythe stood in the doorway and watched the tiny light from Deanna's flashlight disappear among the trees. She was bone tired after the eventful day and decided to take care of the dishes tomorrow morning. Tonight, she wanted to curl up in bed and think about the extraordinary woman who was her neighbor for the autumn.

CHAPTER FIVE

Deanna stood on her deck and looked out across the calm lake. The moon's reflection glittered in the water, and only a jumping fish disturbed the surface occasionally. Sipping another black coffee, Deanna didn't care that it would keep her up all night. She was glad it would, since she had to work. She ignored the small voice that suggested she was afraid she would have heated dreams about Faythe.

As beautiful as her new neighbor was, the way she looked at Deanna was more appealing than her brilliant green eyes. Faythe seemed keenly interested in other people, but an opaque glossiness covered her real self.

Deanna had tried to peel this perceived layer off when she did the drawings of Faythe, working with a frenzy throughout the afternoon that surprised her. She even brought out her oils, which she hadn't used since she did a painting of Miranda two years ago. She simply didn't have enough time since one assignment followed right after another.

Deanna was grateful to have work. Many struggling artists had to find one or two other jobs to keep afloat financially. The fact that she lived in an inexpensive cabin and didn't have any costly passions, except reading, made it possible to buy her materials and set aside money in a trust fund for Miranda.

Their mother, Angela, and her husband paid for Miranda's school, but Deanna planned for the day when Miranda would be old enough to graduate. "Graduate. Huh." Deanna took a large gulp of coffee. "Calling it graduation doesn't mean a thing."

Deanna had cried furious tears the day her mother and stepfather decided to send Miranda to a facility, which they glamorized by calling it a school. Their motive was obvious. Get rid of the autistic kid; make room for the new husband's spoiled little preteen brats. "Damn them. They don't know her anymore. Not like I do."

Their mother lived two hours from Grantville in the house where Deanna grew up. Percy, her husband, bought half of it when they sent Miranda off to school and Deanna moved out. Receiving a quarter of the value of the house, Deanna used the money to buy the lakeside cabin and put the rest in Miranda's trust fund. She didn't want anything else to do with her mother or Percy, and certainly nothing to do with what she regarded as their blood money.

Deanna placed the empty mug on the rustic wooden table on the porch and slid her hands up inside the sleeves of her sweater. The autumn days were still warm, but the nights were getting colder. Above her the trees swooshed and whispered as the wind played with the fire-colored leaves. Deanna didn't know of any place where autumn could possibly be more beautiful.

She bent her head and found that the solid beating of her heart blended seamlessly with the cadence of branches clattering against each other. "Being one with nature" was a cliché she normally wouldn't think to utter, but as she stood on the deck, feeling raw and strangely emotional from her dinner with Faythe, she knew it was a cliché for a reason. "This is insane," she murmured to herself. She remained where she was for a few moments longer, then grabbed her mug and walked back inside. She had work to do.

❖

"But darling, you can't possibly mean that!" Faythe's mother's voice pierced the cell-phone towers from Manhattan to Vermont with surgical precision. "Why wouldn't you have us out to the cabin?"

"Because I'm on vacation. I don't want to see anyone." Examining herself in the bathroom mirror, Faythe knew if she said that she *especially* didn't want to meet her mother and Chester, all hell would break loose, but it was true. She had nothing against Chester, and on good days she could ignore her mother's nagging, but right now, she couldn't muster the energy to listen to Cornelia's endless monologues about her own love issues.

"You can't isolate yourself like this." Cornelia Hamilton made her signature huff-turned-growl, which signaled that she was highly unsatisfied and wanted the world to know. "You know I love you, Faythe, but I would never have thought you'd be so stubborn. It's one thing that you decide to put your career on hold, which no one does in the media business, especially at your age. You also isolate yourself from the people who love you."

"People? You're talking about you and Chester?" Faythe rubbed night cream on her face with one hand while pressing her cell to her ear with the other. "Unless he's changed, he's not that fond of me. Probably because I refused to let his firm do my personal PR."

"Which was another mistake on your part." Cornelia didn't miss a beat, and Faythe regretted that she'd opened that particular can of worms. "All the Broadway crowd and the soap stars use Chester's agency."

"Then he doesn't need me."

"It wasn't a matter of need. He was trying to do you a favor."

"Favor. Huh." Faythe got some cream in her left eye and blinked repeatedly. "He wouldn't have hesitated to use me as a poster child for the 'all-American girl next door turned overnight star.' Or did I misunderstand when I overheard him telling his CEO that? He was obviously name-dropping."

Cornelia was quiet for several seconds. "He said that?"

"Yes." Lowering her hand, Faythe softened her voice. "I'm sure he meant well, Mom. He probably wanted to impress you too. I simply wasn't interested in being anyone's show-and-tell project, you know?"

"I see." Cornelia's frosty tone was unmistakable, and Faythe tried to guess if she or Chester would catch her resentment.

"And this is why you don't want us to come?"

"It's not that I don't want you to come. I want to be alone."

"Just over the day? Please, Faythe?"

Faythe sat down on the stool by the makeup dresser with a thud. A completely new, almost pleading quality in Cornelia's voice, something Faythe could never remember hearing, made her give in. "All right. Why not? But just for the day, okay, Mom? Bring Chester. Bring the dogs. They'll have a blast getting away from Manhattan."

"You sure?" Cornelia sounded strong again, and Faythe wondered if her mother had played her for the umpteenth time. "We won't overstay our welcome. I just want to visit you."

"All right. See you in a few weeks." Suddenly exhausted, Faythe said good-bye and disconnected her cell. She set it to mute, knowing her voice mail would pick up any missed calls. After brushing her teeth she slipped into a large T-shirt before climbing into bed. She tried to not overanalyze her mother's state of mind, but the more she pushed the conversation out of her mind, the more her dinner with Deanna sneaked back in.

Faythe could easily picture her, so brooding and aloof. With her black bangs framing her stark blue eyes, Deanna's strong features were enough to make Faythe's heart thunder. The fact that it clearly wasn't easy to get under Deanna's skin—frankly, the woman seemed to have her fair share of *issues*—made her only more interesting. This was surprising, since Faythe's normal rule was "no complications," and she'd rather go without than set herself up for hassles and heartache. Deanne could readily provide both. "Wonder if she even likes me?" Faythe whispered to the bleak moonlight streaming in through the small holes in the blinds. "Probably not. I'm so not her type."

It was only human to speculate if Deanna could possibly be gay, or even bi. Just because she was ruggedly handsome in a sleek, classy way and made Faythe's thoughts travel down seldom-taken routes didn't necessarily mean Deanna was sexually interested in her own gender.

Faythe thought back to her last relationship. It had been two years since she dated anyone more than a few weeks, and almost a year since she dated at all. *This can't be true. Am I turning into a hermit?* Clearly Faythe wanted more than what she'd settled for so far. She wanted a career that fulfilled and challenged her, and she wanted a life outside of her career. A family.

Faythe shrugged at her own wishful thinking. Was it even remotely possible for someone with genes like hers to find love and have kids? Her parents had blatantly switched partners after their divorce and had even cheated on them in between switches. Granted, her aunt Nellie didn't act like her brother, but she was a confirmed bachelorette. As far as Faythe knew, Nellie had never entertained the idea of being in a relationship other than close friendship. *So, promiscuous parents and a perpetually single aunt.* As role models went, Faythe preferred the eccentric Nellie's example. But she didn't want that lifestyle either. Deep in her heart she knew she wanted…someone. Someone special.

A faint sob worked past her vocal cords and broke the silence of the dark bedroom. The long, festering yearning for change, for something more, had never made her become this emotional, and she tried not to read too much into the fact that her bout of vulnerability coincided with her dinner with Deanna.

She refused to cry and buried her face in the soft pillow for a few moments, which helped compose her. Then, utilizing the technique she'd learned years ago while suffering from terrible stage fright, she breathed slowly in and out with measured, even breaths. Eventually she became relaxed enough to begin to fall asleep. This time when images of Deanna surfaced, they only made her smile.

❖

Deanna closed her tubes of acrylic paint, rinsed the brushes under lukewarm water, and glanced back at the picture she'd worked on until dawn. A fuzzy bunny sat under a mushroom, surrounded by a semicircle of mice and squirrels. This was her third children's book in a series with this particular writer. With the publication of the second book, Bunny Buttercup had become a bestseller. The readers, which translated into the parents of the kids in the three- to seven-year-old demographic, were practically banging on the publisher's door for the third book to come out. Deanna had two more major illustrations to finish, and four smaller ones. She was pressed for time, but the thought of bringing that kind of money into Miranda's trust fund made her stress worthwhile.

Bunny Buttercup was a philanthropic rabbit who hiked through the forest helping any animal in need, often in hilarious ways, but always with heart and passion. Deanna delighted in illustrating the exploits of this furry little superhero. She had read the two first stories to Miranda, who couldn't get enough of them. She had insistently brought the books to Deanna when she stayed until bedtime while visiting. Clearly Miranda wanted her to read. For her to be this focused was nothing short of a miracle, and in Deanna's eyes, this was yet another of Bunny Buttercup's accomplishments.

Bunny Buttercup represented goodness, and for Deanna, illustrating something so innocent, completely without dogma or moralizing sentiment, was very satisfying.

She placed the brushes on a towel to dry and stretched slowly, her neck crackling unpleasantly. Soft purple light crept through the windows and she stumbled into her bathroom. Unforgiving fluorescent light and a large mirror revealed that pulling all-nighters like this was perhaps not so clever. Dark circles and fine lines around her eyes told the tale of sleep deprivation. She rushed through her bathroom routine and fell into bed, exhausted. She couldn't wait to show Miranda the illustrations of Bunny Buttercup. The expression on her sister's face when she saw her favorite character was worth any loss of sleep, past or future.

CHAPTER SIX

During a week of working her way through a multitude of creative-writing exercises, Faythe carried her laptop from the house, to the deck, and even down by the lake. She was more than ready for a break. After closing it with a resounding snap, she popped a CD into the player, eager to end the silence.

Her cell phone rang before she managed to choose the right track. Cursing, she flipped it open, forgetting to check the display.

"Hello?"

"Oh, God Almighty. Bad time?" Suzy's strong voice was husky, thanks to too many cigarettes, and carried easily over Madonna's.

"Damn. Hang on." Faythe set the cell phone on speaker mode and walked toward the kitchen. "What's up, Suzy?"

"I know what you said, and it has only been a week." Suzy spoke fast, as if hoping to keep Faythe from protesting. "I have a fantastic offer for you, something you really should consider."

"I'm not interested—"

"It's not the network. It's a short stint as an awards host."

"Awards host. Which awards show are we talking about?"

"Don't sound so apprehensive. It's not the Oscars. It's a literary society with an ambitious charity program. This year it will benefit children and young people with special needs."

Her interest tweaked, Faythe poured coffee into the high-tech machine and pushed the button for a double espresso. "Sounds interesting. When is it?"

"Beginning of November. They need your response ASAP, preferably within a week or two."

"E-mail me the information and I'll get back to you in a few days."

"All right!" Suzy sounded as excited as if she'd found an oil well in her office. "This type of serious work should keep you in the public eye if you're still sure about this career move."

"Dead sure."

"Well, then, we're on a roll. Ciao." A definite click ended the call and Faythe shook her head. Suzy could be as exasperating as she was efficient, but under her gruff exterior, she was as loyal as they came.

Faythe's mind whirled back to her dinner with Deanna as she steamed the milk for her espresso. Every time she took a break during her marathon writing exercise, she'd thought of her enigmatic, gorgeous neighbor.

Out on the patio she started the hot tub she'd filled yesterday and watched the jets create whirls everywhere. She could sort her jumbled thoughts a lot better if she had a good soak. Inside, she switched into her black swimsuit, tugged her hair back into a ponytail, and grabbed a bath towel. Tiptoeing across the deck, she dropped the towel on a chair before she slipped into the busy water. It was almost too hot, but the chilly autumn air cooled her neck and shoulders as she sat up a little, making it bearable.

As usual, the hypnotic massage of the hot tub sent her thoughts scurrying and she sorted them into clearer paths. Why had Kitty-with-a-heart, the woman working at the supermarket, warned her about Deanna and called her *that woman*? And why did Deanna act so strange when Faythe mentioned her trip into town? Something really weird was going on.

Deanna knows what they say about her. Well, how could she not know? Faythe leaned back and watched some leaves break from the maples nearest the house and ride the faint breeze. Deanna had probably saved Faythe's life when she helped her to shore last week. She'd risked her life by swimming in the cold water to assist a total stranger. What contemptible person would do such a thing? It didn't make sense.

The drawing Deanna had made of her was probably the truest glimpse into Deanna's character she had ever seen. How had Deanna pulled it off, since she really didn't know Faythe? She had depicted Faythe the way nobody had seen her, or wanted to see her, in years.

"That looks comfortable."

Was the husky voice a memory? She was focusing so hard on figuring out Deanna's mystery... A quick glance to her left showed the outline of her neighbor as she approached the Jacuzzi. "Deanna." Faythe sat up.

"Sorry. Didn't mean to startle you." Deanna shuffled her feet and shoved her hands into the back pockets of her jeans. "I haven't seen you around and thought I'd...eh...thank you for dinner. I didn't intend to be impolite. I've been busy with a deadline."

"Oh, yeah? Another book?"

"Yes. A children's book. Bunny Buttercup."

"Oh. Really. It sounds adorable. I've heard about the author. Wasn't it shortlisted for an award?"

"Yes. It didn't win, but it gained a lot of attention and has done well." Deanna looked preoccupied.

"I'm happy for you." Faythe felt unusually shy, but wasn't about to let the awkwardness stop her. "Want to join me?" The words left her lips before she knew what she meant to say.

"What? Oh, no. That's all right. I should get back to work. Would you like to go on a more reliable boat trip on the lake with me?"

"I'd love to." The heat from the water must have caused the hot flush up her neck and cheeks. "When did you have in mind?"

"Early tomorrow, in my canoe. I usually take my camera and stay a few hours."

"I haven't paddled a canoe since I was twelve and at summer camp, but I think I remember how." Faythe laughed. "At least I know better than two friends there who always insisted on facing each other while they paddled, which didn't work so well."

"You're kidding." Deanna's deliciously throaty laugh made Faythe's nipples harden despite the hot water. Displaying even white teeth, Deanna gave a broad smile that transformed her strong features into sheer beauty, and Faythe softened inside. Kitty-with-a-heart's comments seemed ridiculous and petty, and Faythe couldn't wait to get to know Deanne better.

"Seven too early?"

"No. I'm used to getting up at four, so seven is fine." Faythe stood up in the hot tub without thinking, but Deanna's roaming eyes made her want to sit down just as quickly. Not wanting to seem even more conspicuous, though, Faythe climbed out of the tub and reached for her towel. "I'm turning into a prune."

"All right. See you tomorrow."

"I'll make us breakfast to take along."

Backing up so fast she nearly hit the railing behind her, Deanna nodded. "Sounds good. Bye." She disappeared along the path and through the trees, and only when Faythe began to shiver did she realize she'd forgotten to wrap the towel around her. Groaning at herself, she hurried inside and headed for the shower to wash her hair.

When was the last time her heart fluttered the way it did now? She glanced at the mirror as she squirmed out of her swimsuit. Even her chest looked flushed. In the shower she tried to let the water rinse the heated thoughts from her mind.

CHAPTER SEVEN

Sitting behind Faythe in the canoe enhanced Deanna's experience of the lake's mirrorlike surface. The birds seemed in awe too; not even the autumn leaves stirred. The air was crisp, but not cool enough to turn their breath into mist, and Deanna realized that the uncommon feeling inside her was peace. Short-lived, it evaporated as soon as Faythe turned and smiled at her. That smile had haunted Deanna for days.

"Beautiful doesn't quite cut it, does it?" Faythe looked reverently at her. "I can't describe how this makes me feel. How can I ever go back to Manhattan?"

"I could never live too far away from nature."

"Were you born here? In Grantville, I mean?"

"No, I'm from Montpellier."

"City girl? I'd never have guessed."

"I'm that unsophisticated?" Deanna raised an eyebrow, delighted when Faythe blushed.

"No. I meant you so clearly appreciate living among…this."

"Actually, I lived a very average suburban life."

"And how did you end up here?"

"Oh, life." Deanna thought of Miranda, how their mother's betrayal and altered loyalties had forced this situation upon them. "Just happenstance, really."

"That's not uncommon. Nothing happenstance ever had the chance to enter my life. Once I left college, I was on the fast track in the media business. The speed blinded me. I thought I was living my dream, maybe because everyone else took that for granted."

"I can see how that might confuse a person."

Faythe turned forward and continued to paddle with long, slow strokes. "The term 'finding yourself' is a cliché, but trust me, that's why I'm here. I lost sight of what I wanted. Some days I lost sight of me." Faythe's sorrowful laugh tore at Deanna.

"I hope you do find yourself. Really."

"Me too."

They paddled along the narrow part of the lake in silence, and Deanna relaxed again, blocking thoughts of her mother and other unhappy parts of her life to focus on the rising sun's rays that played with the highlights in Faythe's hair. She wore it in a low ponytail with a Tilley hat hanging on her back. Dressed in jeans and a red windbreaker jacket, and devoid of makeup, she looked years younger than during dinner a week ago.

Deanna itched to draw her again and looked with longing at the backpack at her feet. She always carried some basic art supplies and sketch pads, as well as a set of dry clothes in a sealed bag, a first-aid kit, a thermos of coffee, and some sandwiches. Faythe had been smart enough to bring something to eat and spare clothes as well.

"A log coming toward us," Faythe said. "Left or right?"

"Right." Deanna guided them around the trunk, which floated slowly with the current as several birds sat on top of it and groomed themselves. Their ruffled feathers and beady eyes pleased her.

Faythe glanced over her shoulder again. "Any particular goal in mind, or do we just paddle until we see a place we like?"

"Let's keep going a while longer, unless you're sore. I know some pretty spots about half an hour upstream."

"I'm okay. I may be a city girl, but I work out." Faythe grinned and kept paddling.

"I could tell the other day."

"What? How?"

Deanna cursed inwardly for speaking without thinking. Visions of lean muscles playing under soft, pale skin surfaced instantly, no matter how she tried to suppress them. "I…I just noticed when you…I mean, when you used my shower after the rowboat sank." That sounded even worse. Deanna kept paddling, hoping the moment of awkwardness would vanish.

"Wow, I'm glad you noticed. I certainly appreciated your strength when you towed me through the water." Faythe wrinkled her nose. "Something tells me you're not much for gyms, though. You're in good shape because you're the outdoorsy type. Am I right or am I right?"

"You're right." Deanna was relieved at Faythe's good-natured response. It was amazing to be around someone who wasn't suspicious or judgmental, and even if a small voice in the back of her mind reminded Deanna to be careful, not to read too much into Faythe's sweetness, it pulled her in, like a wasp to strawberry shortcake. "I don't do gyms, but I take long walks, paddle the canoe, and chop my own wood in the winter."

"Thought as much. Perhaps you could show me how to chop wood? I'm staying at least three months. That's what it should take, minimum, to 'find myself.'"

Deanna's heart twirled. "Three months. That's almost till Christmas."

"Yeah. If Aunt Nellie is coming here for the holidays, I might even spend them at the cabin. Who knows? My parents always start bickering about where I should spend Christmas or New Year, and I'd rather skip their massive parties."

"Your aunt is a nice person. I've talked to her briefly and appreciate her kindness."

"She's the sanest one in my family, trust me."

"Including you?" Faythe seemed completely sane and very nice.

"Hmm. Don't know. I guess I'm all right, but Nellie is so much wiser. She has it all together, you know?" Faythe's tone sounded longing, tinged with distress.

"She's older." Deanna knew her comment sounded a bit lame but wanted to reassure Faythe. "For what it's worth, stepping off the carousel to follow your heart when you're on the fast track to fame and fortune says a lot."

"It does?" Faythe's shoulders relaxed visibly. "I thought it spoke volumes about how indecisive and confused I am."

"We all become confused. You've got enough courage to act, and you will get un-confused soon enough."

Faythe's laugh carried over the lake and stirred up a flock of birds on the other shore. "Thanks. You're good for my self-esteem."

"Glad to hear that." Deanna had been mysteriously upset when she sensed pain in Faythe, and comforting her warmed her belly. Deanna cleared her throat and glanced to the right. "How about over there? That's a gorgeous spot and easy to pull the canoe ashore."

"Beautiful. Let's get going. I'm starving."

Deanna's broad, rare smile stretched unfamiliar muscles. "Me too."

❖

Faythe leaned back on one elbow and sipped her coffee. The caffeine seemed to diffuse directly into her veins and rejuvenated her. Or perhaps it was the fresh air, she mused, but changed her mind. Usually the crisp air made her go to sleep. She looked around the area Deanna had chosen for them to enjoy their breakfast.

"I've never seen anything so beautiful," Faythe murmured. "I truly enjoy the scenery once I do get outside."

"Guess Central Park isn't exactly outdoors."

"Not exactly, even though I love jogging there every morning. I try to go super early, though, which is a bummer since I love to sleep in." Faythe shifted her gaze to Deanna, who lay on her side in a position that mirrored her own. "How about you?"

"I'm a night owl. I can stay up so late it's early morning before I go to bed. Guess that spills over to being a morning person. I don't sleep much."

Faythe knew from Deanna's sad tone that this wasn't a subject she should pursue. Deanna moved forward enough for her black hair to cover her face, a familiar gesture. But why did she hide?

"I change depending on my mood," Faythe said casually. "If I'm swamped with work and running in circles, I'm grumpy in the morning. If I'm doing something interesting, even if it's stressful, I'm annoyingly cheerful, according to my colleagues."

Deanna's hair fell back over her shoulders and she grinned. "Annoyingly cheerful? Really. I'm trying to picture that, but I can't."

"Oh, I can get overenthusiastic. I'm like a dog with a bone. Once I'm excited about a project I never let go until I've sorted everything out, unraveled every part of the mystery, no matter what it is." Deanna's expression became somber, and Faythe realized she'd stepped into a minefield.

"Guess that's the mark of a good reporter."

"Yes, it is."

"To keep digging."

"To find the *truth*." Faythe finished her coffee and placed the mug in her backpack. "That's the reporter's job. No, their duty. To find the truth and report it to the public."

"No matter whom it hurts. No matter if the truth is not what it seems." Rigid, her eyes cold, Deanna gripped her mug with a white-knuckled hand.

Faythe refused to take the bait and spoke softly. "Someone hurt you?" She didn't want to add to Deanna's pain, but she refused to accept responsibility for what someone else had done. "A reporter printed something that wasn't true?"

"Not exactly. Anyway, it's ancient history." Deanna jerked her shoulders again in what looked like her trademark way of dismissing a topic. "Forget about it."

"It's a little hard when you obviously expect me to turn on you and do the same. Look, you don't know me, but I don't know you either." Faythe tucked a few errant strands behind her ear. "And I promise, I'm not here on this gorgeous morning to dig up some dirt on you. I'm on vacation."

Deanna's taut body relaxed marginally. "Guess I'm a bit paranoid."

"You might have every reason, I don't know, but not with me." Faythe didn't know how else to reassure Deanna. But the advice from the woman in the grocery store and Deanna's aversion to reporters tickled Faythe's curiosity. She wanted to ask Deanna about the warning but couldn't, especially after assuring her she wasn't there to pry. She would have to be patient.

"All right. It's not fair to be so secretive and expect you to walk on eggshells, but I've been burned and I have to be careful." Deanna rose to her knees and packed the leftovers of their breakfast without asking if Faythe was ready. "I'm simply not used to socializing, which shouldn't surprise you."

Faythe decided to be honest. She might burn her bridges, but she refused to bend over backward to accommodate anyone, not even Deanna. "Here's what I know." Faythe took Deanna's hand, making her stop brushing breadcrumbs off the blanket. "That woman in town, Kitty-something, said I should stay clear of you. She didn't give me any details, and she seemed genuinely concerned. I figured if you were an ax murderer, you'd be locked up. But I don't let anyone sway my opinion or determine my friends."

"I see." Deanna squeezed her hand, her voice a whisper. "And I'm not what they say I am."

CHAPTER EIGHT

Deanna paddled the last few yards and jumped up to pull the canoe ashore. She wished she hadn't asked Faythe to join her and knew the jerky movements of her hands betrayed her feelings as she helped Faythe onto the grassy slope. Why did she let Faythe draw her into a conversation that opened doors that should stay closed? And she was furious that she couldn't find a single harmless topic to break the silence on their way back. *"I'm not what they say I am."* Faythe would surely ask follow-up questions, especially after Deanna said, *"It's nothing. Nothing I want to talk to you or anyone else about. This was a mistake. Let's go home."*

Faythe had stared at her with her beautiful green eyes, and if Deanna had read any sort of accusation in them, she could have used her pent-up anger and resentment to write her off. Instead, Faythe's eyes held equal parts pain and compassion, and the sight killed her. Once Faythe became more familiar with Grantville and its townspeople, this compassion would turn to dismay.

"Deanna…" Faythe stood rigid, clinging to her backpack. "Deanna, please. I don't know what I did, or said, that made you so angry, but no matter what it was, I'm sorry. I didn't intend to."

"Not your fault. I'm not good with people. Or around people. The fact that I work from home and live out by the lake by myself should tell you something." It hurt to speak. Her vocal cords felt as stiff as the rest of her body.

"I wasn't prying. I thought we were getting to know each other." Faythe took a deep breath and stepped closer. "Please."

Deanna hated her own weakness, which twisted her throat into a hard knot. She swallowed repeatedly to avoid the treacherous tears, searching for the anger and resentment that had saved her so often. Instead, something inside her softened. She didn't know if it was because of Faythe's gentleness or because of the undeniable attraction. *For heaven's sake! Am I getting totally spineless because of some damn onslaught of hormones?*

Faythe fiddled with the drawstring in her windbreaker. "Can't we beach the canoe and talk?"

"I don't have anything else to say." Deanna meant to sound dismissive, but instead the words came out as a husky whisper. "You don't know me. You don't want to know me. Take my word for it."

"No. I've done the 'right' thing for ten years and followed all the good advice the well-meaning people around me have dished out. Look where that's gotten me. Stuck in a media circus doing news stories about everything from juggling poodles to the best freaking treatment for athlete's foot." Faythe gestured emphatically.

Deanna laughed, surprised. She hadn't expected to find humor in Faythe's words, and certainly not in her own. "Juggling poodles?"

"Yup. Three of them. All were true divas."

"They demanded champagne in their dressing room?" Deanna couldn't stop her silly smile.

"How did you know?"

Faythe grinned back, and suddenly Deanna could breathe again.

"Here, let me help you." Faythe pulled on the opposite side of the canoe and together they dragged it farther up and turned it upside down. "Ah. There."

Deanna brushed a few wet leaves off her jeans and pushed the hair out of her eyes. "Thanks."

"You're welcome." Faythe lifted her hand, palm up, to Deanna, who took it hesitantly. "Want to catch a movie, perhaps later in the week?"

Deanna could hardly reply. The sensation of Faythe's soft, slender hand in hers drowned out everything else. It wasn't the first time they had touched. When she'd held Faythe in a firm grip as she saved her from the water, she hadn't felt this bittersweet tenderness. Shaken, Deanna gently pulled her hand back. "All right. Absolutely. Why not?" She didn't think about her words. She just wanted to escape these startling feelings and the innocent touch that caused them.

"Tomorrow night? I can check which movies are showing. Or would you rather rent something? Aunt Nellie has pay-per-view."

"Sounds good. I mean, renting." Deanna finally realized that going into town to the movies with Faythe would be impossible.

"I think so too. At seven or thereabouts?"

"Sounds good.'"

"See you then." Faythe stepped closer and hugged Deanna. "Thanks for taking me canoeing. Take care."

"You too," Deanna managed. The unexpected full-body contact depleted all of her oxygen, and she stumbled backward. "Bye."

"Bye." Faythe waved and headed toward her house.

Deanna stood frozen, making sure Faythe was not about to say something more, then spun around and hurried to her cabin. She dumped the backpack on the kitchen table and continued into the bathroom, where she closed the door. She needed as many walls and doors between herself and the outside world as possible. Gasping, she studied her reflection, not recognizing the wild look in her eyes. Normally she kept a cool façade, her temper carefully subdued and controlled. Two years ago, she had let her temper flare, which cost her dearly. Nothing could take away that pain, and she had restrained herself since then, determined not to rock the boat again.

Faythe was a variable Deanna hadn't counted on. Although a woman of the world, well dressed, knowledgeable, and with a fantastic career already despite her youth, Faythe possessed a soft innocence, something genuinely *good* that drew Deanna in despite her best efforts to keep Faythe distant.

That hadn't worked, since Faythe had stepped right up and hugged her. Deanna leaned her forehead against the cool mirror. How was she supposed to keep someone as lovely as Faythe away? Every time Deanna tried to create some distance, either by being cold or dismissive, the pained expression in Faythe's eyes wouldn't let her follow through.

"I may have to tell her the whole ugly story." Deanna grimaced at her reflection, looking at herself cross-eyed since she was so close to the mirror. "Then again, she might be so stubborn that she'll try to save me from myself."

Deanna stalked out of the bathroom and over to her work area. Tossing her jacket on a pile of books on a chair, she switched on the light, then opened her sketch pad and grabbed a charcoal pen. She drew a scene from memory, the canoe in the foreground and the lake framed with maple trees in the background. Before she knew it, a slender figure sat in the front of the canoe. With long hair framing her face, the woman glanced over her shoulder at the dark outline of another woman who sat with a paddle resting just above the waterline.

Deanna stared at the drawing, half finished and sketched in such a frenzied style. Faythe seemed to have invaded every part of her existence, and Deanna could think of only one place where she would find no trace of Faythe. She glanced at her watch. It was time to go see Miranda anyway. She had never needed the comfort of being around her beloved little sister this much. Miranda, the gentlest soul in Deanna's life, never questioned her. Perhaps that was why Faythe's sweetness was so compelling?

Not about to speculate a second longer, Deanna grabbed her bag and car keys and was out the door in record time.

Opening Google on her laptop, Faythe typed in "Deanna Moore Grantville Vermont." She had to find out what the hell was going on. The computer mulled over the entry and found more than ten thousand hits. The first ones were about Deanna's work, her illustrations and paintings. Deanna had her own section at one of the publishers where Faythe found a small bio, with thumbnails of her Bunny Buttercup illustrations. A guest book was attached, and Faythe clicked on the link, curious what readers thought of Deanna's work.

The comments were appreciative and endearing, competing with each other to express how much they loved and adored the illustrations for Bunny Buttercup. Faythe felt proud of Deanna when she read how parents seemed to enjoy the stories and the illustrations as much as their children did.

Returning to Google, Faythe found another link, this time to a discussion forum for books and their authors. Eventually she was staring at the long row of messages in a thread called "Deanna Moore, illustrious illustrator." Faythe had stumbled upon vile remarks on the Internet before, but never been personally involved. She read several of the messages but couldn't manage any more.

> I know what U did. I know the girl U hurt. I don't think U should work with kids ever.
>
> You are an immoral bitch who should be locked up!
>
> You f*cking wh*re!
>
> Why don't you move away from Grantville? You're not wanted here!

The occasional messages from appreciative readers were lost in the flurry of flames against Deanna. Stunned, with a thousand questions forming in her head, Faythe did the only thing possible. She tracked down the webmaster and requested that he purge the derogatory comments.

Faythe continued to other sites, and even though she didn't find such foul language, she discovered similar comments with a clear message. Other people than Kitty-with-heart, probably Grantville residents, clearly felt the same way she did. Frowning, Faythe decided not to log on to the local newspaper's site. It would be wrong to read what she knew would be written there. She had to ask Deanna herself. She owed her that if she wanted to be her friend.

Friendship was important, but the concept left her antsy and she twirled a lock of hair around her finger, over and over, as she thought about the situation. She had no idea if Deanna found women sexually attractive, but her response to the handshake and the hug earlier spoke volumes—mostly about strong, if repressed, emotions. Faythe had held Deanna's hand long enough to feel her racing pulse. She had no clue how she had dared to simply hug her, but as brief as the contact was, Deanna had trembled against her. It had taken all her willpower to let go and merely smile.

Faythe closed her eyes and thought of Deanna's tormented features when she tried to push Faythe away... She snapped her eyes open again. That was it. Deanna was trying to push Faythe away, *before* the reverse happened. Whatever people were up in arms about, Deanna was certain Faythe would side with them. Stubborn and with a journalist's desire to find the objective truth, Faythe straightened her back and began to type. She wouldn't go behind Deanna's back and dig up dirt on her, that wasn't fair, but she would write down everything she felt and knew about her. She'd write it like a novel, like a drama documentary, and add little by little. This way she would get to know the true Deanna. She could still write down her own subjective—*no, heated*—thoughts about her. This was for her own eyes only.

Faythe's fingers flew across the keyboard. This was the second best thing to actually spending time with Deanna. She would discover the truth.

CHAPTER NINE

D ee." Miranda rocked back and forth on her bed, her arms wrapped around herself. "Dee-dee-dee-dee…"

"Honey. Honey, listen to me. I'm here now." Deanna forced herself to sound calm and reassuring. Her little sister had regressed into a behavior she had displayed the first semester at the Tremayne Foundation and School. She looked so small and young where she huddled, barely coherent. Touching Miranda when she was this distraught was dicey at best. Either Miranda would cling to her or she would recoil like a wound-up spring.

Carefully, Deanna placed a hand on Miranda's shoulder. The rocking stopped for a moment, and she didn't push Deanna away.

"There you go, honey." Deanna slid closer and wrapped both arms around Miranda. "You're fine. You're more than fine. You're okay now. I've got you." She kept murmuring in the monotone voice she knew calmed Miranda's frayed nerves. That, together with slow, circular caresses along Miranda's back, stilled the rocking motion, and eventually she curled up almost on Deanna's lap. Her sister's fresh scent of soap and mint toothpaste was familiar, and Deanna focused on that fact to keep any angry thoughts from showing. "There, you see. You're doing fine."

The young man working nights at Miranda's dorm had apologized profusely for disturbing Deanna in the middle of the night. Afraid that something serious had happened, Deanna had begun to dress with one hand while she was still on the phone. The night staff member told her that Miranda had been upset ever since her surprise visitors left earlier in the evening.

"What surprise visitors? Why the hell didn't you call me right away?" Deanna asked as she struggled into her jeans. "You know I'm only twenty minutes away."

"We thought we were handling it, Ms. Moore. Miranda looked calmer just before bedtime. But when she woke from some nightmare or something, we couldn't reach her. She won't let us near her, and I don't want to have the nurse on call medicate her if we can avoid it."

"No, you're right. Don't give her anything. I'm on my way out the door as we speak. Tell her Dee's coming."

Deanna drove as fast as she could through the empty streets of Grantville, her mind whirling with questions. Sometimes her mother decided to spring a surprise visit on Miranda, and this time she might have had her husband and any or both of his brats with her. Usually Miranda tolerated her stepfather fairly well, but the two teenyboppers were too much for her. If Deanna had been on speaking terms with her mother, she would have demanded that the superficial little horrors be banned from visiting, as well as making any *surprise* visits. As things were, the only communication between her and her mother was the notes they both made in the binder in Miranda's room. Staff and next of kin communicated via the binder when it wasn't possible to have a face-to-face meeting. It also functioned as a diary of Miranda's progress. They were well into their twelfth binder after nine years now.

"Dee?" Miranda pulled back. "Read."

"What, honey? You want me to read to you?"

"Read." Miranda removed a book from the shelf and placed it between them. She never gave anything directly to anyone, but it was still clear what she wanted.

"Which one is this?" Deanna examined the book. "Aha. One of our favorites. *Charlotte's Web*."

"Friend."

"Yes, that's right. It's about true friendship."

Deanna helped Miranda crawl back into bed, as always feeling utterly protective of the girl. Anyone who gave Miranda a quick look would probably guess her age to be about twelve. Deanna tucked her in beneath the soft down duvet and moved up to sit next to her, one hand on Miranda's cinnamon-colored hair, while she opened the book with the other. She began to read the story of the loyal, intelligent spider that saved the life of her friend, the pig, and as she kept reading the classic story, her own anger began to dissipate.

She couldn't help Miranda if she allowed her temper to rule. Her sister needed her calmness as much as she needed love and affection. Deanna refused to give her mother's actions another thought. She would do what she always did—write a no-nonsense message in Miranda's chart. Nine years ago she vowed never to speak to her mother again, and she had kept her word.

Angela Moore decided to place Miranda in this facility when she was only seven. Though it was progressive and cutting-edge, Deanna was infuriated because their mother had betrayed both of them. Angela had sworn they'd always be together, be a family, after their father passed away when Deanna was eighteen and Miranda was two.

Five years later when she met Percy, that all changed. He was a widower with two daughters Miranda's age, and it didn't take him long to convince Angela that Miranda was better off in an institution. Deanna did everything possible to keep her original family together, and when Angela wouldn't listen, but talked on and on about how the staff at Tremayne's worked miracles with autistic children and that it would be good for all of them, Deanna gave her mother an ultimatum.

She could still see the pained, angry expression on her mother's face. Deanna told her mother that unless she reconsidered sending Miranda away, she would leave and never talk to her mother again. Ever. Angela pleaded with her, but also refused to budge. The incident ended in total chaos. They shipped Miranda off to Tremayne's, and Deanna left without saying another word to either Angela or Percy.

Determined to keep her anger at bay, Deanna focused on the story. Miranda's head rested on her shoulder and grew increasingly heavy as the story of Charlotte, the spider, unfolded. After only forty-five pages, Miranda's breathing was even and she had slid farther down under her duvet.

Deanna carefully dislodged her arm and rose from the bed. She made sure Miranda was comfortable and carefully brushed the silky hair out of her face. Her sister was the epitome of cuteness, with her slightly freckled, upturned nose and huge blue eyes. Deanna wanted Miranda to have every opportunity—not only the ones available for anyone with her diagnosis, but *any* chance possible for happiness and fulfillment. Did Angela see how amazing her youngest daughter was and the progress she had made the last few years? Miranda's language skills had picked up enormously when Tremayne's enrolled five of their students in a trial program devised by the University of Vermont.

Deanna had to admit that Tremayne's *had* been good for Miranda, and that the feud between her and her mother didn't benefit her sister at all. Still, they reached total gridlock nine years ago, and after the nightmare two years ago when all hell broke loose around Deanna at Grantville High, she saw no end. If not for the all-consuming sisterly love she felt for Miranda, Deanna would have disappeared a long time ago. She would have changed her name and moved to another state, perhaps even to Canada. Instead she was stuck in a life that revolved around her sister and her work.

Deanna grabbed a binder from a shelf, browsing through the latest entries jotted down by the staff, to see if they had recorded anything the last few days to explain what had happened. Irene Costa had made a short entry the previous day, written in dynamic letters, and Deanna's trained eye immediately detected that Irene had pressed the pen hard against the paper, a sign of her displeasure.

Miranda's mother and stepfather visited and brought Miranda's stepsisters. I tried to advise against it, since it has yet to benefit Miranda to be around children her own age, especially if they show very little concern or appreciation toward her. Angela Moore Bodell insisted that it is in Miranda's best interest to learn to interact with her entire family, and when I tried to suggest that it might be too much for her to meet both girls at the same time, Mr. Bodell interfered, clearly feeling I had criticized his daughters, which was never my intention.

It didn't take the Bodell teenagers long to make Miranda mute and fidgety. She eventually started rocking and tugging at her eyelashes, a familiar sign that she's

under significant stress. Luckily, the Bodell family left before things escalated, but I had to remain isolated with Miranda in her room for an hour, brushing and braiding her hair over and over to calm her. I've seen her sister Deanna do this on several occasions, and it seemed to work after a while. Miranda is still not talking now when my shift is over, which is never a good sign.
Irene Costa

Deanna set her jaw and gripped the pen hard in turn. She had to force herself to not use the harsh language and profanities that first came to mind as she wrote.

I received an emergency phone call from Tremayne's tonight, when they risked having to sedate Miranda if I couldn't manage to calm her down. I held her and later read to her, and it is obvious to me that our mother's selfish way of thinking, and her husband's all-too-great faith in the benevolence of his daughters, caused Miranda to regress into old behavior when subjected to stress. If our mother can't see this and keeps acting in ways that are not in Miranda's best interests, I'm afraid that Miranda will suffer further setbacks that will ultimately become obstacles she can't overcome. This type of spur-of-the-moment visit cannot be allowed to occur again.
Deanna Moore

Deanna replaced the binder on a shelf and tiptoed out of Miranda's room, leaving the door slightly ajar and the nightlight on, as always. She walked up to the day room where the two young men who had the night shift were watching TV with the sound barely audible.

"Hi, guys. She's calmed down and gone to sleep now." Deanna put her jacket on. "Can you make sure Irene Costa knows about what happened tonight?"

"Absolutely, ma'am. She's working the day shift tomorrow, so she'll get the report right away."

"Excellent. Well, don't hesitate to call me if Miranda has another setback. Good night." Deanna nodded briskly and walked down the corridor. The night air cooled her temper somewhat, but now she had room for other, more confused feelings—about Faythe. Their morning together, paddling the canoe, and the way Faythe managed to coax words out of her that Deanna never thought she would utter. The entire experience flooded her senses as she drove back to her cabin. They had almost alienated each other.

At one point, Deanna felt so cornered she lashed out, *wanting* to distance herself from Faythe, to go back to the status quo where she felt safe. She hadn't counted on Faythe's innate ability to bypass her apprehensions. Why did her smile make Deanna forget everything about her resolve—*about my need for self-preservation*—and go completely mushy?

The empty streets did little to distract Deanna as she drove through Grantville. The way Faythe hugged her when they said good-bye after their picnic preyed on her mind. Meant only as a hug between friends, it had been like pouring water on a withering plant. Afterward, in her panic, Deanna pulled back quickly, since she knew in her heart that such touches would endanger her peace of mind.

The sweetness of the memory overshadowed any discomfort. Faythe's aura of innocence and goodness drew Deanna in. Faythe would never be unfair or unjust about anything; she obviously possessed a strong moral code. This quality should have been reassuring, but instead it made Deanna uneasy. If Faythe ended up believing and siding with the people in Grantville who pegged her as an immoral cradle robber...

Deanna gripped the steering wheel harder. Faythe was practically a stranger to her. It shouldn't matter what she thought. She had hardened herself against Gloria Mueller and her posse of "ladies-in-waiting" for two years now. Their method of making sure every person who counted in Grantville knew their "truth" made it hard to pretend she didn't care, but she managed. Now she should be able to jut her chin out and disregard anything Faythe might think of her.

When Deanna considered that possibility, the pang in her chest told her she was kidding herself. What Faythe thought of her was beginning to matter a lot, and ultimately that vulnerability might undo her.

CHAPTER TEN

Faythe opened the door, a broad grin on her face. "Jeez, can you believe this weather?"

"I can." Deanna removed her rain coat and looked around. "Where can I hang this so I don't mess up the floor?"

"Here. Hand it over." Faythe took the coat and carried it quickly to the mud room on the opposite side of the kitchen. Returning, she noticed that Deanna had placed her rubber boots on the small welcome mat and now stood hesitantly in the doorway to the living room. "I have everything ready. Popcorn, Coca-Cola, unless you're a Pepsi kind of gal, and extra pillows and blankets."

"Extra pillows?" Deanna raised an eyebrow. "Don't tell me. You need something to hide behind if we watch something scary."

Faythe felt her cheeks flush. "Eh, well, so I'm a chicken."

"Any thoughts on what to rent?" Deanna sat down on the far end of the couch.

"I browsed the pay-per-view options, and since I'm a sucker for romantic comedies, I looked up their current selection of those first." Faythe sat down next to Deanna. She supposed she should have opted for the other corner of the couch, but she wanted more physical contact with Deanna. She hadn't been able to get the quick hug out of her thoughts.

"Romantic comedies?" Deanna flipped through the list of films available. "Not really my cup of tea. What do you think of Bogart and Bacall?"

"As in Humphrey and Lauren?" Faythe wrinkled her nose. "They were brilliant, but the movies are a bit dated."

"They're not dated. They never could be dated—they're classics." Deanna shook her head. "All right, look here. They have *Lawrence of Arabia.*"

"God. Another ancient one. How about *Love Actually,* or that new one, *Miss Pettigrew Lives for a Day?*"

"Let me read the blurbs." Deanna's tone wasn't encouraging, and Faythe wondered if they'd be able to figure out something to watch. She should have pegged Deanna for being a deep person even when it came to movies.

"Oh, boy. *Love Actually* is apparently one of those romantic comedies that has barely enough substance to hold it together. What's with you and these no-brainer romances?"

Faythe slammed the popcorn bowl down. "They're not no-brainers! *Love Actually* happens to be brilliantly put together with a great message. *Miss Pettigrew* got fantastic reviews and the actress playing Miss Pettigrew, Frances McDormand, is an Oscar-winning character actress." Faythe glowered at Deanna, feeling as if her taste in movies had put another nail in the coffin when it came to proving how shallow she was.

"No worries, I didn't mean to upset you. I was just teasing. We like different things, that's all."

"So you're not being snobbish about my taste in movies?" Faythe inhaled deeply and slowly let the air out through her nose.

"Perhaps a bit." Deanna looked apologetic. "I'm sorry."

Faythe knew a sincere apology when she heard one. "God, Deanna, I'm overreacting. You can pick any movie you'd like. You're my guest."

"Actually, I'm curious about this Frances McDormand movie."

"You're not just saying that, are you?" Faythe eyed Deanna suspiciously.

"No." The short-cropped answer spoke more than any lengthy explanation.

"All right. Next time we'll watch *African Queen* or something. I like that one."

"Or *Casablanca.* Very romantic." Deanna winked as she pressed a button on the remote, starting the movie. Faythe reached for the popcorn and moved closer to Deanna so they could easily share the big bowl. Several times their hands touched by mistake as they reached into the bowl, each time sending tingles up Faythe's arm.

When it looked like Miss Pettigrew was going to miss out on love, Faythe felt the familiar longing deep inside, genuinely sympathizing with the character in the movie. She leaned her head against Deanna's shoulder, knowing instinctively that the closer proximity would ease the pain.

"You all right?" Deanna murmured, briefly touching Faythe's hand in the popcorn bowl.

"Yeah, I'm fine. Thanks." Faythe grabbed a handful of popcorn. She didn't move away from Deanna's shoulder. It felt too good. The domestic scene was so appealing that she indulged herself, even knowing it was temporary. Rubbing her cheek against Deanna's arm, Faythe pretended they were a couple. She knew she was being silly, but she had gone without companionship like this for far too long. "This is cozy."

"Cozy." Deanna seemed to echo Faythe's own feelings.

"Yeah. I've missed just hanging, just being home doing nothing."

"Can't remember the last time I watched a movie with a friend like this."

"Me either." Faythe glanced up at Deanna. Her eyes seemed even darker blue than usual, and were her lips fuller too? "I'm so glad you're here."

"Oh." A faint tremor in Deanna's arm concerned Faythe.

"My time to ask. Are you okay?" Faythe slid even closer, placing a hand on Deanna's knee. "You can tell me."

"I'm fine."

Faythe could have perceived the words as a brush-off, but the tone—longing, with a tinge of desperation—kept Faythe from being offended.

"Deanna…" Faythe cupped Deana's cheek and rubbed her thumb over her cheekbone. "You look very fine to me." She wasn't sure where her audacity came from; she had never acted this forward around anyone. *It's not like I'm coming on to her. I just want her to know… what? That I find her irresistible? Or that I'm ready to listen to her if she wants to talk about what's bothering her?* All of the above was probably true. Deanna was on her mind most of the day and visited her dreams at night.

"Thank you." Deanna's throaty voice reverberated throughout Faythe's body, creating unmistakable physical reactions.

She let her thumb slide down Deanna's cheek and trace her generous jawline to her determined chin. It rested, hesitated, just below her lower lip. Deanna licked her lips, her eyes narrowing as she gazed down at Faythe.

"You play dangerous games." Her voice was thick.

"I'm not that much into games," Faythe whispered. Her heart pounded in her chest. "I never win at anything."

"No?" Deanna kissed her palm. "You seem like a winner to me."

"Nah, just good at keeping up appearances." Faythe grimaced at how serious the initially flirtatious conversation had turned. "I've learned from the best."

"Your parents?"

"Yeah."

Amazingly enough, Deanna kept Faythe's hand in hers. "What did they do? Or didn't do?"

"They stuck together in what seemed like the perfect marriage until I graduated from high school. The day after graduation, my mother moved to a condo in Manhattan. My father sold our house in the suburbs and moved to Florida."

"The day after? What about you?"

"I was already signed up to work at a summer camp with kids. My parents assumed I would be cared for there until I went onto college." Faythe sighed. "And I was. I had a good summer, full of distractions, and learned tons about kids, especially young teenagers. I also learned I wasn't the only kid from a broken home."

"Still, it must've been a shock." The understanding in Deanna's eyes made Faythe want to curl up against her shoulder again and simply be held. She had forgotten all about *Miss Pettigrew* and focused solely on Deanna's husky voice and the guarded kindness in her eyes.

"It was. But not as much as the way they've acted during the last ten years." Faythe cringed. Her words sounded so stilted. "I shouldn't be shocked. I've seen worse in the media realm and show business since then."

"What happened?" Deanna laced her fingers between Faythe's, sending pleasurable vibrations up her arm.

"They decided to make up for lost time." Faythe shrugged. "Both my parents began to hook up with multiple partners—some overlapping, some even simultaneous. Though I'm free-spirited, their behavior still bothered me so much that my mother called me a prude in public." Faythe smiled joylessly. "Imagine living the suburban idyllic existence one week and then having your parents turn into completely different people, dating individuals even younger than you are. When I asked them if my entire childhood and adolescence had been a lie, they admitted it was. It was that important to them to keep up appearances while I was still under age. Once I was on my own, they went through some freaking metamorphosis." Faythe moved closer to Deanna, seeking comfort in her body's warmth. Deanna was wearing her trademark knitted gray sweater, and the worn yarn was soft to the touch.

"They have an unusual moral code," Deanna said. "Parents do things we never thought they would, that's for sure."

"Oh, sorry. I'm just blabbering about myself. I should be asking you—" Faythe tried to sit up, wanting to look into Deanna's eyes.

"Hush. You're fine. Relax." Deanna held Faythe in place against her side and tucked her closer. "Are you in contact with your parents?"

"Yeah, every week. They do love me, but it's embarrassing when they're either on the rebound from a lover ten to twenty years younger, or if they're caught cheating. Still, my mother is back with Chester, who's not *that* much younger. She really seems to like him." Faythe shuddered. "She wants to spend a few days with me here."

"With Chester? Could be interesting."

"Not sure. Probably. Why would that be interesting?" Faythe managed to tilt her head back and was only a breath away from Deanna's lips.

"You can ascertain if this Chester is made of the right stuff. You're an interviewer, right? You're used to reading people, feeling them out."

"Well…yes."

"You probably have a really good eye for anyone trying to pull a fast one on you."

"Usually. Actually, I do have a good eye for people who aren't on the up-and-up. Good radar, you could say." Was it her imagination or had Deanna stiffened? Faythe patted Deanna's thigh reassuringly. "Just like I feel that you're a good person."

"You do?" Deanna's voice sounded oddly strangled.

"Yes." Faythe moved her hand to cup Deanna's neck. "And I *think* I have you pegged as being just like me." She massaged the tense muscles under the black hair. "Am I way off base to think that you're a lesbian?"

❖

Deanna had guessed that Faythe was gay, but hadn't counted on her directness. *I should have known she'd be this up front. She hasn't been anything but open since I pulled her out of the water.*

"No." Her throat ached too badly to say more. Deanna stared at the unwatched movie still running on the TV.

Faythe slid her hand down to Deanna's chin and forced her to look into her eyes. "Are you okay with it? I haven't put my foot in my mouth, have I?" She didn't see any judgment, only kindness and something that very much resembled desire.

"Yes, I'm all right. I've been out for a long time. Just not…eh… dating, right now."

"Bad experiences?"

"You could say that."

Faythe caressed Deanna's jawline, making her shiver. "I'm not dating either. It's been…let me see… Goodness, it's been more than a year since I even went to a restaurant or a movie with anyone."

"Really. You should have a lot of opportunities to find exciting dates, considering the circles you move in." Deanna couldn't imagine anyone passing up the chance to spend time with Faythe. But Faythe's face darkened.

"It can be a pretty superficial world. I get enough shallowness when I deal with my parents." Faythe sat up and Deanna let her go, straightening up at her end of the couch too.

"I'm sorry. I never meant to imply that you—"

"No, no. It's all right. I can understand that show biz seems like the proverbial smorgasbord for anyone not in the business." Faythe's broad smile contradicted the dark clouds in her eyes. "And I admit, if casual sex was all I was after, I wouldn't have to look far for a temporary lover. Those days are over for me, though."

"Just so you know," Deanna said, then wrapped an arm around Faythe and held her firmly against her shoulder, "the words 'superficial' and 'shallow' don't apply to you. I'm a pretty good judge of character—these days." Deanna clenched her teeth after the last telltale sentence, hoping Faythe wouldn't latch on to it.

"I...sometimes I wonder," Faythe whispered. "I messed around a bit in college, after my parents' divorce, but when I figured out I was mimicking their behavior, I pulled myself together. Still, I did run with the in crowd, and we got into quite a bit of trouble before I saw the light."

"And when you saw the light?"

Faythe sighed, her body softening against Deanna's. "I told myself I wasn't meant to have a relationship. The short ones were unfulfilling, and obviously I don't have the right genetic makeup for a long-term one." The wistful tone in her voice belied the casualness of her words.

Deanna wanted to object, but something desolate in Faythe's eyes stopped her. She disagreed wholeheartedly. No one was more suited for a long, healthy, happy relationship than Faythe. *Unlike me. She doesn't realize it, but she's way out of my league.*

Indulging in a moment of guilty pleasure, Deanna held Faythe as the movie played on. This was more than she could hope for, and she was too spellbound by Faythe to pass up the opportunity.

CHAPTER ELEVEN

Deanna cursed her old car, specifically the radiator that was threatening to boil over unless she drove with the heater on max. The warm Indian-summer day made it too hot to risk driving to the neighboring town to buy groceries, like she usually did. She would have to pull on her emotional armor and go into Grantville with its potential whispers and comments. She felt queasy.

The large Stop'n Shop was preferable to the smaller ones in the center of town. In fifteen minutes her old Saab hiccupped and nearly jumped into the parking lot. She stayed in her car for a few minutes, telling herself she needed to make sure the radiator didn't burst. Eventually she got out, locked the car, and grabbed an abandoned shopping cart. As she pushed it toward the entrance, she ignored the impulse to pull up the hood of her gray sweatshirt jacket.

It was early. Relieved not to see many shoppers, Deanna focused on the list she'd put together last night when she couldn't sleep. During the three days since she'd spent the evening with Faythe, their interplay was constantly on her mind. But she couldn't let thoughts of how Faythe felt in her arms slow her down. Deanna moved quickly through the aisles and thought she would escape when she spotted trouble ahead.

Three young women stood at the end of the cereal aisle, blocking her way. Glancing back, Deanna refused to take another route to the cash registers. Instead she jutted her chin out, determined to sail by them.

As she approached them, a small blonde spotted her and whispered loudly, "It's her. It's Ms. Moore! Savannah!"

Savannah turned her head and seemed like she wanted to

hide behind her river of black hair. Her deep-set gray eyes looked apprehensive. "Ms. Moore."

Deanna wasn't sure if Savannah was greeting her or gasping in dismay.

"Savannah. Ladies." She was coolly pushing the cart by the girls, when one of them, a tall, gangly brunette, snickered.

"Must be harder to pick up girls when you're self-employed and nobody wants to talk to you, eh, Ms. Moore?"

"What?" Deanna pivoted and stepped back toward the girls, putting a hand on her hip. "Lara, isn't it?"

"Yes." Lara looked defiant.

"Care to repeat that to my face?" Deanna spoke in a low voice, knowing how ominous she sounded. Frankly, it was a relief to confront someone rather than have them gossip and snicker behind her back.

Lara glanced at her friends, apparently reluctant to meet Deanna's eyes. "You know what I mean. After you broke Savannah's heart, you *should* have lost your job. It's not right for a teacher to pull something like that. You used your position."

As dead wrong as Lara was, she showed more guts and misguided loyalty than any of the grown-ups she'd come across since the incident.

"Care to comment, Savannah?" The young woman Deanna turned to was pale. "No? I can't correct the facts that Lara bases her assumptions on, can I?"

"What's she talking about, Savvie?" Lara looked bewildered.

"Let's get out of here. I can get this stuff later." Savannah tugged at Lara's sleeve. "Bye, Ms. Moore."

Lara seemed rooted in place. "Wait a minute." She seemed to sense something, her intelligent eyes narrowing. "Savvie?"

"Let's just go, Lara. Please?"

"Okay." Lara placed a protective arm around Savannah's shoulders, and Deanna stood motionless as the three young women abandoned their baskets and hurried through an unmanned cash register. Lara glanced back once, the hostile expression changed to one of confusion.

As Deanna paid for her groceries she couldn't shake the sensation that something important had happened. She wished she could talk to Faythe about it. That was impossible, though, because it meant pulling every sordid detail out into the open, and Deanna didn't want to tarnish their relationship. Friendship, she corrected herself. Faythe was not interested in relationships. *And I'm not exactly the catch of the year.*

Deanna was hoisting the heavy bags into the trunk when a voice startled her. "Ms. Moore. Deanna?" When Deanna turned, Savannah Mueller stood four feet away, tugging at the sleeves of her cashmere sweater. Deanna remembered the familiar sign that she was nervous.

"What do you want, Savannah?" Deanna stowed the last bag. "You know, if anyone, especially your friends, see you talking to me—"

"They drove back to Lara's place in her car. I came in my own." Savannah cleared her throat and continued breathlessly. "I'll be quick." Savannah took a tentative step closer. "I know this isn't the place, but I really need to talk to you."

"You and your mother have caused me a lot of trouble. You're actually the last person I want to talk to. Ever." Deanna wasn't in the mood for a heart-to-heart with Gloria Mueller's daughter.

"I know." Savannah's eyes filled with tears, and Deanna thought she saw true remorse, mixed with something resembling panic. "It's just…I don't have anybody else to turn to."

"You belonged to the most popular clique in high school." Deanna snorted. "Surely those gorgeous young ladies that you used to hang with would be there for you in a heartbeat?"

"I don't want to talk to Lara or Brandy. They wouldn't understand."

"Or you would look less like Ms. Popular in their eyes? They're still devoted to you, their born leader, aren't they?"

"Ms. Moore. Please. Won't you just hear me out? I'm begging you," Savannah whispered, even paler now.

"I don't know." Frustrated, and wanting to retain her anger toward this spoiled brat, Deanna shoved a hand through her hair. She couldn't ignore Savannah's obvious distress. "I don't want you coming to my cabin," Deanna said sternly.

"I won't." Savannah reached into her purse and handed over a pink business card. "Here. It's my cell-phone number. If you figure out a way to see me, just text me. I should go. Don't wait too long. It's really important." Savannah hurried toward a Miata as pink as the business card and drove off.

Deanna tucked the card in her back pocket and got into her car. The engine had cooled some and started willingly. Knowing how fast the radiator started to boil, she put the heater on max again. With the windows down, it was bearable inside the car, though still a bit hot. When the mechanical issues couldn't keep Savannah and her pleading out of Deana's mind, she tried to imagine why Savannah was so adamant about seeing her. Two years ago, she had begged to see Deanna too, but under very different, upsetting circumstances.

As she drove home, her mood sank below freezing as she relived some of the humiliation. Seeing Savannah, no matter how pitiful she looked when she nearly cried in the parking lot, would obviously be a mistake.

❖

Faythe looked up from her laptop, amazed. She hadn't taken a break for coffee, let alone lunch. She stood from the couch where she'd been sitting with the laptop resting on her knees. Her shoulders were stiff and her joints sore. Hard work certainly had its disadvantages.

She hadn't slept well the last few days, but her writing was going better than she expected. Faythe entered the kitchen and opened the fridge, then stared at the empty shelves. "But I went shopping." Ah, Faythe thought. That was several days ago. She'd had a great appetite after she came to stay by the lake, but the last days had been about writing, not eating. That had to change. She glanced at her watch. Six thirty. It would be dark before she finished grocery shopping, if she went out.

She looked longingly at Deanna's lights. It might be coincidental that she had been so productive since her movie date with Deanna, but she didn't think so. She had woken up the next day rested and full of ideas that begged to be written down. She'd written six ideas for proposals and one novel synopsis. *Even my fingertips ache.* She'd never quite pictured herself as a nonfiction writer, but the storyline about an old man's journey through to his hometown, and the lives he touched and forever changed, had come to her when she sat down to write something completely different.

Reluctantly, Faythe had started to type the words as they entered her mind, and once she was done, two hours later, she read through a synopsis neither she nor anyone else would ever have pegged her writing. The old man in the story felt so real to her; Faythe was dying to see if she could expand the eight pages of the synopsis into a novel-length story. She had connected so deeply with the character that it was with grief she'd finally closed the laptop and rubbed her aching hands. How she'd love to find the ability within herself to bring that story to some readers. She had a fan base who loved her morning show, and some of them might be faithful enough to buy a book by her. Nobody at the network or any of her family members or friends would expect something like this. *Not even I think I can really write like that.* And still, she had de facto written the synopsis, the first step to completing the story.

Faythe shook her head and opened the door to the patio. Soft jazz was barely audible from behind the trees. Faythe squinted and thought she could see a faint outline of someone moving about in Deanna's cabin. Impulsively, she yanked her windbreaker off the hanger and stepped outside.

The autumn wind was warmer than usual, even at this hour, and Faythe didn't bother to zip her jacket. She hurried between the trees, stopping only when she was ten feet from Deanna's deck. Suddenly self-conscious and hesitant, she shifted where she stood, not sure what she would say if she knocked on the door.

"Faythe?" Deanna's voice, coming from behind her, startled Faythe and she spun around too quickly.

"Deanna!" Pressing her hand against her chest, Faythe was sure she looked silly.

"Are you okay?" Deanna stepped closer, looking concerned.

"I'm fine. Actually, I just thought I'd pop over and say hello. Um, I mean, I heard the music, and we haven't really spoken since…well, since movie night." An annoying blush warmed Faythe's cheeks.

"Come inside." Deanna gestured toward her cabin. "I'm microwaving some interesting stuff from Lean Cuisine, and I have enough for two, if you're hungry."

"Starving, actually." Faythe was relieved she wasn't making a big deal out of her unannounced arrival. Inside, the music wrapped around everything, creating a cozy atmosphere.

"I was planning to have my dinner on the couch. That all right with you?"

"Sure thing." Faythe stopped in the doorway to the kitchen. "Anything I can do?"

"If you'd grab two glasses over there, and some mineral water from the fridge, that'd be great." Deanna nodded at one of the top cabinets.

"On it." Faythe carried the items to the coffee table and sat down. Deanna joined her with two plates of steaming pasta, and Faythe's stomach growled in delight.

"Hungry, eh? Me too." Deanna handed Faythe one of the plates and eyed her as she wolfed down the food. "What've you been up to?" The question was casual, but her eyes were not. Nearly black, they bore into Faythe's, as if she was looking for the ultimate truth.

"Writing, mainly." Faythe tried to sound equally laid back, but couldn't because her heart pounded harder and faster at the sight of Deanna sprawled next to her on the couch.

"Anything you can share yet?"

"Just tidbits. Anything and everything that comes into my head, but not worth sharing, really. I mean, it's so fragmented that only I can make any sense of it. Whatever happened between us during movie night seemed to unblock me." Aghast at how openly she spoke about that evening, Faythe tried for a quick save. "I mean, we cleared the air a bit, didn't we?"

"A bit." Deanna nodded. "We also complicated things."

"You regret that we snuggled." Faythe groaned at her vocabulary. *Jeez, that sounded really mature. Not.*

"No, no." Deanna looked surprised. "That was the best part. As I told you, it's been a while." She grabbed the bottle and poured them some mineral water. "The closeness…felt great."

Stunned by Deanna's unexpected openness, Faythe relaxed. She finished eating and placed her plate on the coffee table before scooting closer to Deanna. "You look like you have something on your mind," she said when she noticed Deanna's distracted expression.

"Just a lot going on."

"And I'm obscuring your path, aren't I?"

"Yes." Deanna spoke softly, clearly wanting to take the sting out of her one-syllable answer.

"I should feel sorry, I suppose."

"No need." Deanna put her plate away also and took another sip of water.

Faythe brushed an errant drop of water off Deanna's chin, her thumb caressing her lower lip in the process. "You're gorgeous." She spoke before her mind could edit her tongue and saw from Deanna's two rapid blinks how her words surprised her. "Well, you are," she murmured.

"Thank you." Deanna looked a bit shell-shocked and drank more water. "I'm not sure how you could possibly find anyone as grumpy and aloof as me attractive."

"Eclectic taste in women?" Faythe suggested whimsically and laughed as Deanna choked on her next sip. "Sorry."

"You're not in the least sorry." Deanna put her glass back on the coffee table and reached for Faythe with lightning-fast hands. Suddenly Faythe was on Deanna's lap, with her strong arms around her waist. "You little minx."

Faythe lost what little was left of her breath. Deanna's hands burned through her white cotton shirt, and surely she wasn't imagining that they moved in small circles against her? Faythe's eyes began to close, and she barely pulled herself together enough to keep from moaning in bliss.

"Faythe." Somehow, Deanna's teasing voice had grown deeper and now sounded just how melted dark chocolate tasted.

"Yes."

"Look at me."

Faythe struggled to open her eyes and gazed at Deanna, whose eyes were dark blue pools of turbulent emotion. "Looking. As I said, gorgeous."

"Oh." Deanna groaned and cupped Faythe's shoulders. "This is crazy."

"I just want to kiss you," Faythe said, squinting as she focused on Deanna's caressing hands that massaged her in the same slow circles. "And don't stop. I really like your hands."

"You do?"

"Yup." Faythe moved near to kiss Deanna and frowned when she withdrew from reach.

"That can be very dangerous," Deanna said.

"I'm not afraid." Faythe smiled before she saw the stark seriousness in Deanna's eyes. "Really, Deanna. I'm not. I just want...*need* to kiss you."

"What if it turns into something more? Something you're bound to regret." Deanna trembled against Faythe.

"I'm a big girl. You don't have to look out for me." She was becoming uncertain even though she desired Deanna. "But maybe you're trying to let me down easy, and I'm too dense to realize it." The thought hadn't occurred to Faythe until now, but that would explain some of Deanna's reluctance.

Smiling broadly to mask her hurt and embarrassment, Faythe began to slide back to her corner of the couch. "Well, no harm done, then." Her constricting rib cage hurt, as did the big lump in her throat as she tried to swallow. Faythe kept her professional demeanor firmly in place. "Silly me."

"Stop it," Deanna whispered huskily, and held her tight on her lap. "You must know that I'm beyond attracted to you. Your laughter, your amazing eyes, your body, and your sweetness." Deanna buried her face against Faythe's neck. "You don't understand. I'm trying to protect you."

"Protect me? From what? From yourself?" Faythe smoothed Deanna's hair because no matter what, she needed to keep touching her.

"Yes." Deanna breathed deeply a few times. "My reputation isn't the best in this town. You may already have heard some of the gossip. I'd be surprised if you hadn't."

"Some."

"Ah." Deanna nodded slowly and only the faintest slump in her shoulders betrayed that Faythe's admission affected her. "I'm not sure what you've heard, but it started two years ago and the gossip is still alive and kicking, so this could backfire."

"Because I'm a familiar face?"

"Trust me. This is a career stopper." Deanna stroked Faythe's cheek. "It was for me."

"Did something happen today that brought this to the surface?" Deanna gave her a startled look.

"How could you possibly know?"

"It's out of character for you to open up like this, so I figured something happened."

Deanna studied Faythe's face in such detail she felt a slow blush permeate her cheeks. "Yes. A former student asked to talk to me, in private, even though she knew it would get both of us into trouble if anyone found out."

"So, I take it this student was part of the original 'sin' that started the gossip in the first place."

"You assume correctly."

"And why does she want to talk to you? And when?"

"Don't know. ASAP."

The short sentences didn't help clarify anything. Faythe backtracked to what Kitty-with-a-heart had said. "Someone mentioned immoral behavior. Did they accuse you of having an affair with a student?"

"Yes. And no."

"Could you elaborate? I don't understand."

"Savannah told her friends that she and I were lovers, that we used the office in the high school art studio for our romantic trysts." Deanna pulled back and pushed Faythe off her lap. Tucking her legs up underneath her, she continued. "She also told them that I seduced her and that we planned to elope to Canada. Needless to say, her parents— the mayor and his wife—were less than pleased. They started a vendetta against me, the local press even ran the story, and I resigned."

CHAPTER TWELVE

Deanna rinsed their plates, not sure how she'd ended up in the kitchen so fast. One minute, she was sitting with Faythe on the couch, spilling everything she'd promised herself not to stain their friendship with, and now she was standing by the sink with her back to Faythe. Thoughts careened back and forth in her aching head, and she wanted to grab her jacket and get out of the cabin. *Just to breathe.*

"Need help?" Faythe's soft voice merely sounded friendly in a non-committal way.

"No. Thanks. I've got it." Unable to speak other than in staccato, Deanna wiped her hands and turned around, determined not to act like a coward. She met Faythe's eyes without blinking. "So. There you have it."

"I want to hear your side of it." Faythe was propped against the door frame, looking calm, though a bit guarded.

"Why? Nobody's ever asked for my version of the truth." Two years' worth of anger simmered just beneath the surface, and Deanna could taste it as she spoke. It wasn't fair to take it out on Faythe, but she was the only one here.

"Often things aren't quite as they seem. I've learned that by conducting hundreds of interviews. If I look at this situation logically, I see clear discrepancies between what I know about you and what you just told me about this Savannah girl." Faythe didn't sound casual and sweet-natured. Her vocabulary and her voice quality had changed. Deanna guessed this was how the professional Faythe sounded when she entered people's breakfast nook from their TV screens. Professional, articulate, shrewd, and stunningly beautiful.

"Guess this wasn't what you had in mind when you showed up on my doorstep, huh?" Deanna motioned toward the coffee machine on the countertop. "Coffee?"

"Yes, please. We could probably both use a mug." Faythe sat down at the small table by the window overlooking the lake. The moon was filtering rays of pale blue light between the maples and creating shimmering sparkles on the water. Deanna was in no mood to appreciate the breathtaking beauty, but sat down across from Faythe.

"Just tell me, Deanna," Faythe said quietly. "It's about time you told someone."

"It's not that easy." Deanna followed a scratch in the old oak table with her index finger. "It's not just about me."

"This isn't an interview." Faythe squeezed Deanna's hand. "It's not even an off-the-record thing. I'm not sitting here in my professional capacity. I'm just me now."

"All right." Deanna could actually feel energy stream from Faythe's hand. She wasn't comfortable with showing any sign of neediness, but clung to Faythe with cold fingers. "I moved here nine years ago, for family reasons. The first two years I barely supported myself as an illustrator, then got a job as an arts teacher at Grantville High School. I loved working with the kids, especially the ones in junior high. I managed to keep my career as an illustrator going at the same time, and everything seemed to fall into place."

"Until…"

"Until two years ago when Savannah Mueller began her senior year. We're talking homecoming queen, the mayor's daughter, the captain of the cheerleader team. And a terrific student, always on the honor roll. Little Ms. Perfect."

"Sounds unbearable," Faythe said. "Go on."

"Actually, Savannah was a nice kid. She was usually far more levelheaded than her mother. I never saw the trouble coming. I really didn't." Deanna rose to get the coffee, but sat down again when Faythe pressed a steady hand on her shoulder.

"I'll get it." She brought two steaming mugs and headed to the fridge for some milk. "Okay, where were we? Oh, that's right. Little Ms. Perfect. Nice girl. Then what?"

"Savannah developed a crush on me. I could tell early on, and she wasn't the first girl to idolize me, so I took it in stride and treated her kindly, but no different than anyone else. I told myself it was a normal, passing-phase thing." Deanna cupped her hands around the mug, warming them, but found it lacking compared to the comfort of Faythe's hands. "As it turned out, I was wrong."

"She pursued you?" Faythe rested her chin in her palm.

"Savannah was probably used to *being* pursued, rather than the other way around. She started out by making herself useful—carrying equipment, cleaning brushes, putting up chairs at the end of the day. When I didn't take the bait, she stepped it up a notch by convincing her parents to invite me to different functions, benefits, that sort of thing, trying to get me involved.

"At first I was impressed when I realized how many charities her mother was head of. It took me a while to understand that Gloria Mueller was not acting out of the goodness of her heart, but because she wanted to be the queen bee. She ran those charities like they were her kingdoms and the employees and other volunteers were her loyal subjects. When I discovered what was happening, I bowed out. That's when Savannah began her siege.

"She seemed devastated that I wasn't impressed enough to keep going to the meetings. One day she stayed after class and burst into tears, clinging to me, telling me that she loved me and that she couldn't bear to be without me." Deanna tried to smile, but her lips trembled too much. "I was shocked. A schoolgirl crush I could deal with, but these raw emotions, the despair. I guess I handled the situation badly."

"What did you do?" There was no judgment in Faythe's voice.

"I told her that what she felt wasn't love. I gave her the generic speech about how common it is for a young person to idolize a teacher, a role model." Deanna shrugged. "Savannah didn't take it very well. I chalked that up to her being a spoiled only child to wealthy, influential parents. I was obviously dead wrong."

"What happened?"

"She was crushed. She'd told her best friends about 'us' and, I suppose, turned some of her wishful thinking into 'facts.' They truly believed that she and I were lovers. Later, Savannah told them that we wanted to elope to Canada, to get married."

"Oh, Jesus."

"Yes. I was shocked. And angry. I lashed out at her, telling her there was no 'us,' and never would be. I explained that I thought she was a nice kid, but that was it. I wasn't in love with her, and it wasn't going to happen."

"Oh, Deanna."

"I know. I broke her heart. And she reacted the only way she knew how. Revenge." Deanna closed her eyes and felt Faythe take her hands and remove the coffee mug. She opened her eyes when Faythe pulled her up from the chair and guided her to the couch. There, she sat down and tugged at Deanna, making her sit next to her, wrapping them both with a blanket.

"You looked so cold. Better?"

"Yes. Thank you." Deanna allowed the warmth of Faythe's body to permeate hers before she continued. Talking about this no longer seemed a choice, but a necessity. "Suddenly, it wasn't just Savannah's best friends who knew about 'us.' Everybody, students and faculty alike, thought that I had seduced my most beautiful pupil and more or less left her at the altar. I wasn't even out at work, then. But I thought, naïve as I was, that the faculty would realize how preposterous this accusation was.

"I was shocked when I realized they'd swallowed everything Savannah dished out—hook, line, and sinker. She didn't have to act heartbroken. She was. But she used her pain to nail me, and once her mother got involved, I was history. It only took Gloria a week to get the word out. Remember, she had all these connections and ran all the major charities and events *and* was the mayor's wife. Her word in Grantville, was, and still is, the law, even if her husband isn't the mayor anymore. So I quit."

"Why? You could have fought them. They didn't have any evidence."

"Oh, but they thought they knew what happened. No smoke without fire, right? And when my colleagues found out, I imagine the fact that I'm a lesbian and that Savannah *confessed* to such a thing made it very plausible. Why would anyone admit to a lesbian affair, which they considered such a stigma, if it wasn't true? Why subject yourself to that kind of gossip?"

"I see. So Savannah had them all believing you bedded her, then abandoned her and broke her heart."

"The school's board of directors called an emergency meeting. They assured all the concerned parents and local media that they had launched an investigation, which was a lie. They'd already made up their minds. The hidden message was that they would make sure that no sexual predator—that would be me," Deanna said, laughing bitterly, "would ever be able to prey on any of Grantville High's pupils again."

"They said that? I can't believe it."

"Oh, did I forget to mention that Gloria Mueller is a member of the public and private school boards, as well as the PTA?"

"Ah. I see. Know thine enemy." Still, Faythe realized that she didn't fully understand. "Something is off. You could have fought this, tooth and nail. It's as if they've got a hold on you."

"You're very perceptive. I should've realized." Deanna shook her head, twisting the edge of the blanket. She squeezed her eyes shut, wrinkles marring her forehead. "I *can't* tell you. Not everything. I've told you more than I've confided in anyone."

"I see." Faythe looked at Deanna with concern, and Deanna wondered what was going through her head. "You obviously have your reasons, strong ones, but you have to understand that it sounds strange. It's out of character that you didn't sue everyone for slander and defamation of character. Your silence must've made you look guilty in everyone's eyes. When I listen to my gut instinct, I can't believe you'd prey on a young girl. No way." Faythe sighed. "I mean, I've heard family members and neighbors of people accused of such things state the same thing, that their loved one would never prey on anyone, that they must be innocent—"

"And then it turned out they were guilty after all." Deanna shrugged. "Can't blame you if you think I'm lying through my teeth. If you think it's possible I could seduce young teens and promise them marriage in Canada—" Deanna went rigid, pushing the blanket half off. Stupid tears ran down her cheeks and tremors reverberated throughout her and made her hands shake, but she refused to even blink when she looked at Faythe. She was caught in this web of lies, but she would not give anyone the satisfaction of breaking down completely. *Show no fear.*

"So, what kept you in Grantville after you were ostracized?" Faythe was obviously not giving up.

"Everyone expected me to, *wanted* me to move as far away from Grantville as possible."

"Why didn't you?" Faythe gently pushed Deanna's hair back

from her face. The touch meant more to Deanna than Faythe could ever guess.

"Because of Miranda, my sister. I could never leave her behind. She's a student at a facility in this town for children with special needs. She depends on me. That's all I can tell you." Deanna's eyes begged Faythe not to force the issue.

"And it's not enough for me to understand. I can't connect the dots between you succumbing to slander, to sacrificing yourself like that for your sister." Faythe took both of Deanna's hands under the blanket. "But you saved my life and I owe you the benefit of the doubt. Still, I can't help you with this new situation with Savannah if you don't keep me in the loop."

"Oh, God. Savannah. I haven't spoken to her, or she to me, for two years. I saw her at the supermarket and she wants to talk to me."

"Really?" Faythe looked surprised. "Any guess as to why?"

"No idea. She seemed genuinely concerned about something and looked very different from the cheerleader teen she was two years ago. Obviously something's going on."

"Any chance of an apology? Preferably a public one with a chance to clear your name."

"Perhaps. But it seemed more than that. And it scares me. If anyone finds out that we've spoken, even in passing, I'm afraid everything will be like it was two years ago. People still hate my guts, and occasionally I run into someone who feels the right to give me a piece of their mind. But compared to how it was back then…" Deanna leaned her head back against the couch. "I suppose everything is relative."

"It sure is." Faythe sucked her lower lip in. "Let me think. Since you're actually considering listening to this misguided young woman, you shouldn't do it here at your house, or in public."

"No, no."

"A motel room sounds even worse."

"Faythe." Deanna winced. "I can't see how we could possibly arrange it."

"Don't you think you owe it to yourself, or to Miranda?"

"In some ways you're right—"

"And you won't tell me in what ways I'm wrong." Rubbing the back of her head, Faythe messed up her hair completely. "Listen. Aunt

Nellie's house might be a good option. I know it's close to your property, but nobody knows that we're friends."

"I can't let you risk *your* reputation like that."

"You're not. You're risking Aunt Nellie's." Faythe wrinkled her nose. "And she's too rich to care. Not even the Gloria Muellers of this world have any impact on Nellie."

"But—"

"No buts." Holding up her hand, Faythe suddenly looked stern in a way Deanna hadn't seen before. "If you decide to find out what she wants, then tell her you can meet at my house and that I'll witness what you two say. I won't have her try to trap you into something worse than she got you into in the first place."

Deanna stared at Faythe. "You—you really seem to believe in me."

"I really do want to believe in you, Deanna."

"Okay, I'll think about your offer. Thank you." Deanna clutched Faythe's hands. "It's been so long since anyone even considered taking my side."

"It bothers me that nobody stood up for you."

"It hurt me for the longest time that my so-called friends among the faculty turned their backs on me so readily. Back then I didn't know what Gloria was capable of." Deanna knew she was explaining too much and cut herself off. "Let's just say I understood why they couldn't—I mean, didn't dare to support me. Neither of them wanted to risk losing their jobs. If you cross Gloria Mueller, it's damn hard to find a new employer in this town within the educational system. It wasn't their fault any more than it was mine." Deanna tried to speak in a matter-of-fact way, but knew her pain still shone through.

"Remember where I used to work," Faythe said softly. "Public opinion doesn't sway me very easily, probably since journalists are experts at putting spin on things."

"Thank you." Deanna slumped back. "I'm so tired."

"Me too. Intense conversations can wear you out."

"Well, try imagining the first intense conversation in more than two years. I'm out of practice."

CHAPTER THIRTEEN

Deanna looked at the pink business card Savannah had given her. At first she had merely tucked it away. Of the many conflicting emotions that flooded her system, anger was the strongest. She was about to tear the silly card in two and forget the whole painful thing when she stopped. The card had a small tear at the top edge, but the phone numbers were intact underneath the swirly font that spelled out Savannah Mueller, Customer Service, Grantville Animal Shelter. *She's working? She didn't go to college?*

Curiosity overshadowed her anger, and she tried to figure out why a young woman from wealthy and politically ambitious parents worked at an animal shelter. Savannah's parents certainly had the funds and the connections to send her to any of the Ivy League universities. Deanna thought about their encounter the day before and what it had ultimately led to when Faythe came over. She tucked the business card away since she wasn't ready to decide what to do and walked over to the couch to fold the blanket she and Faythe had huddled under. Faythe's scent lingered on the fabric, its clean freshness reminding her of oranges and ginger. She inhaled deeply, then caught herself and placed the blanket on the armrest. She had a lot to do today, and she couldn't waste time standing around feeling sentimental.

In the part of her cabin used as her studio, Deanna turned on the overhead light. She had many times dreamed of a loft condo or apartment with huge windows that let in the north light. Instead she'd settled for several blue-colored bulbs that mimicked north light passably. She placed a new sheet of paper on her workspace and made sure she'd sharpened her pencils. Sitting on her stool, she felt almost physically comforted by the feel of the pencil between her fingers. When she began to draw, she knew this would be a productive day. Bunny Buttercup and his friends seemed to appear out of nowhere and take up residence on her paper, and she felt genuinely happy as she added the details.

She couldn't wait to start blocking in the colors. It was like being a child with a coloring book again, and she loved that part as much as the drawing itself. The entire process was meditative, and this project had kept her going these last two years. The image of Gloria Mueller spewing her acidic words, her voice well articulated and refined, surfaced. Gloria supposedly came from humble beginnings, but marrying a much older man who became a successful politician paved the way for her own career as the First Lady of Grantville.

"To think I admired that woman," Deanna said. "And even tried to impress her once. Damn, I can be such a fool." She worked more focused with the pencil, forcing her frustration out of her body and mind. Working creatively like this could exorcise even the darkest feelings.

When her thoughts migrated to the topic of Faythe instead, Deanna's hands created the lovely forest around Bunny Buttercup, with intricate flowers and trees. She could still feel Faythe's soft, tender kiss on her cheek. It was meant as a kiss of support and friendship, but for the first time in years, Deanna experienced a clear element of desire. Faythe's external beauty was obvious, and to feel attracted to her was a healthy sexual reaction, but Deanna felt much more. Deanna was wary of several things about Faythe—her profession, coupled with her celebrity status, and her declaration that she wasn't relationship material. Deanna stopped drawing, her hand hovering a fraction of an inch above the paper. Why did Faythe prey on her mind so much? They weren't lovers, or even considering becoming such. Were they? *Am I?*

Deanna quickly drew a row of small mushroom streetlights that lined the forest path where it disappeared among the trees. No matter what, she needed to decide soon whether to call Savannah. Faythe would keep asking her about it, she was certain, and it really bugged Deanna that Faythe might think she was a coward. "Head-on," she whispered as she added fireflies to help light the mushrooms. "There isn't a helmet strong enough for that."

❖

"Suzy!" Faythe stared in surprise at her agent, who stood on her doorstep, chic and well coiffed as usual. Suzy Connelly was in her early fifties, but with the help of surgical augmentation and restoration, she looked like she was in her early thirties. Her hair short and chalk-white blond, Suzy always dressed in black, no matter the occasion, which suited her, even though her husband often complained about it, which Suzy ignored.

"I thought I'd stop by." Suzy beamed, hoisting her briefcase, which held all of Suzy's important documents in digital form, and some even in hard copy. Once Suzy had dropped her briefcase on Faythe's couch and the contents had spilled out. The most unexpected object, considering Suzy's laconic remarks about her husband and his traditional point of view, was an eleven-by-eight picture of him in a silver mesh frame.

"Stop by? Where are you going? You live in Manhattan, for heaven's sake."

Suzy grinned unabashedly. "Well, I have two reasons for being in the neighborhood. One is a great offer you simply can't refuse, and the other one is…Cornelia called me."

"My mother called?" Faythe realized she was starting to sound like a parrot. "Whatever for?"

"If you ask me inside, I might just tell you." Suzy looked pointedly behind Faythe. "It looks like a nice house."

"Oh, sorry. You surprised me." Faythe glanced at her watch. She had slept late, tired after her evening with Deanna. Something in her midsection suddenly glowed at the thought of how she and Deanna had sat so close on the couch. "Come in, Suzy."

Inside, she gave Suzy a tour of the house, knowing she would appreciate it, and finally they ended up in the kitchen where Faythe brewed fresh coffee. "Why don't you get to the point?" She wasn't being impolite. She and Suzy had always been candid with each other. Too many secrets in Faythe's family as she was growing up had made her demand it. Was that why she'd persuaded Deanna to tell her the truth? Or part of the truth. She still didn't have one major piece of the puzzle that was her neighbor.

"Faythe?" Suzy's voice broke through Faythe's musings. "You went vacant on me."

"Sorry," Faythe said again. "What were you saying?"

"God Almighty, you must be breathing too much fresh air out here," Suzy flicked her wrist, "in the sticks."

"Grantville, Vermont, is hardly the outback." Faythe snorted. *Trust a super-urban personality like Suzy to consider this beautiful place the sticks.*

"Whatever. I have the best news for you."

"You do."

"Yes. Yes." As if a genie had breathed new life into Suzy, her cheeks suddenly glowed and Faythe could have sworn that even her hair glistened more. "CNN wants you!"

"What?"

"You heard me." Suzy pulled out her BlackBerry. "Wait. Let me show you the e-mail. Hang on." She pressed several buttons, scrolled the wheel on the side of the phone, and mumbled impatiently as her eyes darted back and forth across the little screen. "Here." Suzy handed the phone to Faythe. CNN had approached Suzy when they heard she was on leave, asking if she was available or already contracted with a network.

"I can't believe it." Faythe scrolled quickly through the e-mail. "They want me to anchor a science program. Science? I'm not even comfortable with the subject as a layman."

"Bah! They've seen you conduct interviews on a *multitude* of subjects and are impressed with how well you do your research and work with your subject no matter what it is."

"I've done my share of crazy interviews." Faythe leaned back and stared at the ceiling, wishing the white boards could provide an answer. "Wow. How long do I have?"

"Two weeks."

"Two weeks. I suppose that's fair."

"They'll offer a terrific salary with tons of benefits and bonuses."

"How can you know this? The e-mail didn't mention anything about money." Faythe eyed Suzy suspiciously at Suzy. "Ah, I see. You were on the phone with someone you know at CNN within minutes."

"I'd be a poor agent if I wasn't." Suzy looked flattered. "So, my dear, you now have two options, and I bet we haven't seen the last of the offers. I know most of the headhunters personally, and they're all scurrying around like rabbits on speed, trying to scare up fresh faces for their slots."

Faythe was still trying to wrap her brain around this unexpected news. "I'm not sure about this." She tapped the BlackBerry's screen with her fingernail. "I've looked forward to shorter workdays with free time. I can't see that happening with a high-profile job in CNN's science section."

"Oh, you can do it." Suzy grabbed Faythe by both shoulders like she intended to shake some sense into her. "You're not happy if you're not working, Faythe. Remember you used to tell me how you dreaded going home to your empty condo after a day at work."

"Right. I *used* to think that. I used to feel nothing else mattered. I was wrong. That's why I'm here. You know that." Faythe recoiled, suddenly upset. Suzy obviously sensed she was pushing too hard and laughed animatedly.

"You'll just have to find a good balance. Now, on to the more delicate matter."

"My mother." Faythe was all for changing the subject, but perhaps not to the topic of her mother.

"Yes. She called me."

"Why would she do that? It's not like you're on each other's Christmas-card lists."

"I asked myself that very question. She was very sweet, asking me about my family, my parents. You know."

"Yes. She was brought up right, my mother." It was really funny to think that Cornelia, so busy living her own life and fulfilling her dream of the perfect partner, would take time away from "landing" Chester to approach Suzy. "So?"

"She's worried about you."

"Is she now?"

"Yes." Suzy squirmed in her seat, lacing and unclasping her fingers several times. As much as Faythe liked and trusted Suzy, she also knew she didn't have much patience and considered anything touchy-feely insufferable mush. "She wants me to talk some sense into you. Her words. She's afraid you'll give up fame and fortune." Suzy paused and took Faythe's hand. "Frankly, so am I. This thought of a vacation came on awfully quick. You're more than just a client to me, after all these years, Faythe. You can confide in me."

Faythe willed herself not to sigh out loud. "And I have. I've told you my motives. I'm not content being the happy-go-lucky morning anchor anymore. If I'm tossed into another interview with a person who's run with the bulls in Pamplona and now needs someone to pity him while he's in a freaking body cast, I'll shoot myself."

"God Almighty. All right, all right." Suzy let go of Faythe's hand. "I hear you. It's just that this transformation from loving your job to hating it came pretty quickly."

"For you. For my parents. But I suppose it's a good sign that they're actually listening at all." Still annoyed, Faythe drew a deep breath. "These feelings have been creeping up on me for a long time. Maybe two years."

"Two years. And you've never said anything?"

"The feelings weren't strong enough until now."

Suzy transformed from the typical eager agent to a pensive human being, intent on trying to understand. "You really are serious, aren't you?"

"I really am."

"I thought it was just a phase because you were bored." Suzy made a helpless gesture, palms up. "Several of my clients constantly need something new, something challenging, but when push comes to shove, they're back doing their soap, or their talk show, looking quite content."

"So you thought that was the case with me?"

"Yes." Suzy smiled gently, which altered her expression completely, and Faythe once again realized why Suzy's husband worshipped her. "But your mother is still up in arms, so to speak, and really concerned you might be making bad choices for all the wrong reasons."

"I'll explain to Mom. Again."

"You better, because she won't settle for hearing it from me." Suzy reached for Faythe's hand again. "So, my dear, favorite client. What's my new mission when it comes to you? I take it CNN is off the table."

"Yes. It is." Faythe squeezed Suzy's hand and knew this woman wasn't only out to make money. She was also a true friend. "As for my future, I have enough set aside to keep me in oatmeal for quite a while. I'm actually writing right now, trying out different styles and topics, to get my bearings. I haven't written long pieces in ages, and I need to get my feet wet. It's fun. It's difficult. But most of all, it's what I want…no, it's what I need to do."

"I can tell. Well, I'll be happy to research literary agents et cetera for you, as soon as you have something you want to show anyone. I have connections in that world, remember?"

"Guess it doesn't hurt to be married to a publisher, huh?" Faythe winked. "Smart move."

"My love for books brought us together."

"Your love of tall, dark, and handsome men brought you together." Faythe corrected her with a grin. "At least that's how your better half tells the story."

"Him? He's a notorious liar."

"Liar? So when he declared his undying love, he was lying?" Faythe raised an eyebrow, laughing at Suzy's wry look.

"He better not be." She glanced at her watch. "Oh, God Almighty, I've got to go. Another pit stop before turning the car around toward civilized territory."

Faythe was about to object, but quieted when she realized that nothing outside Manhattan would ever feel like anything but the boondocks to Suzy. "Drive safely," she said as they stood. "You never know what creatures you may run into this far from civilization."

"Funny." Suzy wrinkled her nose in a less than ladylike manner and snapped her enormous briefcase closed after tucking away her BlackBerry. "Actually, I have a date with my husband at a bed and breakfast in Barre."

"Oh, cool. Enjoy your stay. It's quite the cultural center." She doubted Suzy would see Barre that way, since she was the essence of a spoiled New Yorker, but Faythe had gone over to Barre many times as a child to attend the opera, among other things, with her aunt.

"Thanks. So I've heard."

They parted after a few more minutes of small talk and Faythe remained at the front door, letting the crisp autumn air into the house. "She must think I'm bonkers to give up such a dream job." She shook her head. *Maybe I'm acting like a spoiled brat, not wanting to play in the same playpen forever.* Faythe knew as soon as the thoughts appeared that this wasn't true. She wanted to write, and she wanted out of the media circus. Strengthened at the core of her being because she was being true to herself for the first time in years, she thought about the next topic close to her heart: Deanna. She hadn't heard from her since last night, but Deanna was probably in shock because she had lowered her guard. Faythe wondered if she would have to coax Deanna out of her foxhole again.

Closing the door to the now almost bright yellow trees, Faythe couldn't wait to get back to her laptop. She knew exactly what to write about.

Just as she flipped her laptop open, her cell phone rang and the display read "Ben." Curious what her father might want since he rarely called her unless he wanted to discuss something practical like money, she answered.

"Hi, Ben." Faythe never called him Dad anymore. Ben Hamilton had asked her to call him by his first name when she was a high school senior. Faythe had felt awkward about the request and wondered that first year if he was tired of being her dad. Ben kept reassuring her it was because her eighteenth birthday had come and gone, and she was an adult now, like him.

"Faythe, I've just heard from your mother. What the hell do you think you're doing?"

Chapter Fourteen

The pink business card lay tucked into the top drawer of the old oak dresser just inside the front door. Deanna glanced at the drawer every time she passed it. Sometimes she shuddered, but it also distracted her and made her pensive. The card represented so much hurt and fear that it was almost like a live entity.

She had worked two all-nighters and slept late, a habit she resorted to while under pressure of a deadline. "Or under any pressure." Deanna sharpened her pencils with a craft knife. She always worked better late evening and night. *I suppose that has to change if I ever strike it big and can afford that studio with the big windows. No use in having windows unless there's daylight.* Huffing at her own sarcastic words, Deanna returned to her work area. She'd nearly completed her illustrations and was surprised that she was far from tired of drawing the cute bunnies and their friends. She'd always wanted to make a name for herself as an avant-garde, edgy artist, and here she was painting rabbits with aprons and tool belts, and dressed as firemen and doctors. Deanna jumped as the phone rang.

"Hello."

"Hi. It's Faythe." Faythe's voice sounded off.

"Hi."

"I know it's late."

"No problem. I'm working late these days."

"Oh, you're working. I'm sorry."

"As I said. No problem." Deanna's thoughts whirled. What could be wrong? Last time they spoke, Faythe was the strong one, the nurturing of the two. Now her voice was stark, but with a certain frailty.

"I didn't want anything in particular, really." Faythe spoke hastily. "It can wait. I mean, I'll talk to you tomorrow. Or later in the week."

"Hey, wait a minute." Deanna thought quickly. "You got some cocoa?"

"Cocoa? Yeah. Why?"

"I'm out, and that's what I drink when I pull an all-nighter," Deanna lied, thinking she sounded completely lame. "And since you're up, and I'm up, and I plan to be up all night working, I figured I need some hot chocolate." *Damn, I'm babbling.*

"Oh. I see. All right." Faythe's staccato voice made Deanna wince, but at least she sounded approachable. "Want to come over here, or should I bring the cocoa?"

"I'm on my way." Deanna hung up and tossed her pencils to the side, then locked up and jogged along the moonlit path to Faythe's house. Only when she knocked on the back door did she realize that she'd passed the dresser for the first time since she tucked the card into the drawer without looking, or even thinking about it.

Faythe opened the door and motioned for Deanna to come in, her face hidden in the shadows. "Hi."

"Something's wrong." It wasn't a question because it was obvious.

"I'm fine." Faythe stalked out of the kitchen only to return. "Damn. Forgot to make hot chocolate." She flipped on a light and yanked a canister from a shelf. With equally jerky movements, she filled a glass pitcher with milk and placed it in the microwave. She stood there staring at the revolving pitcher, unmoving. "What am I forgetting?" she murmured.

"Mugs?" Deanna could see Faythe trembling and now she was really concerned.

"Mugs. Yeah. Good idea." Faythe placed two blue ceramic mugs on the counter. Suddenly she spun around, nailing Deanna with her green eyes. Like a cat's, they seemed fluorescent in the dim light.

"Faythe. What's wrong?"

"Wrong?" Faythe smiled, a professional, broad, and very white smile, which Deanna figured she'd perfected to use at work when her interview subject was not her forte. But in the setting of a cozy kitchen, the smile was almost scary.

Deanna knew better than to push verbally, but also saw how small

Faythe seemed in her oversized white T-shirt and black leggings. *She looks so cold.* Not thinking about any repercussions, she strode over to Faythe, who merely stared up at her. Taking her in her arms, Deanna merely held her as the microwave oven pinged and stopped revolving.

"Really, I'm fine." Faythe talked directly into Deanna's shoulder. "Honestly."

"I know you are." Deanna refused to let go. If she did, she might not get a second chance. "You're very fine."

"Deanna."

"Shh. I've been self-absorbed lately. Thinking of very little but myself and what's going on in my life. I never meant you couldn't share your feelings, your problems. Just give me a chance and I'll show you that I'm actually a good listener."

"I don't need a listener." Faythe stood rigid in Deanna's embrace. "I don't need any more words."

"I think you do. Something's got you worked up. What?"

"Please, Deanna. I know I called you, and I'm grateful that you popped right over. I know you made up the stuff about the cocoa." Faythe leaned her forehead against Deanna's shoulder. "I just don't want to talk."

"I won't make you." Deanna rocked Faythe gently. "But you'd be the first to tell me it's better to talk about things."

"I'm such a bitch."

Stunned, Deanna stopped rocking. "What?"

"I'm not exactly practicing what I'm preaching, am I?" Faythe sighed against Deanna, her warm breath penetrating Deana's sweater.

"I'm not sure. You'll have to tell me."

Faythe half laughed, half sobbed. "You just don't give up, do you?"

"No. Not in my nature."

"You'll think I made a mountain of a molehill, that I exaggerate and am totally oversensitive."

"There's no such thing as being oversensitive. Either you're sensitive or you're not."

They stood still in the kitchen, Faythe shielded in Deanna's embrace, until finally Faythe cleared her voice. "My mother is worried that I'm throwing my life and my career away."

"By taking time out?" Deanna tried to understand.

"Yes and no. My agent was here a few days ago, with a fabulous offer from CNN. I turned it down because it's the direct opposite of what I want. You know, long hours, no social life, no room for anything but work."

"I understand."

"So, my agent had an ace up her sleeve. My mom had called her. Suzy, that's my agent, is a pro and would never break confidentiality, but she delivered Mom's message."

"Which was?"

"Get your act together, or else. I'm kidding. She said she was concerned and asked Suzy to talk some sense into me."

"And that's when the CNN job showed up."

Faythe pushed away from Deanna a little. "Yes. I'm sure Suzy would have placed that on the table anyway—but it sure was timely."

"It was."

"And then someone else butted in. My father. Ben." Faythe's lips were a pale, fine line. "He's called every day for the last few days."

"Something tells me he wasn't calling to show his support."

"You're very astute." The sarcasm was obvious.

"Want to talk about it?" Deanna kept Faythe's hands in hers, reluctant to lose her touch.

"Oh, he agreed with Mom for the first time in over a decade. Told me just how worthless and stupid my career move is."

"Good Lord."

"Yes, and every day, he's become more agitated. I can't seem to do anything right these days. And it bothers me that I'm so upset! I'm a grown woman, for heaven's sake. I'm only accountable to myself. He's always been shallow, so I know better than to take his words seriously."

"But he's also your dad, whom you want to please and be praised by," Deanna said quietly.

"Yeah, that's what I figured, and that's why I told him about what I've been writing for nearly three days straight. I was so *sure* he'd be interested and excited, since I really do have a good idea for a book. I honestly thought he'd eventually see things my way and not be so hung up on my last glossy, glamorous job." Faythe grabbed a paper towel from a roll. "I should've known better, but I can be so damn naïve."

"What happened?" Deanna didn't let Faythe's reluctance bother her. She hugged her close and kissed her temple.

"He laughed. He laughed out loud and told me it was time to get my head out of the clouds. Saying that books like the one I want to write are boring and nobody reads such things anyway. He went on and on."

"Oh, honey." The term of endearment was out before Deanna could stop it.

"You must think I'm such a wimp." Faythe closed her eyes and drew a couple of deep breaths.

"I don't think that at all."

"It's just that everything he said confirmed my worst fears—that I should stick to what I know and not aim for the stars."

"You're embarking on a whole new voyage. It's only natural to feel intimidated." Stroking Faythe's back, Deanna thought about how different she felt while holding Faythe compared to comforting Miranda when she was upset.

She was out of her element, though, since she hadn't held anyone other than her sister in more than two years. She tried a rocking motion, which seemed to work. Faythe buried her face into Deanna's shoulder, whispering words nearly impossible to hear.

"I'm...silly...I should just...not give a shit." Faythe sounded exhausted.

"You're not silly." Deanna guessed that her father's daily phone calls had made her brood instead of sleep.

"Why do we always want our parents to validate us, no matter how old we get?" Faythe looked up at Deanna with tears in her eyes. "It's counterproductive!" Her beautiful face became even more so when her feelings radiated from it.

"I agree. I have some parental issues too." Deanna couldn't stop staring at Faythe and detected something beyond the obvious beauty, something unique. Faythe's innermost self seemed to be laid bare because she was so upset.

Faythe gazed back up at Deanna, apparently seeing something in Deanna's eyes that stunned her. "Deanna."

"Yes?"

"You're so good to me. And you're so beautiful."

The unexpected words made Deanna tremble. Faythe was so much better and beautiful than she was. Her hands trembled, and she steadied them by holding Faythe even closer. She stroked Faythe's back in slow circles, telling herself she was comforting her, but Faythe wasn't crying. The tears still clung to her eyelashes, and it felt far too good to touch her to be purely altruistic in motive.

"Deanna." Faythe whispered her name again. "I need to kiss you."

Fire erupted inside Deanna and she lowered her mouth to Faythe's. With incredible softness, and with a tenderness she never imagined possible, she pressed her lips against Faythe's, then slipped the tip of her tongue inside Faythe's mouth. Groaning, she tasted the sweetness of the woman in her arms, her name echoing in her head. *Faythe. Faythe.*

"Mmm, you taste so good," Faythe murmured into the kiss. "And you feel good, too." Her hands mimicked Deanna's movements on her back. She tucked her hands into Deanna's back pockets and pulled her closer. The kiss became hotter, deeper, and Deanna was dizzy from the onslaught of emotions. This was more than a physical reaction.

Deanna nudged Faythe backward and stopped only when they reached a closed door. Grateful for solid support, she held Faythe tenderly against the door, sliding her hands up and down her sides. She was dying to touch her breasts and to cup her sex so she could feel the heat through her leggings, but she didn't. Deanna didn't want Faythe to think she was some unfeeling brute out to score. Her own wetness flooded her sex, and when Faythe pushed against her, touching the front of Deanna's lower abdomen, she groaned and slid her lips down Faythe's neck.

"You feel so...you're so sexy, so beautiful." Deanna held Faythe by her waist, her thumbs just beneath her breasts.

"And you feel so right, so good." Faythe clung to Deanna's neck, inviting her to kiss her again by nipping at her lower lip. "I've wanted to do this for days and it feels better, *is* better, than I ever dreamed."

Deanna murmured agreement against Faythe's mouth. She'd watched Faythe's lips intently for what felt like an eternity. Now when she closed her mouth over Faythe's and ran her tongue inside the velvet lips, she knew this was not just any kiss or any woman.

Faythe's hands were in her hair now, holding Deanna close by lacing her fingers through it. Her eagerness and obvious arousal fueled

Deanna's desire, and she caressed Faythe's collarbones underneath her big T-shirt.

Suddenly Faythe grew still and slowly withdrew. She stared up at Deanna, her lips trembling and her nipples so hard they were clearly visible through the shirt. "I never thought I could feel this way, this much. You take my breath away."

"You drive me crazy when you look at me that way." Deanna smoothed Faythe's hair back from her face. "I'm sorry if I came on too strong." She was so winded it was hard to speak.

"No, no. You were just perfect. If I allowed my body to call the shots, I'd drag you to my bed right away."

"Really?" Deanna had to smile at the imagery. "What a sexy thought."

"Sexy thoughts about a sexy woman." Faythe didn't look haunted or upset anymore. Instead she had a gleam in her eye that was hard to decipher.

Deanna suspected that she had a similar look. She hugged Faythe close, afraid to kiss her again because she knew it would be a mistake. She had no problem thinking of Faythe and her needs first. She put Miranda before anything else, and now Faythe. Deanna wasn't ready to examine the significance of her behavior too closely.

"How about that hot chocolate?" She kissed the tip of Faythe's nose, wanting the physical nearness to remain, but also trying to lessen its intensity.

Faythe looked bewildered, but then she slid her hands from Deanna's jeans pockets and patted her bottom. "Why not? I'd say you've earned it."

As they walked toward the kitchen, Faythe held Deanna's hand, apparently unwilling to let go completely. Deanna was happy to oblige, and only when Faythe needed both hands to make the hot chocolate did they let go.

CHAPTER FIFTEEN

Faythe ran faster than usual, and she was apparently running from something. Her feet hammered against the forest path, and she was glad she'd picked a new route. She was dying to see Deanna again, though afraid to. Not because of the kiss, which had been the wonderful part of the emotionally upsetting evening two nights ago. "I acted like a total wimp," Faythe muttered under breath. "I sounded like a total loser." The next morning after she had sobbed on Deanna's shoulder, she woke up with a hangover-like headache and tons of remorse. This was not how she wanted Deanna to see her. Accomplished, together, and in charge of her life—those were the attributes she wanted the world to see. Not Ms. Misery. Faythe had to laugh at her own choice of words. "Yeah, that's it. I'm pitiful. Witty, but pitiful. Maybe I'll invent a new word for it. Wittiful."

"Hi." A bright female voice to her left made Faythe nearly stumble. "Oh, sorry," a young woman chirped and extended a hand between them. "I'm Pammie."

Pammie. Awfully cute. Too cute. Faythe had never shaken hands with anyone while jogging, but tried to keep her pace while doing so. "Faythe." A quick glance, so she wouldn't fall over a tree root, proved that the girl looked more tough than cute in her black outfit.

"First time I've seen you on this track." Pammie's waist-long blond braid swung merrily.

"Could be because it's my first time running here." Faythe assumed what she hoped was a friendly expression to take the sting out of her words. "Nice to meet you, Pammie."

"Likewise. I live over there, across the lake. I drive over here to run. The paths are much better."

"I see." Faythe didn't mean to sound so short, but she was becoming winded.

"I still live at home. Well, I'm in college, but I'm an intern right now, in Grantville."

"Enjoying it?" Faythe managed and turned her head to look at Pammie again. Suddenly her left foot folded underneath her and she plummeted to the ground.

"Oh, God! You okay, Faythe?" Pammie was at her side immediately. "That was a nasty fall."

"I'm fine, I'm fine." Faythe rose on one knee, but when she tried to put some weight on her left foot, she slumped back onto the ground. "Damn it. I must've sprained my ankle. So damn stupid." She blinked tears of pain away as she removed her sneaker and watched her ankle swell up.

"You need ice. And a doctor. Can you get up? Lean on me." Pammie looked around them. "And not a soul in sight."

"Calm down. It's probably just twisted. I'd appreciate a hand to see if I can stand."

"Sure. How do you want to do this?"

"Let me get on my knees and then steady me as I get up, okay?"

"Okay."

Moving very carefully, because her foot did hurt, Faythe managed to get up on her knees and then, with Pammie's help, she stood on one leg. As soon as she tried to put weight on her foot, she whimpered. "I can't believe this. I've never sprained anything before. It's really painful." She inhaled deeply and tried to breathe through the agony.

"Oh, I've done it several times," Pammie said. "And if you've done it once, it's likely to happen again if you're not careful. Something about the muscles and ligaments being stretched too much and then your foot gets unsteady. Or something like that. The doctor explained the details to me, but it was pretty elaborate medical mumbo jumbo. Oh, I'm babbling and you're in pain. Sorry."

"Don't worry. I'll be fine. I just have to figure out how to get home." Faythe's foot was beginning to throb with every beat of her heart. She needed to elevate it as soon as possible.

"I'll help you. If you can hop on one leg and hang on to me as your personal crutch, I'll help you to my car at the parking lot by the barbecue pits."

"Is it far?"

"About three hundred yards behind us."

Three hundred yards. It might as well be three hundred miles. Deciding to tough it out she said, "All right. Let's go for it."

"Hold on tight." Pammie wrapped Faythe's arm around her shoulder. "Ready?"

No. "Sure." Faythe hopped next to Pammie, trying desperately to ignore the pain in her other foot that seared through her leg with each thud. *Think about something else.*

"College, you say? You a senior?"

"No, junior." Pammie seemed to understand the urgent need for small talk. "Can't believe only two years ago I was just a high school kid in Grantville."

"Time flies."

"Sure does."

"Where did you go to college?" Pammie had wrapped her arm tightly around Faythe's waist and was supporting more of her weight.

"Columbia."

"Wow. Me too! What a coincidence. And you majored in?"

"Journalism."

Pammie whistled. "Cool. You work on a magazine or newspaper?"

"TV."

"Ah."

"You don't sound impressed." Faythe chuckled despite the pain. Clearly Pammie would have been more in awe if she'd been a print reporter.

"Oh, I am. Of course I am. Working for television must be a dream job."

"It's a job. Not my dream job. I want to write."

"Then that's what you should do."

"Thanks."

"What for?" Pammie tried to glance at Faythe, who shook her head in warning.

"Watch it. Ground seems uneven here."

"Sorry." Pammie took a better hold around Faythe's waist. "Only about fifty yards now."

"Really?" The small talk had really distracted Faythe, and she was grateful.

"There. See that blue between the trees? That's my car."

Faythe tried to look, but all the hopping was taking her breath away, and she could only focus on moving forward and ignoring the pain. "I'll take your word for it."

Minutes later, Pammie unlocked her Toyota and helped Faythe into the backseat. Finally elevating her burning ankle, Faythe leaned back and moaned. "Damn, it fucking hurts."

"You need a doctor. Perhaps an X-ray."

"I hate to admit it, but I think you're right." Faythe stared gloomily at her swollen leg. "I better go home and clean up—"

"Are you nuts? You need to be seen right away. Your foot is swelling. I'll drive you to Grantville Memorial."

Faythe had to laugh. "All right. Thank you." She remembered Aunt Nellie driving her to the ER there once as a child when she stepped on a board with a rusty nail. *Same foot, come to think of it. Wonderful.*

It took Pammie about fifteen minutes to drive through town and into the ER admissions area. She jumped out of the car and grabbed a wheelchair for Faythe, who was grateful and self-conscious. They were in luck. A doctor was available, and soon a nurse's aide whisked Faythe away to be X-rayed. Pammie had insisted on staying, apparently not about to let Faythe out of her sight.

When they were waiting for the doctor to read the X-rays, Faythe found herself directly across from Pammie for the first time. Pammie wore black leggings and a hoodie over a gray T-shirt. Her left eyebrow was pierced, and both her upper arms boasted small, intricate tribal tattoos. "You've been really sweet to me," Faythe said. "You really don't have to stay. I can catch a cab home."

"This is a small town. Not *that* many cabs around." Pammie shook her head. "I don't have any plans today. I want to stay and make sure you're okay."

"Ms. Hamilton?" The doctor, a woman in her late fifties, said, "The good news is no fractures."

"And the bad news?"

"You have a bad, painful sprain, but I think you've already figured that out."

"Yeah, pretty much."

"It doesn't need a cast. The nurse will give you an Ace wrap, an icing schedule, and PT advice. You need to keep your foot elevated and iced. Stay off it for a few days. If it doesn't improve in three or four days, come back and we'll examine you again and perhaps opt for a cast, all right?"

"I'll do that. Thank you, Doctor."

"You're welcome, Ms. Hamilton." The doctor colored faintly. "Um, I always watch your show when I'm off duty and enjoy it a lot. Just what I need to wind down and relax. Not all days are as quiet around here as today."

"Thank you," Faythe repeated. "Glad you like what we've done over the years." Faythe had never thought about her job from the doctor's perspective. Every time she was sent out on a job that seemed especially silly, she felt the network wasn't enlightening and informing the viewers. Looking at this accomplished woman, Faythe realized entertainment news had another side. Sometimes people needed something light, distracting, and fun to help them make it through their busy, difficult lives. *Maybe I helped save someone through this doctor, if I helped her make it through another watch?* She felt better thinking about it this way.

"You got a ride home?" the doctor asked, looking over at Pammie.

"She sure does." Pammie grabbed the wheelchair's handle.

"Good. Remember, stay off your foot and elevate it."

"And ice," Pammie filled in.

"I'll remember," Faythe said, distracted by Pammie's attentive glance. *Okay. So she's recognized me now. Oh, well.*

Faythe waited inside the glass doors while Pammie got the car. After climbing into the passenger seat, she glanced over at Pammie, who gazed back at her with open curiosity. "Well, you did tell me you worked in TV. I suppose it's nice when not everyone recognizes you."

"It is."

"And you're here on a break." Pammie chewed her lower lip.

"And you let it slip that you wanted to write again, before. Guess you've escaped, haven't you?" Pammie didn't seem to be judging her at all. Instead, she sounded reflective, like she was trying to figure out a riddle, but without any preconceived ideas.

"You're right. Thanks for not gushing. Or the opposite."

"What's the opposite of gushing?" Pammie winked.

"It involves people so upset because of something you said or did seven years ago, they spit when they talk."

"Ew. Really? I've always told a friend of mine that fame is highly overrated. She didn't believe me until a few years ago."

"She famous?"

"Infamous. Trust me. Living in a small town like Grantville and being infamous is not a small thing. It can nearly kill a person."

Faythe was wondering if Pammie knew Deanna. Suddenly it dawned on her that she had to know *of* her, at least, having attended Grantville High. But was she talking about her? She was talking about a friend. Deanna would not be *friends* with a former student. Would she? Was this the part Deanna had left out the other night?

"What do you mean, kill?" Pammie's choice of words seemed a bit overly dramatic to Faythe.

"Literally. My friend, she's this gorgeous, talented girl. She got into trouble and she's paying for it now. Big-time."

"She has you on her side, I can tell."

"Yeah, she does. She has a few other friends, but they're totally in the dark about things, and it's been like that for years now. She's not having an easy time at home, and she even dropped out of school. She's the best, I mean, she truly is a great person, but she needs someone to talk to. Sometimes I worry she'll do something stupid."

Taken aback, Faythe realized she had opened up for this type of serious conversation and couldn't avoid it now. She was in pain and tired, but she wasn't about to blow Pammie off. "Take a right over there." She pointed at the dirt road that led down to her aunt's house.

"There?" Pammie stared at her.

"Yes. I'm staying in number eleven-fifty-two."

"Oh. Really. Wow." Pammie turned and they soon pulled up behind Faythe's Crossfire.

"Nice ride." Pammie sounded impressed, but preoccupied. "So you live here."

"I do. It's my aunt's cabin."

"Some cabin." Pammie opened the door and walked over to the passenger side. Helping Faythe to her feet, she steadied her before giving her the crutches the hospital sent her home with. Faythe hopped to the kitchen door, felt around for the keys in her jacket pocket, and opened it. "Please, come in. Can I get you something?"

"Tea or coffee would be great, but I'll make it. Just point me in the direction of the...oh, there's the kitchen." Pammie arranged two kitchen chairs for Faythe, the second one for the sprained foot. "Here. Elevate."

"Bossy, aren't you?"

"So I'm told." Pammie grinned and walked over to the coffee machine. "Oh, look! Am I glad I work part-time at Starbucks or what? That's some machine." She fussed over the built-in espresso machine and expertly made two lattes. Faythe directed her to the drawer where she kept her favorite cookies, and soon they were munching away and sipping the hot drinks.

"So, your friend needs a counselor."

"Hmm. Not so sure. She needs more than that. I thought—" Pammie interrupted herself and played with the rim of her coffee mug. "She needs to talk to someone other than me. Someone who'd understand and advise."

"You sound just like the friend she needs. You really care, and you're there for her, right?"

"Right. It's just that we're kind of more than friends. I mean, I want us to be, and I know she does too. She's just so messed up that she can't be with anyone. All she does is work. If she's not at her day job, she's working every charity known to man."

Tears were forming at the corners of Pammie's eyes.

"And you're in college, away from Grantville."

"Yes. When I'm out of college, I plan to look for a better apartment in Manhattan. Right now I'm sharing a tiny space with another girl. I'm not going to be stuck in Grantville for the rest of my life." Pammie broke a cookie in tiny pieces before eating them. "Or at *least* out of my parents' house." Something in the way she spoke, a sudden harshness to her bright voice, hinted at untold issues between Pammie and her parents.

"It's only natural to fly the coop."

"Trust me, at my house, flying the coop is something a girl does when she meets the guy she's going to marry." Pammie glowered as she spoke the last sentence. "You should've heard my folks when I told them that as far as I can see, I'll never marry."

"Not popular with your parents, huh?" Faythe sipped her coffee, pondering how up front to be with her new acquaintance. "I've come to a similar decision." The words were out before she could stop them.

Pammie's eyes lit up. "Yeah? Well, I hope your parents didn't have half as many cows about it as mine did. They're coming around, though. Slowly."

"Cows?" Faythe laughed and soon Pammie joined her. Pammie had all but come out to Faythe with her talk about marriage and shocked parents. Faythe, who remembered her own parents' indifferent attitude to her own nervous step out of the closet, felt her heart reach out to the girl.

"Yeah. Mom is an expert on having cows when something bothers her. I love her to bits. I just wish she'd stop worrying so much."

"It's what most mothers do. Worry, I mean." Faythe couldn't remember her mother being concerned about anything but appearances, but she supposed that did qualify as a worry.

"I don't mean to be nosy, Faythe," Pammie said slowly, a shy expression on her face as she shoved her hands into the pockets of her hoodie. "It's just so easy to talk to you, and I…God, this is going to sound so presumptuous."

Faythe, not wanting Pammie to feel awkward, spoke quickly. "Ask away," she said. "I can't guarantee a favorable response, but I don't mind questions."

"Could you talk to her? You're a familiar face, you know, credible from TV and such. She'd listen to you. And maybe you could look at the situation with fresh eyes and see a solution we don't."

Faythe swallowed the last sip of the excellent latte so quickly she choked on it. She coughed several times and Pammie patted her on her back.

"Now, now. Don't breathe in the java. I don't want to have to load you in the back of the car and haul you off to the ER again, this time for drowning."

Faythe laughed, and coughed again. "Okay, okay. You can stop loosening my lungs now."

"You'll do it? Fantastic!" Pammie pumped a fist in the air, seeming so delighted that Faythe didn't have the heart to tell her she'd taken her "okay" as meaning she'd talk to this friend of hers. Then again, what harm could it do?

CHAPTER SIXTEEN

Deanna took out the pink business card and held it as if Savannah had coated it with poison. She tried to ignore the surging bile in her throat and instead focused on the mystery of Savannah's choice. Or was it a choice? Had her parents, her mother especially, cut her off financially? Or was she merely sick and tired of studying? Savannah was a straight-A student, always heading the honor roll. It was admirable to devote herself to saving runaway dogs, abandoned cats, and so on, but this girl had enormous potential and the money to back her up. She could do anything she wanted.

Wanting Faythe's opinion about this situation, she reached for the phone, then hesitated and, her heartbeat elevated until it drummed like distant thunder, put on her jacket and stepped outside. It was late afternoon. Hopefully Faythe was home. When she rounded the corner of her cabin, she saw Faythe's car through the trees. *Good.*

Deanna knocked on the kitchen door, but nobody came, though she did hear a faint voice inside the house. Frowning, Deanna tried the door handle, which wasn't locked. "Hello? Faythe?"

"Deanna? I'm in here, on the couch." Faythe sounded a little sleepy and Deanna pushed off her sneakers and hurried into the living room.

"The door was unlocked. That crazy— What's happened?" Deanna saw the elaborate bandage wrapped around Faythe's left foot.

"I sprained it while I was running." Faythe told Deanna how Pammie had driven her to the ER.

"Thank goodness you weren't alone." Deanna frowned. The name sounded familiar. "Wonder if I know her, at least by name. One of the high school kids."

"Sounds possible."

"You were lucky. You could have been lying in the woods all night."

"Hardly," Faythe said with a grin. "I was running in an area with designated paths and streetlights."

"Still…" Deanna shook her head. "And you're crazy for not locking your door."

"I know. I thought about it when Pammie left, but I was too tired to get up." Faythe still looked tired, with faint blue circles under her eyes. "Glad you came, though."

"Me too. You can't hop around all alone over here on one leg. Did they at least provide you with crutches?"

"Yes. I'll have to practice, though. Aunt Nellie's hardwood floors are slippery." Faythe blushed. "Could you help me to the bathroom while you're here? I haven't been since this morning."

"Sure. Here, pull yourself up." Deanna steadied Faythe and gave her the crutches. At the bathroom door, she held it open while Faythe hobbled through. "I'll wait outside, okay?"

"Thanks." Faythe looked determined as she closed the door.

"Don't lock it."

"I won't."

Faythe was in the bathroom for quite a while and came out smelling like soap and toothpaste. "I'm so glad you dropped by. I didn't have a chance to wash up while Pammie was here, and I had been running for a while before I fell." She wrinkled her nose. "Felt a bit stinky."

Deanna couldn't imagine Faythe ever stinking. "It didn't bother me," she quipped, and eyed the bandaged foot. "How are you feeling?"

"Throbbing, mostly. It hurts, but it's a dull ache, so not too bad right now."

"Got any Tylenol?"

"I do, but only the PM version. Saving that for tonight."

"I can swing by the pharmacy for you."

"No, that's all right. I know you have to get back to work. Oh, wait a minute. Did you want something in particular, or was this just a social call?" Faythe used the crutches carefully and hobbled over to the couch again. She elevated both her legs and leaned back against the armrest.

"Ah, yes, but it can wait. I had no idea that you'd taken the self-destructive route."

"Tell me." There was sweet command in Faythe's voice as she looked calmly at Deanna.

"I can't get Savannah and her damn business card out of my mind," Deanna blurted. "I've kept it in the back of a drawer, and it's been crawling out of there and into my head every time I pass the damn dresser."

"Wow, sounds bad," Faythe said. She pushed a small pillow behind her neck and leaned back farther. "So you're considering doing something about this stalking business card of yours?"

"No, I'm more inclined to tear it up in minuscule little pieces, but then it will probably come back to haunt me from business-card hell." Deanna could hear a near pout in her voice and reeled herself in. "All jokes aside, I think I have to endure this discussion that Savannah wants to have. She obviously needs closure. She wants to blame me once and for all for what's happened."

"Are you sure?"

Deanna blinked. "You weren't there. You don't know what she told her friends and what her parents later repeated to me. I saw unforgiveable sides of Savannah. She fought dirty and she lied. Her mother, Gloria, took over after a while, and hammered the nails in my proverbial coffin neatly into place."

"Hey, Deanna, it's me you're talking to. I'm sure you're not exaggerating, but people and memories change, whether we recognize that fact or not. You aren't the same as you were then, and I imagine she isn't either. From eighteen to twenty is quite a leap for some kids. And, besides, it's not like things can get any worse, is it?"

"Actually, it can," Deanna said darkly, picturing a furious, saliva-spitting Gloria Mueller. "It can get a whole lot worse."

Faythe looked like she would object or ask questions, but instead she beckoned Deanna to sit next to her on the couch. Deanna was mindful not to end up too close but failed, since Faythe wrapped her arms around her neck in a fierce hug. "I'm so sorry they hurt you so badly." She kissed Deanna's cheek. "And for whatever reason you're afraid they can do even more damage…" Faythe placed a line of incredibly soft kisses along Deanna's jawline, then pressed her forehead against Deanna's, their noses touching briefly. "Mmm, you smell good."

"So do you."

"Toothpaste and soap. As in Colgate and Dove."

Deanna laughed. "Same here."

"Really?" Faythe buried her nose against Deanna's neck. "Oh, yeah. I can tell."

Deanna inhaled deeply, feeling her cheeks warm, no doubt to a hot pink. "You can?" She tipped Faythe's head back and looked down into her green eyes. They were the color of maple leaves, translucent in the sun. Faythe's lips parted—such sweet, full lips. Pink and moist, they beckoned her, drew her in. Deanna kissed Faythe's half-open mouth and received a soft whimper. Faythe kissed her back, her tongue caressing Deanna's over and over in slow circles. Nearly whimpering too, Deanna pushed her hands gently into Faythe's hair, lacing her fingers through the silky masses of caramel-colored strands. "God, you're so soft, so sexy," Deanna murmured into Faythe's mouth.

"Mmm." Faythe purred. Deanna couldn't think of any other word for the sound that emanated from her throat. Faythe felt lithe and supple in Deanna's arms, and she couldn't believe that anyone could feel so wonderful. She kissed a new trail from Faythe's lips to her barely revealed collarbone, where she nudged the V-neck T-shirt out of the way. The small indentation above the collarbone was irresistible to kiss, then lick, just because it was there. Deanna cupped Faythe's shoulders and held her tenderly while she tasted the velvet skin there. Faythe was gasping now, drawing one trembling, shallow breath after another. "Jesus, Deanna. It's been so long, and I can't remember…"

"What to do?" Deanna laughed against the damp skin under her lips.

"…it ever feeling this way. This good." Faythe moaned and moved restlessly against Deanna. "I swear you set me on fire."

"Mmm, you are quite a combustible woman yourself." Deanna blew yet another trail, this time deep into the V-neck, seeking out the valley between Faythe's breasts. The skin there was damp and fragrant, making her mouth water. Nibbling along the faintly visible veins, Deanna reveled in hearing her moan again. "So you like this."

"Yeah. Oh, sweet Jesus, I do."

Deanna lowered Faythe to the small pillow leaning against the armrest. She slipped her fingers under the white T-shirt and felt Faythe's stomach muscles jump when she touched them. "Ticklish?"

"No. Nervous, I suppose." Faythe's eyes were several shades darker now and enormous in her finely chiseled face.

"Nervous?" Worried, Deanna touched Faythe's cheek. "How come?"

"As I said, it's been a while." Faythe's lips trembled.

"For me too."

"Exactly."

"Huh?" Deanna couldn't follow Faythe's logic, then realized what Faythe was hinting at. "Oh. You're afraid I can't control myself since I've gone without for so long."

"No, well, not put like that. No." Faythe colored. "I don't mean to suggest—"

"You just about did, didn't you? You think that it's been so long since I've lured anyone into my bed that I won't be able to control my urges."

"No!" Faythe sat up too quickly, cried out, and fell back against the pillow.

"You all right?" Deanna forgot her wounded pride and rose to cradle the sprained ankle in her hands. "What did you do?"

"I flinched. Remind me not to do that anytime soon."

"Okay. No flinching." Deanna lowered Faythe's foot slowly and tucked an additional decorative pillow underneath it. "There. Better?"

"Yeah." After a few deep breaths, Faythe looked up at Deanna. "I never meant to imply you couldn't control yourself."

"I know."

"I only meant...you do?"

"When I quit acting like an ass, being so self-conscious, I understood." Deanna stroked Faythe's cheek softly. "I'm so used to being accused about anything and everything concerning my sexuality, I became defensive instantly."

"Oh, Deanna." Faythe held out her arms.

"Can we just hug a bit?" Deanna kissed Faythe's temple. "You're in a lot of pain, aren't you?"

"Sounds heavenly. I must have been desperate to prove I'm not a lame lover because I never have any dates." Faythe plucked at Deanna's shirt sleeve. "Which in itself is sort of lame, isn't it?"

"Shh." Wrapping her arms around Faythe, Deanna merely hugged her and admitted to herself that it felt damn good. Her body calmed down, but her desire simmered just beneath the surface. The scent from Faythe's hair surrounded Deanna's senses, engulfing them with its freshness. She would always associate Faythe with the scent of clean soap, minty fresh toothpaste, and something resembling vanilla sugar, which she suspected was Faythe's very own scent.

"So, how about the business card?" Faythe nuzzled Deanna's neck as she spoke softly. "Want to call the kid and sort things out?"

Deanna couldn't answer right away. She tried to sort her conflicting emotions into her usual neat little compartments. Checking off each imaginary box, one after another, was the only way she knew how to proceed. Would her method work this time?

"Deanna?" Faythe pressed her soft lips against Deanna's neck.

"I just want this to end," Deanna whispered hoarsely. "I just want everything to end and go back to the way it was." Stupid, hateful tears ran down her cheeks, dripping off her chin and ending up on Faythe's cheeks.

"Oh, honey." Faythe tugged Deanna even closer.

Afraid that she'd hurt Faythe's foot, Deanna shifted them so Faythe was cuddled up on her lap now.

"Wow, you work fast," Faythe said, in a mock-admiring tone.

"I do." Smiling through her tears, Deanna didn't feel quite so silly. "I don't know what's wrong. I never cry."

"That's probably it."

"What?"

"That you never cry. Not good to bottle up. I know. I do it all the time."

"Cry?" Deanna was trying to keep up with Faythe's reasoning, a few sobs still making her shudder.

"No. Bottle up." Faythe made a big production of rolling her eyes. "Pay attention."

"Oh, trust me," Deanna muttered. "You've got my full attention." She ran her hands over Faythe's back. "Any more attention from me and you'll find yourself on your back in bed."

"Really?" The teasing tone quickly changed to a breathless one. "How decisive. And greedy."

"You bet." Deanna buried her face in Faythe's hair and inhaled deeply. "You're irresistible, you know."

"No. That's just it. I don't know. It's been too long. Last time I was on a date, a friend at the network set me up. Major disaster."

"She was boring? Mediocre? Ugly as sin?"

"Worse. I would have been able to work around a boring, mediocre, ugly woman."

"So what was the problem?" Deanna kissed Faythe's temple.

"She was a he."

"A cross-dresser? Transgender?"

"I could have had a great evening with a cross-dresser or a transgendered individual," Faythe said with exaggerated patience.

"Then *what*?"

"He was a man. A super-duper hunk. A God's-gift-to-woman, if you like the type."

Deanna straightened and looked at Faythe. "You're kidding."

"Nope. He sat there, long hair and all, a Fabio look-alike, and I think he must've attended a 101 course in how to entice women. He pulled no punches when it came to charming me. When I finally got a word in, it took me half an hour to make him listen. I don't know if it's happened to you, but when you warn some guys off with the 'Sorry, but I'm a lesbian' explanation, they get this glow and become all dewy-eyed. I know they're picturing themselves with two—or more—women in a scenario where they convince the 'lesbians,'" Faythe enunciated the word slowly and carefully, "that they're mistaken about their sexuality. They only need this stud of a man to show them what they're missing."

Deanna had begun to giggle at Faythe's antics, and now she was howling. "Oh, yes, I've met one or two of those. So this Fabio wannabe tried to charm you into bed?"

"Well, he actually tried to charm me into picking up the tab, since he'd 'forgotten' his wallet." Faythe made vigorous air quotation marks. "I wanted to bolt so badly, I was ready to write him a blank check. I was also ready to shoot my colleague, who was probably dying to hear all the sordid details." Faythe pushed her hair back and leaned her head on Deanna's shoulder. "I'm not too heavy for you, am I?"

"Huh? No, no. You're fine." Deanna kissed Faythe again. "You're very fine."

Faythe returned her kiss. Deanna paced herself and this time it wasn't hard at all, even if she was still aroused. She explored every part of Faythe's mouth. Finally Faythe's moans became whimpers, thoroughly sexy sounds that Deanna was glad to capture with her mouth. Suddenly she realized her left hand had slipped under Faythe's shirt and was drawing circles up toward her breasts. *God, I want to touch her so badly.*

"Touch me. I need it so badly."

Deanna froze momentarily at Faythe's echoing words. "Are you sure?"

"Yeah." Faythe arched her back, as if trying to reach Deanna's hand.

No more stalling. Deanna slid her hand up and cupped a lace-clad breast. "Oh."

"Oh." Faythe shivered and placed her own hand on top of Deanna's, outside the shirt.

Faythe's stone-hard nipple prodded Deanna's hand. She flicked her thumb over it, twice, and heard more moans. "Like this?" Deanna whispered.

"Yes." Faythe was barely audible. "Like that."

"Like this?" Deanna took the whole breast in her hand, weighing it carefully before she caressed it.

"Oh, yes." Faythe was trembling now, and she grasped for Deanna. "You're driving me crazy."

"Good."

"Kiss me?"

Deanna was more than happy to do so. She took Faythe's sweet-tasting lips, brushing her own across them. Faythe surprised her by entering her mouth first, her hot tongue insistent. A dark, molten place inside Deanna, a place she barely remembered being there, came to life. It connected with her limbs and sent moisture to her sex and dried out her mouth. Nobody had ever kissed her like this, so hotly and with such abandon. Deanna was aroused and afraid. This wasn't about a one-night stand with an attractive, pleasurable woman; this was too much, too soon. So many emotions were surfacing. She panicked and finally withdrew, gasping for air. "I'm so sorry. I'm so, so sorry."

"What for?" Faythe took one of Deanna's hands and pressed it between her breasts.

Her heart thundered beneath it, convincing Deanna that things were happening too quickly. If she were less scarred or more hardened, she would have taken Faythe immediately. But as things were, she couldn't. "For rushing this. For letting my body rule my head."

"So, when you think about it, you don't want this."

"Wrong. When I think about it, I want it more than ever. I'm afraid of screwing up. And believe it or not, I'm trying not to screw this up."

A shadow passed over Faythe's face. "What do you mean, screw up? We were just cuddling, Deanna." She gestured casually with her free hand.

"Oh." Deanna considered Faythe's choice of words. "I see. I suppose I overthought it again. It seemed…felt, more to me."

Faythe lifted Deanna's hand to her lips and kissed each knuckle softly. "Deanna, I've told you I don't think in those terms. Not at all. And besides, I did tell you I'm not relationship material. Why can't we just enjoy each other? We can be really good together, I can feel it. I mean it. I'd love to be with you, Deanna. You're amazing, beautiful, and sexy. There can't possibly be anything wrong with that. We're both adults, after all," Faythe said encouragingly.

Deanna's heart slammed to a halt, skipping beats until she felt entirely numb. Why was she so surprised that Faythe thought like this? Faythe was right. She'd told Deanna that she didn't intend to settle with anyone. Ever. *How could I be so stupid that I forgot that?* It was ironic that she, who shied away from contact and people, was the needy one. Deanna forced a polite smile and carefully freed her hand. "Of course we are. And you know, we should be careful with your foot."

Faythe gazed at her intently. "Are you okay? You're not upset with me, are you?"

"No, no, no," Deanna said quickly. "I'm fine. It's good that you're the voice of reason. I mean, it just goes to show the old adage, never assume."

"Deanna—"

"I'm leaving now. I'll just grab the tiger by the tail and call Savannah. Better get this over with."

"And you can meet here, if you like." Faythe tried to get up from the couch and fell down with a moan. "Damn it. Stupid foot."

Forgetting some of her confusion and hurt, Deanna knelt next to Faythe and felt along the edges of the bandage. "This feels too tight. Your toes are pale and feel cold."

"My toes are always pale. Not usually cold, though."

"Let me unwrap it just a bit." When Faythe nodded, Deanna proceeded to do so. "Ah, as I thought. Feel the circulation start up again?"

"Yeah," Faythe answered. "Now, *that* hurts."

"You can't stay here by yourself," Deanna said, shaking her head. "Do you have anyone you can call to come stay with you? Your mom or dad?"

"No. I don't want them here." Faythe's face darkened. "Especially not my parents."

Faythe obviously had a long way to go before she was ready to confront her parents about what their recent behavior. *And who am I to judge that sort of thing? I haven't spoken to Mom more than twice in nine years.*

"Can't you stay here with me? There are plenty of bedrooms, all with their own bathroom. You wouldn't have to spend more time with me than necessary." Faythe didn't sound pleading, but she looked dark and brooding. "Unless you're too upset with me about us making out."

"I'm not upset."

"I think you are."

"I'm just feeling a little bit silly that I forgot about your attitude to relationships and also for making such a big deal about it. We're adults, like you say. It shouldn't matter. I ought to be able to enjoy being with a beautiful, talented, intelligent woman like you and be happy with what's offered." Deanna wanted to explain, but she could see from Faythe's expression that she was missing her mark.

"You've just confirmed what I suspected all along. Nobody's ever had the guts to tell me to my face, but I'm grateful you did. Honestly."

"What are you talking about?" *What did I just say?*

"I'm not sensitive enough, and frankly, I'm probably too shallow anyway, to be a suitable girlfriend or partner. I haven't had any role models to speak of, which is an understatement, and I've worked and played the last ten years paying attention only to my own interests and goals. I've dated, but rarely the same woman more than a few weeks.

After the inevitable breakup, which is an odd expression since we weren't exclusive, I've felt liberated and free. Happy to get back to my routines and my job."

"And now you want me to stay here with you."

"Yes." Faythe patted Deanna's hand carefully. "Please? I promise not to jump your bones."

Deanna would have walked through fire and chopped through ice to stay with Faythe when she said "please" with such feeling. "All right. I'll go back to my cabin and get some stuff. Clothes and my art supplies."

"Oh, damn, I didn't think about your work. I'm a selfish bitch." Faythe looked so upset at this minor oversight that Deanna started to laugh.

"You're not a bitch. I'll be able to work just fine here. The view from the panoramic window is breathtaking. The light in here is good."

"So you'll stay a few days?"

Deanna knew she was setting herself up for trouble, but she couldn't have answered any differently. Leaning forward, she tucked a loose strand of hair behind Faythe's ear. "I'll stay as long as you need me."

CHAPTER SEVENTEEN

Faythe fumbled for her cell phone, but it landed on the hardwood floor in her bedroom. She glanced at the alarm clock, saw that it was ten a.m., and nearly bolted out of bed before she remembered her injured ankle. Carefully she leaned over the side of the bed to try and reach the ringing phone, but couldn't. The bed was too high, and she was afraid she'd fall off if she stretched any farther.

"What's the noise about?" Deanna asked, coming through the door and making Faythe forget the phone. "Ah, let me get that for you." Deanna picked it up and handed it to Faythe, then mimed she was going back to the kitchen. Faythe nodded and flipped the cell phone open.

"Hello?"

"Darling," Cornelia Hamilton nearly shouted. "Did Suzy stop by? What a delightful woman. I never knew how understanding she could be. Such a successful agent and all."

Faythe was in no mood to deal with her mother. "Yeah, she did stop by the other day, Mom. Can't talk right now. In the middle of work."

"Working? On a Saturday morning? Oh, you signed the contract after all." Cornelia sounded genuinely happy. "I was so worried that your new plans would fester and screw with your mind. Besides, I wanted you to know that Chester and I have other plans for the day we planned to visit you."

Faythe was ready to throw the phone across the room. *First she nags and gives me the guilt trip from hell because she wants to come here no matter what—and now I'm being stood up.* It would've been hilarious if Faythe hadn't been in such agony with her foot. She wasn't in the mood to argue with her mother or get into a long discussion.

"I've got work to do, Mom. Say hello to Chester for me. Bye." She shut the cell with a click that resonated between the walls. She wished Deanna hadn't left, but couldn't really fault her politeness while she was on the phone.

Grabbing her crutches, Faythe visited the bathroom, then headed for the kitchen where Deanna was expertly flipping pancakes.

"Smells wonderful." Faythe sank down on one of the chairs. "Blueberry pancakes again?" Deanna had served them two mornings ago, and Faythe's mouth watered at the thought.

"Yes. You said you liked them."

"That's an understatement. Who would've guessed you'd be such a terrific cook?"

"Who indeed?" She flipped a pancake expertly. "Ready for your first stack?"

"First? I can't exercise yet, remember? At this rate, I won't be able to fit into any of my clothes."

"You're fine." Deanna put a plate with six pancakes in front of her. She made them thicker than their diner counterparts; blueberry syrup ran down the sides of the stack, and a big glob of whipped cream sat on top.

Deanna fixed an identical plate for herself and sat down across the table from Faythe. They ate in silence, until halfway through the meal, when Deanna jumped up to bring coffee. Faythe inhaled the fragrant aroma and sipped it carefully. "This is life restoration at its best," she said. "I can't tell you how many interviews, preparations, and research I've carried out with a mug of coffee in my hand. Even coffee from the workplace's stinky old coffee machine is better than no coffee at all."

"I agree. My first children's book, which I was so incredibly apprehensive of illustrating, was christened in coffee. As it turns out, it became a great success, both for the story and the illustrations."

"How come you were particularly nervous about illustrating for kids?"

Deanna looked surprised. "Do you remember your childhood books? The ones with pictures in them?"

"Sure I do. I still know several of them by heart."

"Exactly. Our children's books are so important to us, and we are influenced by them when it comes to our reading as adults. Kids will take these books to their hearts, cherish them, and learn from them. We shape each new generation with the books we provide them." Deanna chased a runaway blueberry around her plate. "So I lived on coffee and croissants and worked around the clock. I discarded at least a hundred drafts before I came up with the right look for Bunny Buttercup."

"I have a confession." Faythe wasn't sure how to tell Deanna that she'd researched her online. Deanna had told her about being wary of reporters, and looking someone up was nothing short of prying. "I found your Web site, well, your publisher's Web site, and saw some of your work on the children's books. I love the Bunny Buttercup illustrations. I also think it's great it hasn't been overly commercialized."

Deanna regarded her evenly over a forkful of pancakes. "I knew you would research me online."

"You did?"

"What kind of a reporter would you be if you didn't check your sources, do your research, and make sure I wasn't blowing smoke in your eyes?" Deanna looked serious, but a small twinkle in her eyes made it possible for Faythe to breathe easier.

"Anyway, that's when I found a few other blogs and sites, where some people called you not-so-nice names and so on. I realized that no matter what I thought I knew, or didn't know about you, you needed someone to look into things impartially."

"Are you still impartial?" Deanna didn't take her dark blue eyes off Faythe.

"No. I'm completely biased now. But, that said, I'm still professional enough to be able to spot the truth. I'm enamored with you, so much that I'm ready to trick you into bed, using bribery if necessary."

Deanna tossed her head back and laughed, the first real laughter Faythe had heard from her. "You're so shameless." Deanna wiped at the corners of her eyes. "You're so shameless and delicious I'm using all my willpower to keep my hands off you."

"Really? So, I'm irresistibly sexy, but it really doesn't matter how sexy I am because I'm just not worth the trouble. I don't know whether to be flattered or insulted."

Deanna looked shocked. "I didn't mean it like *that*. I'm sorry."

"No need to be." Faythe blinked rapidly, fighting stupid tears at Deanna's description of her.

"Oh, darling." Deanna rounded the kitchen table, pushed the empty plates away, and lifted Faythe up on the table. "Listen to me. Listen." She smoothed Faythe's hair back from her face. "I realize you think you're not relationship material, you're afraid you're shallow, and you see your past track record of breakups and so-called romantic failures as proof."

"So?" Faythe sobbed, then tried to quit crying. She couldn't, and Deanna ended up wiping her face for her.

"So you're wrong. You're a fantastic friend, and you'll make someone an equally fantastic partner." Faythe was about to object, but Deanna placed her finger over Faythe's lips. "Shh. I know you don't believe me, which infuriates me…" She held one hand up, palm forward. "Damn it, I'm talking as if I don't have any social skills. I'm not mad at you, but I'm furious at whatever your parents said or did to make you think you're like them."

"But they're right." Faythe shrugged. "They were my role models until I was eighteen. Then they divorced and settled with their new partners."

"So they acted shallowly and convinced you that you were a chip off the old block. You're not shallow at all."

Faythe drew a deep breath. She wasn't shallow when it came to other her values: work ethic, friendships, moral and ethical dilemmas. What concerned her was her track record with women. Most of the time she hadn't wanted to go beyond the first date. A thought dawned on her. "Uh, Deanna. I know this may sound silly, but I may have given you the impression that I've had tons of lovers."

"Not tons, but you've apparently searched for love in quite a few places. That's none of my business. I can't judge you for that. I was a little wild in college myself."

"Well. Wild and wild." Faythe looked down at her dangling legs. "Oops. This position wasn't what the doctor ordered. I need to elevate my foot again. It's throbbing."

"All right. Here." Deanna helped Faythe to her feet and gave her the crutches. "Why don't you hop back into bed? You'll feel better with that foot elevated. I'll bring you more coffee."

"Good idea. Thanks." Faythe limped back to her bedroom and slid into bed. The down duvet nestled softly around her and the smell of lavender took Faythe back in time to when she'd stayed with Aunt

Nellie as a child. Of course she was in one of the guest rooms then, not the master bedroom suite, but the linen smelled the same and the luxurious duvets hadn't changed either.

"Here you go." Deanna handed over more coffee.

"Mmm." Faythe sipped it and hummed at the rich taste. "Jeez, you're good at this."

"Thanks. How about elaborating on what you were talking about before." Deanna curled up at the foot of the bed and didn't take her eyes off Faythe.

"Oh. That. Well, I have dated quite a few women. More than I can count. The thing is, I'm not the experienced vixen you might think. I can count my sexual partners on one hand. Most of them my girlfriends in college."

Deanna listened to Faythe stutter. "Are you apologizing for not being a wide-eyed virgin, or for not being a sex connoisseur?" She winked, and Faythe gaped, then laughed.

"Neither!" She fell back against the pillows, still laughing. "Sweet Jesus, woman, you're crazy."

"Yeah. I am. Pretty crazy about you, actually." Deanna had saved Faythe's coffee and now placed both mugs on the bedside table. "I don't care about any past partners, lovers, girlfriends, or whatever. Whoever you interacted with helped make you who you are. You're terrific, and if you think I was expecting a sexual acrobat who would orgasm while swinging from the rafters…well, that's something we'd have to practice, I suppose."

Faythe nearly lost her breath completely. Deanna slid up to her and looked her over seriously. "You seem a bit flustered, my dear. Can I assist you somehow to regain your composure, and your breath?"

"No. No, I'm fine. Honestly." Faythe eyed Deanna carefully. She hadn't expected Deanna's new playful side. "And I can't help but wonder how come you're so witty and chipper today."

"Oh, that's easy. I've met a deadline. I took digital pictures of my illustrations for the next Bunny Buttercup book, e-mailed them off, and the publisher and the writer both loved them."

"That's fantastic. We should celebrate. As long as I can keep my foot off the floor once in a while, I'm open to suggestions."

"Yeah?" Deanna hesitated. "Would you like to go on a picnic?"

"That sounds wonderful."

"It's a community picnic, of sorts, at my sister's school. Miranda and all the other students will be there."

"Your parents too?"

Deanna still looked friendly, but her shoulders stiffened. "No, not this time."

"Ah. Well, I look forward to meeting your sister. Is she as talented artistically as you are?"

"I don't know. She's not able to concentrate on things long enough for us to notice any particular gifts." Deanna looked seriously at Faythe. "Miranda has autism."

"Oh, I see." Faythe knew quite a bit about autism, having done a series about childhood disabilities for the network. "How old is Miranda?"

"Sixteen."

"Is she enrolled in a good school?"

"The best, according to my mother and stepfather." Her contempt was almost palpable.

"Well, I look forward to meeting Miranda. When's the picnic?"

"At four o'clock."

Faythe decided to be completely honest. "I look forward to it. I've spent time around kids diagnosed with autism. I won't approach Miranda until she's ready."

Deanna's expression softened, a welcome change that Faythe thought she'd never grow tired of seeing. She stopped in mid-thought and couldn't remember feeling this confused since her parents' divorce. She shoved the disturbing comparison out of her mind.

"So, how about we order one of those take-out picnic baskets from the bakery on Main Street?" Deanna asked.

"Sounds good."

"I'll go make the call. You rest, okay?"

"Bossy, aren't we?" Faythe thought her broad grin would crack her face. "Okay, okay, I'll rest." She leaned back against the pillows and sighed in relief when Deanna left the room. Still, she wanted to call out to Deanna to come back and hold her. She grimaced. "Ain't gonna happen," she mumbled to herself. "I'm not her type. Sometimes I wonder if I'm anybody's type."

CHAPTER EIGHTEEN

The day promised to be one of the last Indian-summer days with a warm, glowing sun in an azure blue sky dotted with cotton-candy clouds. Deanna carried the basket with bread, fruit, and a thermos of coffee in one hand and a cooler full of sodas, brie cheese, and slices of roast beef. There was also a surprise in the basket for Miranda. Faythe had asked if Miranda had a favorite food, and Deanna thought immediately of oatmeal cookies. Miranda would do just about anything for one.

Faythe had hobbled into the bakery with Deanna and picked out some oatmeal cookies and insisted on paying for them. "They're a present for your sister," she said stubbornly. "They're big enough, you think?"

"Any bigger and they'll fill her up like a three-course meal," Deanna said. "Once she gets going on those types of cookies, she goes crazy. She's supposed to stay away from sugar, since it boosts her energy too much, but she'll need a lot this afternoon, so she should be fine."

"So if I get three of them? With or without raisins?"

"Without," Deanna said, remembering when she'd bought oatmeal cookies with raisins a year ago. Miranda thought the raisins were little bugs and it took Deanna and Irene Costa over an hour to calm her down.

Faythe limped back to the car with the small bag of cookies, looking expectantly at Deanna as they strapped themselves in. "Is it far? The school, I mean?"

"No, it's on the other side of town, in a beautiful park, overlooking open countryside." Deanna pulled out into the nearly empty street. She was driving Faythe's Crossfire since her old piece of junk was at the garage having the radiator fixed.

"Sounds like a perfect place."

"I suppose." Deanna knew she sounded short, but it was hard to think of the school as beneficial.

"You don't sound sure."

"Oh, the school is great. Their autism program is cutting edge, and they've just opened a new wing for children diagnosed with severe neuropsychiatric disorders."

"You mean like ADHD?"

"Yes."

"Sounds good. Disorders can really handicap a kid socially."

"So true."

"I still get the feeling something bothers you about Miranda's situation."

"Nothing to do with the school." Deanna sighed.

"All right. I won't pry. For now. I'll attack when you have your guard down, or when I've distracted you with my naked body."

"What?" Deanna jerked the wheel slightly.

"Hey, watch the road, driver." Faythe pointed out the windshield. "Innocent bystanders at two o'clock."

"What were you saying about naked body?" Deanna refused to let Faythe off the hook.

"I'm a ruthless journalist, remember?" Faythe wiggled her well-plucked eyebrows. "I'm not beyond using my assets to get my hands on a story."

"Did you just say 'using your ass,' Faythe? I'm shocked." The friendly banter, spiced with sexual innuendo, made Deanna feel liberated.

"I said 'assets' and you heard me." Faythe stuck her nose in the air and huffed theatrically. "I've never used my *ass* in *that* manner, my good woman."

"Really? You don't know what you're missing."

"Deanna!" Faythe snorted. "You're as naughty as I am. Actually, I think you're worse."

"What do you mean? Did you think I was kidding?" Deanna deadpanned. "I was entirely serious."

"I think not."

Deanna couldn't stop a wide grin from forming. "No?"

"Nope."

"Well, my dear, we're both saved by the bell. The school bell, as it were." Deanna turned and drove through some gates where she waved at the guard on duty. She'd been coming here three times a week for nine years, so they recognized her on sight.

"Just so you know," Faythe said as Deanna maneuvered the car into the nearly full parking lot, "I may let you go for now, but I have a good memory for details." She uttered the last word an octave lower, obviously joking, but Deanna shivered.

"Duly noted."

They walked and hobbled respectively toward a big lawn where tables formed a U-shape. People were unpacking baskets and coolers while they were chatting.

"Deanna. Over here! Look, Miranda. There's Deanna now."

Irene Costa came up, holding Miranda's hand. Miranda was dressed in blue jeans and a red and white sweater. At first, she looked like any teenager, but up close, her vacant look, mixed with fear and suspicion, told a different story.

"Deanna," Miranda said. When Miranda spoke her name, which she rarely did, Deanna choked up and merely hugged her. She wasn't surprised or offended when Miranda immediately tried to break free. She didn't like to be touched and could become annoyed quickly, even throw a temper tantrum.

Deanna gestured for Faythe to follow them to the table Irene had reserved. Miranda had set the table and made the decorations, so Deanna fussed over everything. The decorations truly were exquisite. Miranda had combined petals from late-blooming flowers and different grasses to create napkin rings and a centerpiece that any florist would be proud to display.

The sight of Faythe clutching her bag of cookies while trying to balance herself on her crutches made Deanna flinch. "Oh, God, where's my head? You've got to sit down and—"

"—elevate." Faythe grinned. "No worries. I'm fine." She sat down with a thud, in spite of her brave words, and Deanna watched Miranda busily rearrange the napkin rings on the other side of the table.

"This is so pretty, Miranda," she said. "You're really getting the hang of working with plants and flowers."

Miranda didn't look up, but nodded with emphasis. "Live material."

"Excuse me?"

Irene explained. "Miranda and I have spent the last few days discussing the difference between live materials and inanimate objects." She smiled encouragingly toward Miranda. "Deanna will be really proud when she finds out how well you understand."

Deanna was stunned. Life, death, and non-living things were abstract concepts that some people with autism had a hard time grasping. It was amazing for Miranda to even care about learning the difference.

"Incredible," Faythe whispered from her side of the table. "That's huge, Deanna."

"I know." Deanna smiled at Faythe. "Pretty darn remarkable."

"Sure is."

Miranda looked in Faythe's direction. Deanna knew she wasn't meeting Faythe's eyes, but looking at her eyebrows or hairline.

"Miranda, Irene, this is Faythe, a friend of mine."

Miranda kept fiddling with the napkin holder, her fingers working faster and faster. When Faythe didn't say anything, Miranda became increasingly curious. Until recently, she'd never displayed curiosity or any other emotion. Now she glanced back and forth, probably trying to judge where Faythe fit into the scheme of things.

Used to waiting while Miranda figured things out, which could sometimes take days, Deanna unpacked the picnic basket. Faythe reached for the cooler, avoiding eye contact with Miranda.

Deanna checked her watch. It had taken Miranda less than ten minutes to come this far. Was this a day for miracles?

"Nice person?"

"Excuse me, honey?" Deanna said, turning toward Miranda again.

Miranda didn't repeat her question, but instead tugged at Irene's shirt.

"What is it, Miranda?" Irene enunciated.

Miranda took more flowers from a plastic bag and pushed them together on the table. She tugged at Irene's shirt again. "Nice person."

"Oh. I see. Well, here you go, Miranda." Irene gave her a plastic ring and some nylon strings.

Miranda stuck the tip of her tongue out the corner of her mouth while she created another napkin ring. When she was done she sat with it between her motionless hands, not looking up at either one of them. Irene caressed Miranda's soft, feathered hair and waited. Deanna held her breath.

"Nice...person." Miranda suddenly pushed the napkin ring lined with flowers toward Faythe. "Here-you-go."

Irene nodded at Faythe.

"Thank you, Miranda. This is beautiful. You're very talented, like your sister."

"Deanna."

"Yes, like Deanna." Faythe grinned and looked at Deanna. "You're both artists."

Deanna watched Miranda mull this over, though anyone who didn't know would think she was lost in her own world. Letting Miranda alone, Deanna arranged the last of the food they'd brought. Miranda wasn't picky about food, but she carefully examined everything she put in her mouth, which was time consuming.

"Good to meet you, Faythe," Irene said. "I wanted Miranda to take her time and finish her initial greeting before I said hello."

"I understand. Nice to meet you too, Irene. You're one of the teachers?" Faythe extended a hand to Irene.

"Not officially," Irene said. "I'm Miranda's special contact between her and the floor staff in her wing. I'm also an assistant teacher in the arts program."

"And Miranda's a natural, isn't she?"

"She is. She perceives space and pays attention to detail extremely well. She can search for hours for the right blade of grass or flower petal." Irene looked over at Miranda, who nodded solemnly. "And when you do, you can create just about anything, can't you, Miranda?" Irene looked proudly at her student.

"Hm-mm-hm-mm-hm-mm..." Miranda drummed her fingertips against the table as she hummed her odd little tune.

"What's the matter, honey?" Deanna asked and looked around.

"Something wrong?" Faythe asked.

"Oh, Lord," Deanna heard Irene whisper. "I'm sorry, Deanna. I had no idea."

"Mother and Percy…and they brought the brats." Deanna spoke between clenched teeth. She couldn't believe her mother would so blatantly disregard everything Deanna had written in Miranda's folder. Determined not to cause a scene that would make things worse for Miranda, she stood as her mother, stepfather, and his two teenage daughters approached. If her mother wouldn't put Miranda's needs before her own, Deanna would make sure she herself would.

"Mom," she greeted her small, elegant parent now less than ten feet away. Miranda focused on a croissant, and hadn't noticed the newcomers. "Why don't we walk over to the parking lot and discuss this initiative of yours."

"Discuss?" Angela Moore stood defiant in front of her. "There's nothing to discuss. I'm visiting my daughter on the yearly picnic as I always do."

"You are unbelievable." Deanna hissed low enough for Miranda not to hear, but everybody else did. "You show up, without even notifying the staff so they could prepare her, and you bring *them*." She snapped her head in the direction of Percy Bodell and his two daughters.

"Pipe down, why don't you?" the closest one, a pretty, but sullen, blonde said. "It's not like we *wanted* to come." Her voice carried easily over the sound of people talking at the tables around them.

"Trista!" Percy growled. "What did we say before we left the house?"

That they'd get another pair of Prada shoes if they came along and played the nice sisters? Deanna was ready to throttle Trista, but the girl backed off when her father glared at her.

"Apologize to Deanna," Percy insisted. Trista blushed furiously and Deanna wished he hadn't pushed it. Didn't he know his own daughter?

"I won't." Trista raised her voice again. "She's not part of our family."

"Deanna?" a small voice said from behind. Deanna whirled and saw Irene Costa there with Miranda in her arms and Faythe right next to them. Miranda was breathing in fast, shallow breaths. "Deanna? Mama? It's Saturday. *S-Saturday*."

"Gawd, look at her. What a waste," Trista said.

"*One* more word out of you..." Deanna said quietly, and her obvious vehemence seemed to find its mark because Trista paled and took a step back. Turning to Miranda, Deanna held out her arms. "Honey, it's all right. Come here. It's all right."

"No...not all right. No napkins. No plates. It's Saturday." Miranda stood there shaking, her mind obviously trying to take everything in.

Deanna looked at her mother. "Why did you have to do it this way? She's working herself up to a state."

"You're the one who started shouting," Angela said angrily.

"Not true," Deanna said so quietly she was nearly whispering. "Lower your voice and Irene might just help her through this without having to sedate her. She's looked forward to this picnic for a long time."

"Sedate her? Is that what you do here? Drug her senseless?" Angela was obviously too angry by now to lower her voice, and Deanna's heart broke when Miranda cried out behind them.

Chapter Nineteen

Faythe had never seen such fury on Deanna's face, or anybody else's. Pale, she pressed equally white lips together as she stalked toward her mother, who stumbled back as Deanna towered over her.

"Angela," Deanna said, "you've caused enough trouble with your thoughtlessness. Take Percy and the kids and *leave.*"

"You're the one causing a scene," Percy chimed in. "If you hadn't, we'd be all having some barbecue by now."

"Percy, shut up." Deanna was trembling visibly as she gestured in Miranda's direction. "Can't you see?"

Miranda had stopped wailing, but was whimpering like a wounded animal. Faythe reacted without thinking and moved closer to Irene and the distraught girl. "Hey, Miranda," she whispered, and plucked a few leftover flowers from the table, while balancing on one crutch. "Here, sweetie. Hold on to these. They're yours, aren't they?"

Miranda, still sobbing, reached out for the flowers and held them gently in her hand. She let go of Irene and cradled her other hand around the flowers in a protective gesture.

Irene came to the rescue also. "Faythe, why don't Miranda and I move to the other side of the lawn? The last wildflowers are still in bloom. Take your time on those crutches. We'll be right over there." She pointed at a small cluster of maples. Nodding curtly toward the Bodells, she guided Miranda across the lawn. Faythe shuffled on her crutches behind them.

When they reached the maples, Miranda simply sat down in the grass, caressing the stems up to the petals.

"Good thinking, Irene." Faythe maneuvered into a sitting position on a stump, trying to ignore her throbbing foot.

"Comes with experience and from knowing Miranda. It was clever of you to distract her with the flowers. Have you worked with autistic kids before?"

"No, only come across them very briefly." Faythe glanced at Miranda. "She's a sweet girl. She shouldn't be exposed to all those rampaging emotions."

"I know. They rarely visit on the same day. I can understand Angela wanting to be part of the picnic celebration, but I never thought she'd blatantly disregard her agreement with the clinic and Deanna."

"Jesus, I thought they would throttle each other." Faythe couldn't forget Deanna's fury. "Will you be okay looking after Miranda here? Now that she's out of earshot, Deanna probably won't hold back. She needs to consider the other kids here too."

"You're right. Why don't you go be the peacemaker and I'll stay with Miranda?" Irene touched Faythe's hand briefly. "Thank you."

"You're welcome." Faythe wanted to caress Miranda's beautiful hair, but knew better. She patted Irene's hand quickly instead, got up, and hobbled back to their table. Nobody was there. Deanna had maneuvered her family back toward the parking lot where the two teenagers, obviously bored, sat on a nearby bench, occupied with a cell phone.

"You'll never change, will you, Deanna?" Angela sounded tired and upset. "No matter what I do, or don't do, you're going to cling to your grudges and blame me."

"I'm not out to cast blame on anyone. You made your choices years ago, knowing full well the repercussions."

"Your vindictive attitude—"

"Vindictive!" Deanna flung her hands up, looking suddenly so hurt and exasperated that Faythe had to act. Using her crutches to lengthen her stride, she stood next to Deanna in seconds.

"Miranda is doing better. No need for any sedation. Irene is helping her pick flowers." Faythe put on her best professional expression, shifted one crutch over to her left, and extended a hand to Angela. "We haven't been properly introduced. No time, I guess." *Before all hell broke loose.* "My name is Faythe Hamilton."

"Oh, shit, Dad. It's *the* Faythe Hamilton. On morning TV!" Trista snapped her cell phone shut and rushed up from the bench, followed by her sister.

"Watch your language, Trista. Ms. Hamilton. What an honor. I can't imagine how you know Deanna." Angela's politeness barely masked her distress.

"We're neighbors and good friends." Faythe greeted the rest of the family the same way. Trista raised her cell phone after flipping it open again, obviously intending to take a picture. "Please, Trista. I'd rather you not. I'm here as a private person, not in my capacity as a TV reporter. If you ask me some other time, I'd be glad to pose with your sister while you take a picture." Pleased with herself for the smooth, reprimand, Faythe glanced at Deanna, who wasn't quite so pale anymore. "You okay?" she murmured.

"I'm fine. Thanks." Deanna took a deep breath. "Angela," she said, her voice low but steady. "I'm not trying to be difficult. This isn't about me. Not at all. We're here for Miranda's sake. It's her school picnic, and the staff have spent months preparing her and the others for this day so they could enjoy it. If Irene Costa or I had known you were coming, we could have both prepared Miranda for this type of change, you on your visiting days, I on mine. As for bringing Trista and Laney, maybe it would've been better to let them stay home and not force them to come. They're not here because they care about Miranda but because you made them come. I can't even begin to imagine why."

"They're part of the family. How can Miranda ever know her other sisters if she never sees them?" Angela sobbed. "All you do is criticize me. You find fault with everything I do." Percy wrapped a steadying arm around her.

"Miranda can't handle two selfish teenagers. If they came here because they care, one at a time on a regular basis, she might be able to cope, but since that's not the case…" Deanna pushed her hands into her jeans pockets. "I thought you read my note last time you put Miranda through a last-minute change."

"There you go again! It's like you accuse me of not caring, of not loving my own daughter."

The conversation was going downhill fast, and Faythe was about to ask a question when a group of people in formal business suits came down the broad steps from the main entrance. Faythe thought she heard Deanna moan and glanced her way.

"Mrs. Moore?" A blond woman stepped away from the group and came up to them. "We've met a few times a while back. Your daughter is making fantastic progress."

"Thank you." Angela shook the woman's hand, looking intimidated yet impressed. "This is my husband, Percy Bodell, and his two daughters, Trista and Laney." Angela glanced at Deanna. "And my oldest daughter, Deanna, and her friend Faythe Hamilton." She blushed faintly. "I'm terrible with names. Mrs. Mueller, isn't it?"

"Gloria Mueller." The smile on the bright pink lips faded marginally. She raised an eyebrow at Deanna. "We've met."

Faythe had to dig her nails into her palms to keep quiet. So this was Deanna's nemesis. Or one of them, at least. Elegant in a frosty sort of way, Gloria Mueller was a stunning woman in her late forties. She wore a dark blue skirt suit, with a crisp white blouse. Her hair was swept up in an elaborate twist, and the makeup was flawless, if a bit bright and too pink. She appeared to be tough, not a person you wanted in the opposite corner. But having Gloria *in* your corner actually sounded worse.

"Faythe Hamilton?" Gloria studied Faythe for a moment and clearly made the connection. "As a representative of my hometown, I want to welcome you to Grantville, Ms. Hamilton."

"Thank you." *Claiming the whole town as yours, eh, lady?* Faythe searched for weaknesses or flaws in Gloria's perfect appearance but couldn't spot any. "I was here many times as a child. I love it here." She stepped closer to Deanna, seeing no reason to explain how well they knew each other and that they lived next door to each other.

"Vacationing, I understand? You must come pay me a visit before you head back. I can arrange for a special tour of the city hall and its surrounding park."

"That's very nice of you," Faythe said cheerfully, trying to make her voice sound sugary innocent. "Deanna and I would love to. Perhaps next week?"

Gloria looked like she had herniated something. "Ah, next week? What a pity." She squinted and shifted her briefcase from one hand to the other. "We're having maintenance before the autumn season kicks off. I'll have to get back to you, Faythe."

Faythe knew no invitation would ever come unless it was for her alone, which was beyond rude. She wrapped an arm around Deanna's waist, smugly satisfied when Gloria's eyes narrowed and she looked like she would be sick.

"How lovely to meet a member of the school board." Angela studied Deanna closely and looked back and forth between her and Gloria. "We can't thank you enough for what the staff at Tremayne's does for our Miranda."

"Oh, that's what we love to do," Gloria said, a half smirk on her lips and a steely expression in her eyes. "I'm honored to dedicate my life to serving our community. It's also a privilege to be able to keep our young safe and out of harm's way."

Gloria's obvious hints would have been hilarious if they hadn't devastated Deanna, who leaned heavily against Faythe. Determined not to let on how this venomous snake affected Deanna, Faythe held her tight.

"Oh, I know," Angela said. "It's so important to find out the truth behind matters like that." She found the nucleus of truth instantly, without realizing it.

Faythe squeezed Deanna's side. *Please, honey, tell this woman off once and for all. You can do it.* But Deanna remained quiet until Gloria said good-bye to Angela and Percy.

"Isn't she a lovely, gracious person?" Angela asked.

"Actually, I thought she was a stuck-up bitch," Trista said from behind her father. "I didn't like her."

"Me either," Laney piped up.

Faythe was delighted. Maybe there was hope for the brats. She turned to Deanna, shaking her arm to get her attention. "Want to go help Miranda get ready for a little picnic with all of us? Maybe if we take a blanket and sit over by the flowers, it'll work out. She loves them and they calmed her once before." The question seemed to stir Deanna out of the personal hellhole Faythe knew she'd just visited.

"All right. Why not? We've already given the other families enough to gossip about." She let go of Faythe and started across the lawn.

Faythe studied Deanna's rigid, squared shoulders and wondered how many times she'd had to grin and bear it over the last few years. Sighing, she turned to the girls. "You two could help by bringing the food over." Faythe turned to Angela and Percy. "And the plates and decorations?"

"Sure," Percy said, and pushed his fingers through his thick, black hair. "We drove all the way here, after all."

"Excellent. See you in a bit. Just give us ten minutes. If we can't get through to her we'll have to call it a day, I suppose, and let Deanna take care of her."

"All right." Angela looked like she would cry, but then she, like her daughter, seemed to pull strength from somewhere and followed her stepdaughters and husband over to the picnic table.

When Faythe reached Deanna, Miranda, and Irene, her armpits and palms burned from using the crutches so much. She approached them slowly, not wanting to trigger another episode. Surprisingly, Miranda looked up, her hands full of flowers with their stems picked exactly the same length. "Faythe," she said. "Nice person."

Tears welled up in Faythe's eyes. Deanna looked just as taken aback, while Irene fumbled for a tissue and blew her nose.

"If you only knew." Deanna didn't say anything else, but those few words made Faythe realize what a significant step this was for Miranda.

"I can imagine," she murmured, and wiped quickly at her eyes. "Now. Do you think this can spill over to your family?"

Deanna's look clearly said she'd rather they leave, but she nodded. "Let's try." She cupped Miranda's chin and quickly let go when Miranda pulled back with an annoyed look. "Miranda. How about we ask Mama over to have the picnic with us?"

"It is Saturday."

"Yes. And it's a special Saturday."

"Mama comes on Sundays."

"But today is a special Saturday. All the other students have all their family members here. It wouldn't be fair if you couldn't have that too, would it?" Deanna flinched after she spoke. Had her own words struck a chord within herself, Faythe wondered. Deanna and her mother had denied Miranda the joy of being a complete family for years.

"Families and picnics." Miranda tilted her head as if she thought about it. "Even on Saturdays."

"Yes. Even on Saturdays."

Faythe intended to ask Deanna if any of them had ever bothered to ask Miranda what *she* wanted. Maybe the family feud kept them too occupied, and they had been trying to keep the hostility away from her.

"Mama?" Miranda looked over at the table where Angela and the others were gathering their things. "Leaving?"

"No, no. They want to come over here and sit on a blanket like you and I sometimes do."

"Yes. Come and sit on a blanket." That seemed to settle things for Miranda. She turned her attention back to the flowers and started lining them up on the grass, color coded and in perfect order.

Faythe caught Angela's attention and waved them over, and Irene offered to run up to Miranda's room and get the big picnic blanket Deanna stored there. She was back before the others had transferred all the items from the table. Soon they all sat on the edge of the plaid blanket with Miranda in the middle, busily arranging the decorative flowers in the empty squares. Grateful for the Indian summer that allowed the flowers to bloom later than usual and the families to enjoy such a sunny day, Faythe bit into a croissant and poured herself some coffee. Nobody spoke much. Perhaps they felt they'd said too much before. Faythe couldn't even begin to guess if this peace would last and lead to some understanding, but for now, it was a very good start.

CHAPTER TWENTY

When Faythe tripped and almost fell from exhaustion, Deanna took one of her crutches away. Wrapping her arm around Faythe's waist, she helped her inside. Faythe's skin was warm—no, hot, under her shirt. Worried that Faythe had overdone it, she hoped Faythe didn't have a fever.

"It ended on a good note, don't you think?" Faythe yawned.

"Yes. It did." Despite the emotions buried so deeply only a drilling rig could find them, the afternoon had been all about Miranda instead of old family feuds. Deanna had even awkwardly patted her mother on her shoulder when she got into the car with Percy and the girls. Angela looked stunned and her eyes were suddenly shinier than usual. Could Angela have missed her as much as she— Deanna tried to focus on Faythe.

Feeling guilty about how Faythe had hobbled back and forth on her crutches on one peacekeeping mission after another, Deanna took a firmer hold of her. Instead of the relaxing event they'd planned, they'd ended up in a major family drama. Once Angela and her family left, Deanna spent more time with Miranda to make sure she was all right and didn't realize how late it was until Faythe nodded off and nearly slipped off Miranda's desk chair.

Faythe waved toward the bed when they entered her bedroom. "Just want to lie down a bit. Can't believe how sore my arms are. And my hands. And shoulders. Ow."

"Why don't I help you get ready for the night? You're worn out."

"I'm fine." Faythe squinted up at Deanna. "Honestly. Just a bit sore and tired."

"You fell asleep in the car before we even passed the school gates."

"As I said. Tired."

Deanna shook her head. "I'm going to run you a bath. That'll help with the soreness." She held up a hand to keep Faythe from objecting. "Don't worry. I'll help you wrap your foot afterward."

"All right." Faythe sat on the bed, swaying. "I don't understand why I'm so tired."

"It's been a long day."

"I'm usually tougher than this." Faythe looked peeved.

"Even the sun has its spots, and you're obviously not that tough today. Actually, you were tough enough for ten earlier today when you stopped me from crumbling." Self-conscious, Deanna hurried into the bathroom, turned on the water, and rummaged through Faythe's bath salts. She loved how Faythe smelled, and when she opened a pink jar with the same scent, she poured some into the bathwater. When the tub was full, she had to quit stalling and face Faythe again.

Faythe was leaning against the pillows, her hand on the TV remote, almost asleep. She'd managed to remove everything but her underwear and the bandage around her foot, and her skin looked smooth and slightly tanned. Wearing only white cotton panties and sports bra, she seemed much younger than her age.

"Hey, the bath is ready. Want me to help you with that?" Deanna pointed at her wrapped foot.

"No, I'll be fine. Just give me the crutches and—oh!" Faythe fell back onto the bed. "Damn it. Why am I so tired? I'm used to working long hours."

"Not on crutches. Trust me. I know how much energy it takes to maneuver those suckers."

"You've been on crutches?"

"When I was sixteen. Fell off a ladder and broke my ankle." Deanna knelt in front of Faythe and began to unwrap her bandage. "I painted houses in the neighborhood on my summer break and misjudged a step. I landed on my left foot."

"Ouch."

"Yeah, but I was lucky. It healed without any complications. Hated the crutches though."

"They hurt your arms."

"That they do." Deanna supported Faythe on the way to the bathroom. Trying not to let her eyes rove too obviously along Faythe's half-naked body, she stopped inside the door, unsure what to do.

Faythe lit up. "Oh, how nice." She looked down at herself balancing on one foot next to Deanna. "Would you feel awkward helping me get in? I've managed this on my own so far, but I really feel light-headed."

"Not a problem." Deanna felt like the world's worst liar. Of course she would feel awkward. She wouldn't be able to keep from ogling Faythe's naked body, but she was pretty sure she could mask her reaction. *I hope.* She moved behind Faythe. "Arms up." Damn if she was going to stand right in front of Faythe and stare at her breasts. She pulled the sports bra over Faythe's head, then stared at her hips where the cotton panties beckoned her. Deanna spoke fast. "If I steady you, can you manage, then?"

"Sure." Faythe steadied herself against the wall with one hand and tugged at her panties with the other. "Hell, this isn't working. Let me sit on the edge of the tub." She turned around and her breasts were the most beautiful Deanna had ever seen. Small, slightly pointy, and with plump, pink nipples, their sway was barely noticeable as Faythe managed to pull her panties down to her thighs and sit in one fluid motion. She swayed, but Deanna held her shoulders. "Careful."

"Trying to." Faythe pushed the panties off the rest of the way and eased them aside with her uninjured foot. "So. There." She turned, holding on to Deanna, and slid gracefully into the large tub. "Jesus, this is heaven." She sank below the foam on the surface, ending Deanna's torment of trying to look everywhere but at Faythe's breasts and the spare tuft of caramel brown hair between Faythe's legs.

"I knew it'd be good for you. You'll feel better soon." Deanna knelt next to the tub and felt the water, making sure it hadn't cooled. "How about some tea?"

"Tea?" Faythe wrinkled her nose. "Have you ever seen me drink tea? Ever heard me *mention* that foul beverage?"

"Eh, no, now that I think about it." Deanna smiled. Faythe looked cute with disgust written all over her face.

"If you're going to bring us anything, I'd love an espresso."

"Espresso? At this hour?" Deanna checked her watch. "It's ten o'clock."

"I'll sleep like a baby. Coffee never keeps me up. Chocolate does, though. Could be good to know."

"Okay, so if I want you awake, I'll buy you some of that dark Lindt chocolate."

"Right." Faythe looked alarmed. "Oh, damn. You're the one with all the emotional upset today and you have to pamper me like this. I'm sorry."

"Hey, don't worry. I'm not that upset. And I actually enjoy taking care of you. It's been a while, not counting Miranda."

"Really? I'm not coming off as a super-pain?"

"No. You're fine." *Damn it, you're fine.*

Faythe blushed and pushed her now wavy hair back from her face. "If you look at me that way, I'll pull you in here with me," she said breathlessly.

"What way?" Deanna thought she'd managed to conceal her arousal.

"Like you want to push all the bubbles away and devour me… with your eyes."

Deanna nearly leaped to her feet, but Faythe's green eyes had mesmerized her.

"I do, but haven't we moved beyond that?" Faythe spoke slowly, as if she carefully considered every word.

"What do you mean?"

"Don't get me wrong." Faythe raised a soapy arm and outlined Deanna's cheek with a wet finger. "I find you very attractive. Honestly, Deanna, you make me so hot sometimes, I forget to breathe. You're stunning, you seem to see only me. You don't undress me with your eyes. You don't have to. It's like you can see beneath my clothes, inside my heart sometimes. That's why I say, this attraction thing…we've come further, haven't we?"

Deanna struggled to take the next breath. "But you don't want that. You're not into relationships."

"Oh." Faythe's hand lingered in the air and then she drew a new slow pattern on the side of Deanna's neck. "I think you misunderstand. It's not that I don't want it. I just don't think I have it in me, I mean, the knowhow."

"So you'd want to if you thought you'd be able to?" Deanna tried to follow Faythe's reasoning, which was damn near impossible when she touched her like this. A few drops of water ran inside her shirt collar and across her collarbone. One ran down to her cleavage and another disappeared into her bra. Shivering, Deanna clasped Faythe's hand and held it to her cheek before kissing her fingertips gently.

"That question scares the living daylights out of me, Deanna, but when you do that... I've never let anyone close enough for the possibility to even come up."

"I'm no great catch," Deanna said, "and it's not like I'm proposing." Her cheeks warmed. "But these last few years have really screwed with my mind, and I need to know what I'm getting myself into."

"Would you find having an autumn fling acceptable?"

"Define 'fling.'"

"You know what a fling is!"

"I know my definition, but I'm not sure that's what you mean. For me a fling is something temporary, feelings you count on will pass, and something shallow." Deanna shook her head. "So, no. I really don't think so."

"What if it was tentative instead of temporary? And with feelings based on loyalty and friendship, with every potential to grow. And far from shallow." Faythe trembled now, and Deanna cursed inwardly for putting her through this emotional workout when she was so tired and probably in pain.

"If that was the case," Deanna murmured, "if that's your definition, then it's something I could understand. Deal with."

"Maybe I'm not explaining myself very well. I've never taken to anyone this fast, and against such odds. I mean, why would you ever want to bet on someone like me?" Faythe shrugged. "I know I look good. I can be fun, and as a friend I'm as loyal as they come. But I've lived a pretty shallow life in many ways, and even if I'm dead-set on changing that—what if I screw up?" Her eyes darkened and Deanna knew it was time to act. She simply couldn't stand by while Faythe took all the "blame" for any challenges they might face if they dared to take another step together.

Deanna cupped Faythe's chin. "Hey, stop it. You were wonderful today. You stood by me when that witch showed up, and you calmed everybody else down and even got the brats to help."

"Don't call them that. Even if they act like it, call them Trista and Laney."

Deanna was about to object when she saw the seriousness in Faythe's eyes. "Okay. You're right, you're right. No name calling." She brushed her thumb across Faythe's lower lip. "Anyway, what I meant to say was, you're selling yourself short. You're amazing. And gorgeous." She kissed Faythe's cheek softly. Faythe turned her head and soon Deanna was devouring her parted lips.

"Deanna." Faythe whimpered. "You taste so good."

"Mmm?" Deanna was lost in the sweet, hot kisses. She gently pushed against Faythe's tongue, and her heart pounded when Faythe reciprocated the intimate caresses.

"I have…an idea." Faythe spoke in short bursts. "Why don't you join me?"

"Huh?" Deanna had hardly heard the words Faythe spoke into her mouth.

"Come into the tub with me. We can run the jets. And…relax." Faythe looked sexy as hell where she sat among the bath bubbles with her hair a total mess.

Before Deanna could think of the right words to talk herself out of it, she pulled her shirt off and removed her jeans. She yanked off her underwear, then stood motionless, uncertain where to climb in.

"Here," Faythe said, extending a hand. "Behind me."

Trembling, Deanna climbed into the warm water, the foam tickling her skin as she sat down behind Faythe. She slid her legs alongside her, completely aware of the fact that her own sex would soon press against Faythe's bottom. That well-shaped, firm bottom now squirmed in front of her, pushing back. Faythe leaned against Deanna, sighing deeply. The feeling of Faythe's wet, smooth skin against her breasts made Deanna's nipples harden until they ached, completely sensitized by the closeness.

"Oh, yes." Faythe murmured something intelligible and squirmed. "Mmm."

"Sit still. Please." She could barely get the words out without groaning from sheer pleasure.

"Why? What's the matt—" Faythe glanced at Deanna. "Oh."

"Yes. Oh."

"Aha." Small devils danced suddenly in the deep green of Faythe's eyes. "I see."

Deanna was afraid to ask what Faythe saw. Instead she focused on where to place her arms. She tried the bathtub edges, but the surface was unpleasantly cool. She let them float in the water, but they bumped into Faythe's sides occasionally. Faythe finally took Deanna's hands and wrapped herself in her arms. She purred and rubbed her cheek against Deanna's right arm.

"Faythe," Deanna said through clenched teeth. "Sit *still*."

"I am sitting still. Pretty much." Faythe turning sideways a bit, snuggling in between Deanna's breasts while pulling up her legs.

With her arms full of one beautiful, cuddly woman that she also cared deeply about, Deanna knew she would lose control unless she did something radical, but she had no idea what that might be. Faythe started the jets, and the overall massage stimulated every nerve ending on Deanna's skin.

"Faythe. Look at me." Deanna hardly recognized her own deep, hoarse voice.

Faythe tipped her head back, her eyes heavily lidded and her cheeks flushed. Deanna couldn't take her eyes off her, yet she had to in order to kiss her. Faythe moaned softly into her mouth as they deepened the kiss. She tasted of berries and something else, something dark and sweet and intoxicating. Faythe's hip pressed against Deanna's sex and their bodies rubbed together in the turbulent water.

"Oh, please, please, touch me." Faythe pressed her face into Deanna's neck, latching on to her skin there. "I'm burning. I swear I'm burning up."

"Show me." Deanna wanted nothing more than to touch Faythe, explore every part of her. She wanted to learn what pleased her, what inflamed her, and what drove her crazy.

Faythe took Deanna's hand and pushed it down between her legs. "There. Touch me. Just your fingertips. Right there. Oh. Yeah."

"All right. I've got you." Deanna felt her way between the folds of Faythe's sex. Faythe's moans guided her, as did her whimpers and eventually her cry of pleasure when she found the exact spot. Deanna slid her fingertips back and forth in an erratic rhythm, patient and eager at the same time, wanting to give Faythe what she needed.

"Deanna," Faythe said, breathing hard. "I want to touch you. Like this."

"You will."

"It can't be…just about me." Faythe trembled and clung to her.

"Oh, my…" Faythe threw her head back, exposing her neck in an ancient sign of surrender when her orgasm hit. She cried out once, a short, husky sound that sent a flood of moisture to the junction of Deanna's legs. She wasn't sure if Faythe wanted her to go inside, but Faythe seemed to ride one wave after another. Deanna pushed her palm hard against Faythe's throbbing sex and reveled in the sensations.

Eventually Faythe calmed down, and Deanna couldn't take the onslaught of the massaging water any longer. She slapped the button with her palm, relieved when the water stilled around them. Listening to Faythe's breathing, she put her own desire on hold for a moment, knowing her time would come. She planned to take Faythe to bed if she wanted to be held all night. "How are you doing?" She squeezed Faythe gently where she lay cradled in her arms.

"I'm in heaven, I think." Faythe's sexy purr was back.

"Good. Now, that said, heaven seems to be getting a bit cold. How about we get up, dry off, and snuggle down into bed. Your bed. It's bigger." Deanna kept her tone light, not wanting to sound like she was begging.

"Sounds absolutely perfect." Faythe struggled to get up. "Just one problem. My knees seem to have lost what little cohesion they had, thanks to you."

"Well, I'll just have to make good use of the first-aid course I took a few years ago and drag you out of the water and toss you over my shoulder. You know, firefighter style."

"Oh. Sounds very sexy. I could learn to enjoy such a scene."

Deanna laughed. "All right, here goes." She moved out from behind Faythe and stepped out of the tub. Large bath towels hung on a heated towel rail on the opposite wall and she retrieved two of them, wrapping one around herself before helping Faythe out and covering her.

"Mmm. Thanks." Faythe held on to Deanna and limped over to the sink. Brushing her teeth, she shivered slightly, and Deanna wrapped yet another heated towel around her. Faythe leaned against Deanna as they returned to the bedroom.

"There. Get into bed. I'll brush my teeth and make sure the door is locked." After she tucked Faythe under the covers she hurried to the guest bathroom. After checking the door, she strode back through the house, shivering. She tugged the towel closer around her, but discarded it next to Faythe's bed and joined her. Faythe lay curled up on her side, seeming to be asleep. Deanna pushed the disappointment out of her mind, knowing how tired Faythe was.

"Mmm, there you are." Faythe rolled over on her back, pulled Deanna close, and kissed her passionately. "I've been waiting and waiting."

"I was only gone half a minute."

"As I said. Waiting and waiting." Faythe kissed her again, moving on top of her. "Now, you must show me. Show me exactly what you want, and how, and I'll be at your beck and call."

Deanna's banked fire suddenly roared. She arched into Faythe's caressing hands. "Just touch me any way you want, any way you like. I'm so far gone…it won't take much."

"Oh. Really. Well, we can't have that. I want to enjoy you properly." The devilish tone in Faythe's soft voice suggested to Deanna that she wouldn't orgasm or sleep anytime soon. Moaning under Faythe's hands, she couldn't remember any of the reasons she'd been so hesitant to take this step with Faythe.

Not a single one.

CHAPTER TWENTY-ONE

Faythe sighed in relief when she cautiously stepped on her sprained foot and, for the first time, it didn't twitch in agony. She looked over her shoulder at the sleeping Deanna. Deliciously naked, except for the parts of her tangled in the bedsheets. She was in a deep sleep, which didn't surprise Faythe since they'd made love several times during the night. The memory of their passionate kisses and caresses so hot she thought she'd self-combust made Faythe's stomach muscles quiver.

Tiptoeing to the kitchen, Faythe thought back to the picnic three days ago, when another piece of the puzzle that was Deanna came into play. Her family had been on a collision course, but the hurt wasn't just one-sided. Faythe had seen as much anguish in Angela's eyes as in Deanna's, but Miranda was doubtlessly missing out the most.

But the entire dynamic had changed when Gloria Mueller entered the equation. If her daughter was anything like her, it might not be a good idea for Deanna to meet Savannah. Gaining closure was a positive step, but when the other party was kin to a barracuda like Gloria, closure could entail a whole new set of problems.

A buzzing noise made Faythe nearly drop the eggs she'd taken from the refrigerator. Her cell phone, which was charging on the other countertop, vibrated its way across the surface. The display said "Unknown" and she hesitated before answering.

"Hello?"

"Faythe? It's Pammie."

"Pammie! How are you?"

"Fine. I tried to call the other day, to ask about your foot, but got your voice mail."

"Oh, shoot. I've deliberately not checked my voice mail lately, but I'm sorry I missed your call. Been off my foot pretty much, which has paid off. I'm walking on it today for the first time without crutches."

"Just don't overdo."

"Yes, *Mom.* So, what can I do for you, Pammie?"

"Eh, well…boy, am I busted or what?" Pammie laughed. "I did call to ask about how you're doing, but I also called to ask if you've thought any more about talking to Nana?"

"Who? Oh, your friend. Nearly forgot that in all the commotion." Faythe thought quickly.

"Commotion? You know, if you're up to your neck in stuff, you sure don't need the extra stress."

"No, no, it's not like that. It wasn't really my commotion. I'm more of a spectator."

"Or an innocent bystander," Deanna purred next to Faythe as she wrapped her arms around her from behind.

Faythe jumped. "Yikes."

"Whose sexy voice is that?" Pammie laughed, sounding surprised. "I sure didn't mean to interrupt anything, Faythe."

"You didn't." Faythe swatted playfully at Deanna's roving hands.

"The one who the commotion's about, I bet." Pammie giggled. "So, don't share all the gory details, then. Be that way."

"Some other time." Faythe closed her eyes as Deanna nibbled her neck with her hot lips. "Why, eh, oh…don't you bring, uh, your friend over this afternoon? Around two-three something?"

"Really? You sure? Oh, you're the best!" Pammie sounded so relieved that Faythe started to worry. What if this friend was seriously depressed? "Hey, you took care of me when I hurt my foot—"

"Ah. About that," Pammie said, her voice barely audible now. "I don't think you would've stumbled and sprained your ankle if I hadn't bothered you."

"Nonsense." Faythe felt Deanna stiffen against her and wrapped an arm reassuringly around her waist. "I'm responsible for using my five, sometimes six, senses. I'm glad you were there."

"Me too," Deanna mouthed before nuzzling her forehead, tickling her hairline.

"I'm glad you see it that way. I just know you'll be able to get through to Nana."

"Let's hope so." Faythe paused as Deanna kissed her neck again. "I, uh, I'm going to try, but if she's feeling that bad, she might need professional help."

"Oh, I've thought about that, but she won't even consider it. It's like this is her Golgotha, you know."

"Absolution?" Faythe looked up at Deanna and caressed her tousled hair. Deanna wore only a soft polar-fleece blanket, and Faythe wanted to pull it off and claim her right then and there. "We'll see how it goes. See you later, Pammie."

"Later."

They hung up and Faythe attacked Deanna's teasing lips, kissing her hungrily.

"I thought…hmm…you were making breakfast. Am I misinformed? Am I to be your breakfast, Ms. Hamilton?"

Loving this playful side of Deanna, so deliciously unexpected, Faythe grinned. "Now that you mention it." She patted the countertop behind Deanna. "Up you go, honey."

"What?" Deanna raised a sardonic eyebrow. "There?"

"Yup. Here let me assist you," Faythe said, and pulled the blanket slowly from Deanna's body. The kitchen was warm and cozy, but Deanna's nipples puckered. Lingeringly, Faythe cupped a breast and let the hard nipple prod her palm. She loved the feeling of it, how it gave away Deanna's arousal, and how it made Faythe feel.

Deanna broke free for an instant and jumped up on the counter. Sitting there with an angelic smile, she gestured to herself. "All right. I'm all yours."

"You may not be smiling so confidently in a little while." Faythe pushed Deanna's knees apart and moved in between them. She placed her hands on Deanna's breasts, squeezing them gently, and then harder, encouraged by Deanna's moans. Leaning forward, Faythe began to lick one nipple while her fingers teased the other one into an impossibly firmer peak.

"Mmm, I like how you think," Deanna said in a low growl. "I like how you act on your thoughts."

"And I like how you sound when I do this." Faythe looked up as she gripped Deanna's hips and let her hands slide back to her bottom.

She squeezed and massaged, eliciting deeper and huskier moans when she took one of Deanna's nipples in her mouth.

"Faythe…"

"Mmm?"

"Oh," Deanna whispered. "You're like fire."

"No, you are." Faythe pushed a hand down between them, slipping inside Deanna with ease. Feeling her own arousal surge, Faythe wrapped her free arm tight around Deanna while caressing her deeper and deeper with the other. "You're so hot, I'm concerned you have a fever," she said teasingly. "You might just need a thorough examination."

"Yes, Dr. Hamilton. Whatever you say." Deanna groaned and shifted restlessly on the countertop. "I think I need your healing touch very, very badly."

Faythe picked up a steady rhythm, pushing into Deanna, rubbing her thumb around her clitoris without actually touching it. Deanna moaned again and spread her legs in a wordless invitation.

"Jeez. You feel so good." Faythe's voice was barely audible even to herself, but Deanna seemed to hear her.

"You make me *feel* so good."

Faythe clung to Deanna with her arm around her waist, burying her head against her neck. As Deanna eventually trembled and pressed her knees together, Faythe knew she was going to come. "Oh, yeah," she murmured, and moved her hand faster, her thumb directly on Deanna's clitoris.

"Faythe, oh yes. Yes!" Deanna clutched at her, her mouth half open as she breathed the words against the top of Faythe's head. She soon became incoherent and Faythe became so turned on by the sounds Deanna made, she nearly came too. Holding Deanna tight, she kissed her temples and cooed softly, which would have sounded completely dorky any other time, but right now, it felt like the right thing. Deanna finally seemed to find her bearings and sat up, smiling lazily at Faythe.

"So, this is how you fix breakfast?"

"Yeah, it's a good cardiovascular start in the morning." Faythe grinned. "Honestly, I'd planned on a conventional mushroom omelet."

"Aha. Well, before you get started, I want to know one thing."

"What's that?" Faythe pushed a damp strand of hair from Deanna's face. She had never looked as stunning.

"Did you come?"

"Eh, no. Not yet. I mean, this was my fantasy, but really, it was all about you."

"So you don't need to come."

"Oh, sure, *eventually*." Faythe felt herself blush. "But you're hungry, right?"

"Oh, yes. I am. Starving, in fact." Deanna leaned back on her hands and looked so innocent Faythe knew she was being facetious.

"What are you talking about?"

"Not what. Whom. I'm starving for you, for that sweet little mouth of yours, to begin with." She tugged Faythe closer again, devouring her lips. The desire that simmered skin-deep erupted and Faythe whimpered as Deanna cupped her breasts inside Faythe's robe.

"So where do you want me? Any fantasy I can help you with?" Faythe gasped as Deanna bit down gently on her neck.

"You're already doing it." Deanna stood and took Faythe into her arms. "You've been doing it since day one."

❖

"When's your friend coming over?" Deanna asked as she poked her head into the living room where Faythe sat with her laptop on the couch.

"In an hour or so. You're welcome to stick around, though." Faythe gazed longingly at her lover, who was entirely dressed in black. Black, slightly faded jeans, black long-sleeve T-shirt, black ankle boots, and a black down vest. She moved with a pantherlike grace. *So sexy. So incredibly hot.*

"I have to make a bunch of calls about the feedback my publisher and the writer sent regarding Bunny Buttercup." Deanna kissed Faythe tenderly. "Then Todd from the garage is bringing the car. He lives just up the road and offered to drive it home for me."

"Sweet of him."

"I know. So I'll be back around seven tonight, okay? Maybe sooner."

"Okay." Faythe didn't want to admit that she wanted Deanna around for backup and knew she'd miss her as soon as she left the room. *Boy, I've got it bad.* She'd fallen fast and hard for Deanna. *I don't understand and I certainly can't explain it.*

"All right. See you later." Deanna kissed her again and hoisted her backpack onto her shoulder. "I have my cell if you need me."

"Thanks."

Faythe returned to her text and let her fingers merely play with the keys, typing the words as they came. She had always worked like that, a fact that drove her study-group friends at college crazy. Usually, when she went through the text later in the evening or the next day, she found quite a few gold nuggets to work with, or at least she thought so. *Mom would probably call me delusional and say that I'm kidding myself. No, that's what Dad would say.*

Her mother would start in on the guilt trip from hell, listing all the sacrifices she'd made during Faythe's upbringing, especially remaining married to a man she didn't love for Faythe's sake. For the first time, thinking about what her mother had "given up" didn't affect Faythe. If Cornelia meant that she had sacrificed sleeping with an abundance of men, she'd more than made up for it later. Faythe had lost count of her mother's lovers by the time she left for college. A new thought occurred to her. Was her high-profile job as a TV personality a way for her mother to keep scoring? Faythe laughed. It sounded too preposterous.

The doorbell rang and she jumped. Carefully, Faythe saved her document and closed the laptop before limping slowly to the front door. Being a city girl, she checked through the side window and was reassured to see Pammie standing next to a slightly shorter young woman. Faythe took a deep breath and opened the door. Pammie looked a little nervous as she wrapped her arm around the girl. She was stunning, with long black hair framing a heart-shaped face, gray eyes, and pink, full lips. *Geez, just my type when I was in college. Can't say I blame Pammie for going the extra mile for her.*

"Nice to see you again, Pammie. As you can tell, I'm fully ambulatory again." Faythe turned to the other girl. "Hello, there. I'm Faythe. You must be Nana."

"Yes. Thank you." Nana looked nervously around, even glancing over her shoulder before she stepped inside. "I didn't realize you lived...out here."

"Oh, I see. Well, this is my aunt's cabin and I'm just borrowing it. Why don't we go into the kitchen? The view is great and I've baked an apple pie, believe it or not." Faythe made small talk on the way to the kitchen, trying to create a more relaxed mood. She told Nana about how she'd decided to take a break from her career so she could try to figure out what to do next.

"I thought you'd be thrilled to be so popular on TV and everything?" Nana sat down at the table, crossing her arms in front of her. "Isn't that a career of a lifetime?"

"Depends on what you really want, doesn't it?" Faythe placed the steaming slices of apple pie on some plates and served coffee. "Ice cream with the pie, ladies?"

"Yes, ma'am," they echoed, smiling at each other.

"You're my kind of people," Faythe said, scooping up vanilla ice cream. "Dig in. We can chat while we eat."

At first the girls seemed preoccupied with the dessert and coffee, and even Pammie seemed a bit shy. Faythe decided it was time to loosen things up. "Want to hear some Hollywood gossip?" She had yet to come across anyone who wasn't interested in a little inside information.

"Oh, yes," Nana said, surprising Faythe by speaking up first.

"Well, I would never gossip about anything anyone told me in confidence, but I can share a tidbit about one of our favorite actresses. It will become common knowledge soon, but you have to keep it to yourself until then." Faythe wasn't kidding herself. They'd be texting their friends the moment they left, but she didn't see any harm in it. The news she was about to share with them had already broken in the inner circles in Hollywood and New York.

"We promise," Pammie said gravely, her grin contradicting her words.

"Hmm." Faythe gave them a mock glare. "Well, you know Carolyn Black, the actress, right?"

"*The* Carolyn Black, who plays Diana Maddox in the movies?" Nana's mouth fell open.

"The very same. Anyway, she's getting married in New Haven, Connecticut, in two weeks."

"Oh." Pammie smiled politely and both the girls' faces lost their wonder, since an actress getting married was hardly a scoop. "That's neat."

"Wait. There's more." Faythe leaned forward. "She's marrying her lover of three years. Annelie Peterson."

"Really?" Pammie's eyes grew wide. "*Really?*"

"Really."

"Carolyn Black's gay?" Nana looked back and forth between them. "For real?"

"For real. It's been a public secret for years, but she's pretty private and so is her partner, so the press has been keeping the lid on. We knew if we spilled the beans, these two women would never give us an interview again, nor would any of their big-star friends."

"That's some news." Pammie glanced at Nana. "Which kind of ties into why we're here."

Nana recoiled visibly, pressing herself against the seat back and folding her arms over her chest. "Pammie," she said in a low, warning voice.

"Nana, quit stalling. I practically had to drag you here, and you know it kills me when you treat yourself like you do."

"It's really not your business how I live my life, is it?" Nana spoke curtly, and even if Faythe sympathized with Pammie, she also recognized the pain behind Nana's words.

"It is my business, because I love you," Pammie said hoarsely. "I'm not ashamed of it, and you can't make me stop."

Pammie's soft voice shattered Nana's defenses, and the young woman gripped the edge of the table with enough force to whiten her knuckles. "But I'm not worth your love. Or anyone's. You *know* that." Her words sounded half accusatory, half pleading.

"No, I don't!" Pammie whispered, her voice intense. "I don't know that at all. *You* think that. You think you don't deserve to be loved, but that's not true!" Pammie looked like she tried to stay calm, but her voice quivered. "And it's the same as saying that I'm doing something wrong too."

"What do you mean?" Nana seemed to have forgotten about Faythe for a moment. She only had eyes for Pammie. "You're perfect. You do everything right."

"Everything apart from being gay, you mean?" Pammie's eyes hardened.

"Those are my mother's words."

"And you must think there's something to them, since you keep on bringing them up."

"I've never said it's wrong to be gay!"

"You've used your mother's opinions as an excuse for a lot of things, which is nearly the same thing."

"Stop. Wait. Hold it." Faythe pushed the ice-cream carton between them. "Have some more ice cream and chill. No pun intended. You won't solve anything by playing the blame game."

"But…" Pammie looked rebellious.

"Eat."

The girls looked at each other and reached for the spoon at the same time.

"Here. Let me." Nana scooped up some ice cream and put it on Pammie's plate. "I'm sorry for yelling."

"Oh, honey, I'm sorry for yelling too." Pammie said. "I knew we needed a referee. We've only reached the yelling stage so far."

"It's my fault." Nana stared at her ice cream and tears rose in her eyes. "I don't mean to sound self-absorbed or melodramatic. It's true."

Faythe sipped her coffee and looked encouragingly at Nana. "Why don't you tell me why you think it's your fault, though I don't even know what fault we're talking about."

"I did something terrible. I lied. To a lot of people. I was such a bitch."

"Why did you lie, and what was it all about?"

"I was hurt, which was entirely my own fault, and I wanted to hurt the other person back. Instead of just causing her to be embarrassed, I destroyed her life."

"Can you tell me more?" Faythe asked, her heart thundering.

"I was eighteen at the time. I'm twenty now. She was my high school art teacher and I had such a crush on her. I'd never been attracted to another woman or girl before, and to me it was obvious she had to feel the same way. My parents wanted me to keep going steady with my boyfriend, but once I realized how I felt about my teacher, I knew I could never feel that way about a boy, or a man."

"You're Savannah Mueller." Faythe stared at the girl who'd caused Deanna so much pain. She'd been prepared to loathe her with every cell in her body, but instead she saw this guilt-ridden, traumatized young woman who'd clearly lost herself in the process.

"How do you know?" Nana stared at her with fear in her wide eyes before redirecting her attention to Pammie. "You said she had no idea about anything. Did you tell her?"

"No. Of course not. Didn't you notice that she lives next to Ms. Moore?" Pammie gestured toward the lake. "And you wanted to meet her, didn't you?"

"Jesus, I can't believe this." Faythe's mind was whirling. "I have to call Deanna. She needs to know you're here. She's been debating whether to call you back. I offered to let her use my aunt's house, so nobody would spot you entering her cabin."

"And now we're here." Pammie looked pale. "I never meant to put you on the spot like this. I had no idea you two were, eh, friends."

"Well, we are, and one way or the other we need to resolve this. Deanna has suffered long enough, and from the looks of it, so have you, Savannah. Or do you prefer Nana?"

"Either is fine." Nana shrugged. Suddenly she flinched, looking shell-shocked while staring at something behind Faythe.

"What the hell's going on here?" a stark voice demanded from the doorway. "So these are your friends?" Deanna stalked up to them and stared back and forth between Faythe and Savannah.

"Deanna—" Faythe began.

"Let me see. What possibilities are there here for you as an author? I can imagine you're getting quite the background to your story. Or were you convinced I was a coward, unable to make up my mind about whether to call her?"

"Of course not! I'd never barge in like that. This isn't for a story. I had no idea Pammie's friend was Savannah Mueller. I only found out a moment ago. She—"

"Oh, please, Faythe. You're a famous TV reporter looking for a new gig. I dropped a juicy story right in your lap, and you figured it was just the right size for you to dig your perfect little teeth into."

"That's not true. I realize how it must look, but please, Deanna. You know me pretty well. This past week, if it meant anything to you, ought to have proven that I'm loyal to you."

"I don't think you know the meaning of the word." Deanna was pale now and she stared at Savannah with nearly black eyes. "I can't imagine what your agenda is, but if you've come to spoil things for me, you've succeeded beyond your wildest dreams."

"It's not true. Faythe didn't know my real name. I swear."

"You've sworn before, and look what happened then." Deanna turned her attention back to Faythe. "I won't bother you any longer.

You're back on your feet, in more ways than one. I'll just get my stuff and then I'll be back in my own cabin." She whirled around and left the kitchen.

Faythe stared after Deanna's disappearing back. When she turned to look at her visitors, Pammie looked completely stricken, and Nana had begun to cry.

Chapter Twenty-two

Deanna found it almost impossible to breathe. She ran back to the room she had been using, grabbed her bag, and began to cram her clothes and art supplies into it. She just wanted to get out of Faythe's house as quickly as possible. Tears streamed down her cheeks and she sobbed, so angry and hurt she could hardly think.

"Deanna. Please."

Faythe's voice from the doorway made her flinch. She wasn't prepared to have any sort of confrontation with Faythe, not now, perhaps never.

Faythe hesitantly entered the room. "I know how it looks, but I had no idea who Pammie's friend was. She calls her Nana. I never made the connection."

"Not now, Faythe," Deanna said, her voice hurting her throat. She couldn't stop sobbing and wiped angrily at her cheeks. "Not even you can be that gullible."

"Don't. Don't say stuff like that." Faythe moved into Deanna's personal space. "I know this is your MO, cutting people out, running off. If I let you go now, I won't see you again. I know because you've done the same to your mother for almost ten years."

"I have done...*I* have done?" Deanna said, speaking louder. "Leave my mother, and my entire family, out of this. You did this behind my back, and it has nothing to do with either of them. You sure played the part of the cute girl next door well. I swallowed every single lie you told, hook, line, and sinker." Deanna knew how sarcastic she sounded, and the stricken look on Faythe's face confirmed it. "You had me fooled that you were this vulnerable, misunderstood woman, and I think you proved once and for all that you're as callous as your parents. A chip off the old block, huh?"

"Deanna!" Faythe's eyes became nearly colorless against her pale face. "I was only trying to help."

"I've had enough of your help, so if you'll excuse me..." She didn't want to physically push Faythe out of the way, but the pain of being in such close proximity made her contemplate it.

"No, I won't excuse you," Faythe said furiously. "I can understand why you'd jump to conclusions, after what you've been through. But I won't accept that you think I lied to you or would sell you out like that. Not after last Saturday, and certainly not after the last few days."

"You're incredible." Deanna blinked at the storm of emotions on Faythe's face. "I come home early because I couldn't stand to be away from you and what do I find? You and Savannah Mueller sitting by the kitchen table having a great time." Deanna hated the image she'd just described. "I had decided to try to communicate with her, you know. I thought, with you here, to chaperone and to help me stay as impartial as possible, I just might be able to go through with it."

"And you still can! Nothing's changed." Faythe looked like she wanted to shake Deanna. "I promise you I'm telling the truth."

Deanna wanted to believe her. Images of Faythe, naked in her arms just that morning, soft and smiling, flickered before her eyes. She had just begun to believe life had something resembling happiness in store for her. She should've known better. *I just can't win, can I?*

"Let go of me," Deanna said coldly. "You can promise all you want. I don't believe you."

Faythe paled further and dropped her hands. Rubbing them on her thighs, she stepped back. "I see."

"So, if you'll excuse me?" Deanna hoisted her bag onto her shoulder and pushed past Faythe, her heart hammering painfully in her chest. If she'd stopped to look at Faythe, even for a second, she would've caved, she knew it. Instead, she stalked through the living room and by the kitchen, where two figures still huddled together at the kitchen table. Deanna was several paces past the doorway when she heard someone crying. She slowed down then stopped. One of the girls in the kitchen was weeping bitterly, and the other made cooing and comforting sounds. Deanna walked back, stopping just out of sight of them.

"Nana, please, you'll make yourself sick."

Deanna didn't recognize the voice and deduced it had to belong to Pammie.

"You saw her. You heard what she said. This was a very bad idea, Pammie." Savannah started to cry again. "I shouldn't have come."

"It was brave of you to try. Faythe might still be able to help you out. She did this as a favor to me, and because she's a nice person."

"Now that she knows who I am, she won't want to help. Don't you understand? They're together. *Together.*" Savannah laughed bitterly. "Of all the people you run into, it's Deanna Moore's lover."

"I didn't know that!"

"Of course not. It just makes sense in a sick kind of way. Like karma, you know."

"No, I don't know." Pammie spoke slowly. "Explain what you mean, please?"

"I'm a bad person. I've done bad things. I'm the daughter of a bigot and a bully."

Deanna wasn't sure what to do. Part of her wanted to escape to her cabin and go into hiding, but another part wanted to hear what Savannah had to say.

"That doesn't mean you're screwed." Pammie sounded patient, but Deanna could hear the pain behind her words. "Just look at yourself, how you've changed."

"Not enough, obviously. Didn't you see how she looked at me? Like I was disgusting." Savannah laughed, a bitter, self-deprecating sound.

"She was shocked to see you. She had no idea you'd be here. If anyone's at fault, it's me. I was so busy protecting you, I kept using your nickname. If I'd told Faythe who you were, she'd have arranged this differently."

Deanna slumped against the wall and let the bag drop to the floor. Her anger seemed to seep out through her pores; she felt cold, lonely, and remorseful for alienating the only person who believed in her. Deanna wanted to bang her head to the wall. Instead she turned around and walked into the kitchen. "Savannah."

The two girls snapped their heads to look at her simultaneously. Savannah stared at her under reddened eyelids. "Ms. Moore," she said. "We...I thought you left."

"I was going to."

"I see." Savannah looked at Pammie. "This is Pamela Taylor. Her friends call her Pammie."

"I remember you, now that I think about it, Pamela, even though you never took any of my classes. After we've talked, I should know what I'm supposed to call you," Deanna said wryly.

"Uh, guess so." Pammie shifted on the chair, her arm still protectively around Savannah's shoulder. "Why don't you sit down? I mean, if you want to discuss things."

Deanna had to admire the young woman's courage. She managed to sound polite in spite of the tense situation. "All right. I'll just get some coffee, if there is any—"

"There's plenty. I'll get it, Ms. Moore." Pammie jumped up and poured a mug for Deanna as she sat down across from Savannah. "Milk, sugar?"

"Black is fine right now. Thank you." *I can be polite in the weirdest of circumstances too, apparently.* "Okay, Savannah. Guess the ball's in your court."

Savannah drew a deep breath and looked gratefully at Pammie when she sat back down and took her hand. "First of all, Ms. Moore—"

"Deanna. You're not my student anymore."

"Deanna." Savannah looked uncomfortable. "I did something unforgiveable. I was a spoiled brat who wouldn't take no for an answer and was more concerned about impressing the crowd I was hanging with, than things like honor and truth." She shook her head slowly. "And I was deceitful too."

"Go on." Deanna pushed carefully. "Tell me why you did what you did."

"I had such a crush on you. It started in junior high. You weren't anything like the other teachers. You dressed in a cool way, you were younger and so beautiful, and when you needed an assistant, I made sure to volunteer first. My mother was impressed, as always." Savannah sniffled, pulled a tissue from her jeans pocket, and blew her nose. "Mother loved the fact that I was getting extra credit and showing what the mayor's daughter was made of. She also approved of me hanging with the crowd I was with. After all, their parents were among the richest people in town."

"So what did all this have to do with me?"

"I fell in love with you. I couldn't figure out what was up, and I didn't have anybody to talk to. You were all I could think of. You seemed to understand me, and you took an interest in things about me that nobody else gave a damn about."

Deanna had preferred to spend time with the students during recess rather than sip coffee with the three women who'd worked at the school for almost thirty years and later became the ringleaders in the campaign against her. They were obviously Gloria Mueller's vassals.

"Why did you assume I had feelings for you?" Deanna clung to her coffee mug as her hands began to tremble.

"I don't know." Savannah lowered her eyes. "You were kind to me, supportive, and I thought... I was so sure at the time that you felt the same way I did. My ego was huge, and it took a long time for me to realize that most people in my gang were only friends with me because of who my parents were. Even my boyfriend at the time turned out to be sucking up to Mom."

"Your mother made my life a living hell." Deanna forced herself to keep the hatred out of her voice.

"Mine too." Silent tears began to fall down Savannah's cheeks. "I'm not trying to blame her for the way I acted. I just want you to know that I understand. She can be very hard to deal with."

That was the understatement of the year. It must be horrible to be her daughter. It might explain a lot about Savannah's behavior.

"Why did you lie about us getting married, and me practically leaving you at the altar?"

Savannah blushed. "One lie ran into another and gave birth to a third lie, you could say."

"Huh? Run that by me again." Deanna leaned back in her chair and glimpsed Faythe enter the kitchen. Her eyes were red-rimmed and her face scrubbed clean of makeup. When she looked up and saw Deanna sitting at the kitchen table, she barely flinched.

"Hi," Deanna said. "I passed the girls and overheard Savannah and Pamela talking." She hoped Faythe would understand her cryptic statement.

Faythe showed no sign of either understanding or caring about anything Deanna said. Instead she sat down closer to the girls than to her. "So we're talking." Faythe's voice sounded unfamiliar—curt, a little strangled.

"Nana's trying to explain." Pammie looked sad. "Not sure we're getting anywhere, but at least she gets the chance to tell her side and apologize."

"Good." Faythe looked encouragingly at Savannah. "Go on, then."

"All right." Savannah seemed to feel a little more secure and continued, speaking a little slower. "My so-called friends kept challenging me for proof of my hot affair with the art teacher, with Deanna. In my mind, I hadn't exactly lied to them, just told them things prematurely. I was certain Deanna was in love with me. I had bought into the myth about myself as homecoming queen, cheerleader, and honor roll student. How could she not love me? What was not to love?" Savannah laughed hollowly. "So when I couldn't get Deanna to admit to her feelings, I assumed she was being honorable and didn't want to tarnish the reputation of a student.

"At the same time I was stalling my friends' questions, I was trying to break up with my boyfriend. He wouldn't listen, and eventually, out of nowhere, I panicked and told him and two of my friends about Deanna and me getting married in Canada. It was only supposed to be a tiny white lie, to keep him away and my friends off my back." Savannah sipped the water Pammie had brought her earlier.

"Surely you must've realized what a mistake you'd made?" Deanna asked.

"Not really. Since I figured your sense of honor kept you from acting on your feelings, I was giving you a way out." Savannah blushed. "I know, I know. It sounds deranged. Completely crazy."

"So, if I sum it up," Deanna said slowly, not taking her eyes off Savannah, "you have been brought up to expect to become homecoming queen, cheerleader, an honor student, the wife of a rich man, and follow in your mother's footsteps, always at her beck and call."

"Pretty much." Savannah sounded defeated. "I'm so sorry for messing up everything for you. I'm even sorrier that it took me this long to own up to it. I owe it to Pammie. She never gave up on me."

"How about the friends with you in the supermarket?"

"They don't know the truth, but they will." Savannah pressed her lips together. "Lara already suspects something's off sometimes. They're going to hate me, but that's my own fault."

"While we're on the subject of fault," Deanna said, "why aren't you in college?"

"I didn't feel like it. I like what I do now at the animal shelter, especially working with the dogs." Her face lit up and for the first time since Deanna had sat down, she caught a glimpse of the Savannah she'd known two years ago, stunningly beautiful with sparkling eyes and a dynamic personality.

"And you're punishing yourself, thinking you don't deserve to go to college or the university because of the trouble you caused. And you're sticking it to your parents, right, sweetie?" Pammie asked softly.

"I suppose."

Deanna sighed. "That doesn't make things right, and it's a waste of a good mind. Don't do this to yourself. Get on with your life, and don't look back."

"It's not that easy!" Savannah sat ramrod straight in her chair. "I've managed to move out of my parents' house and get a small apartment. I support myself. I even have money to give to my mother's charities. I've found a way to not despise myself all the time." Intense and trembling, Savannah was obviously not about to move on.

"What about me, Nana?" Pammie asked, her voice low.

"You know I love you." Savannah looked away.

"I'm not sure. You lock me out. You won't even talk about certain things. You let your mother's bigotry rule your life. You speak like you're independent, but you live a life of perpetual guilt, endlessly punishing yourself."

"I thought you understood!" Savannah stared at Pammie as if she was a perfect stranger. "Haven't you been listening? I did something unspeakable to someone who was nothing but nice to me. That should tell you something."

"It tells me you were a screwed-up kid two years ago, but you're not the same person now."

"I agree." Deanna couldn't stand to see Savannah beat herself up.

"You do?" Savannah asked.

"You're a different person, and so am I."

"Of course you are," Savannah whispered. "You've had to live with the false rumors and innuendo all this time."

"Yes." There was no point denying facts.

"Why?" Faythe asked calmly. "Why you didn't press charges, or at least leave town?"

Deanna shook her head. "That's got nothing to do with Savannah's issues."

"I think it does." Faythe spoke casually, but something in her eyes made Deanna suspect that she knew the answer, or had guessed it. *If she's guessed it, she ought to know why I can't say anything now.*

"I can't." Deanna tried to convey her dilemma to Faythe with a glance.

"Oh." Savannah covered her mouth with her hand. "Oh, my God."

"What? Are you okay?" Pammie wrapped her arm around Savannah's shoulders.

"Yes. No. Oh, damn it." Savannah stared at Deanna, her eyes welling up with new tears. "I know. Please, I want to be wrong, but I think I know."

"Tell us what you think you know, Savannah." Faythe sounded concerned, but placed a steadying hand on top of Savannah's clasped fists.

Savannah closed her eyes and large teardrops ran down her pale cheeks. "She must've read my diary. I should've known."

CHAPTER TWENTY-THREE

Savannah's pain and frustration seemed to ooze out of every pore on her flawless skin, creating an aura of despair. She didn't take her eyes off Deanna, but clung to Pammie's hands as she spoke.

"Mom must've read my diary and that means...she knew the truth all along. Or at least, the last year and a half." Savannah hiccupped.

"Here, let me get you some water," Pammie said, and tried to gently pry Savannah's fingers from her own.

"I'll get it," Faythe said. "I think we all need something to drink. Juice, water, soda?"

"Orange juice, please. I'll help you," Deanna offered.

Sensing Deanna needed a few moments to digest the latest tidbit of information, Faythe nodded and they walked to the other end of the kitchen. Faythe opened the refrigerator. "We're in luck, two cartons of orange juice." Faythe filled one pitcher with iced water and a second with juice and ice cubes. "Glasses?" she prompted Deanna, who stood staring out the window.

"Oh, right." Deanna took four glasses from a cabinet and carried them over to the table. Faythe followed suit with the pitchers and sat down. She moved her chair closer to Deanna's, concerned by her stunned expression. They all sipped their drinks in silence, evidently regrouping.

"Feeling better?" Pammie asked Savannah. "You looked so pale."

"I'm okay." Savannah played with the rim of her glass. "Just trying to come to terms with what my mother did. I don't know why I haven't thought about it before. Why did she let this go on?"

"Oh, I can think of a few reasons." Deanna had a knowing look on her face.

"Far too many people with hidden agendas here." Pammie sighed.

"Speaking of that," Deanna said, "I don't remember you being part of Savannah's clique in high school."

"I wasn't. I worshipped her from afar. Once we graduated, I mustered enough courage to make my move." Pammie grinned at Savannah, who blushed. "She was still pining for Deanna."

"Pammie!" Savannah hid her face in her hands."You're making it worse."

"Sorry."

"I made such a mess of things. I must've been out of my mind."

"Well," Deanna said slowly, "you seem to be back in charge of your mind right now. You've figured out that your mother is a lying, manipulative—" She stopped herself. "I could go on, but I won't."

"So if Gloria knows you're innocent, Deanna, I don't think it's hard to figure out why she kept the illusion going." Faythe counted on her fingers. "She doesn't want to have her daughter branded a liar in this little town. And she can still claim that Savannah really isn't gay, but an innocent caught in an Evil Lesbian's yarn."

Savannah winced, but remained quiet.

"Third," Faythe continued, "she doesn't want her peers to laugh at her and call her a gullible fool, and finally, she honestly seems thrilled to be able to rally her peers against Deanna. Makes you wonder which of these motives might be the main one."

"Losing face." Savannah straightened in her chair and spoke clearly for the first time. "My mother is all about appearances. She'd go through fire and water to maintain her position in Grantville. When my father was elected mayor two terms in a row, she was the happiest she's ever been. Of course, when I created the scandal of the year she must have been really let down."

"And we still don't have all the pieces of the puzzle," Faythe said. "Until you decide to trust us enough to share *your* motives for not pressing charges for slander, et cetera, we'll keep on guessing."

"It's not just about me." Deanna looked sad, but less tormented now.

"All right." Faythe looked around the pale faces. She felt like a television moderator as she tried to get the others to sum the situation up. "What have we accomplished here today?"

"We've broken the silence." Savannah smiled carefully. "I've come clean about my part in this. I have no more secrets… Well, maybe something I want to tell Pammie later, but nothing that concerns this."

"I feel like Nana. Nothing can make a rumor fester like not facing it."

"And you?" Faythe turned her attention toward Deanna.

"I appreciate Savannah taking full responsibility for her actions. It doesn't change anything, from a practical point of view, but it does emotionally."

"I wish I could redo everything when it would've mattered." Savannah reached out a tentative hand and Faythe held her breath. When Deanna took Savannah's hand, squeezed and held it for a moment, she exhaled so loudly the others looked questioningly at her. "Faythe? You okay?" Savannah asked.

"Fine. I'm fine." It was only partially true. No matter how much she hoped Deanna and Savannah would figure things out, Faythe still felt as if she'd left part of her soul scattered on the floor where she and Deanna had yelled at each other so bitterly.

"We should come up with a plan how to clear Deanna's name." Pammie looked resolute.

"No." Deanna looked even more stubborn. "We shouldn't. Nothing can be done about it now."

"But why ever not?" Faythe blurted. "You've been wrongly accused for years, and now that Savannah's come clean with you, what reason could you possibly have to refuse?"

"I just do. Take my word for it, and please…if you care…if you can forgive what I said earlier and still care about me, don't pursue this. Please." Deanna wasn't pleading, she was virtually begging, and Faythe couldn't refuse.

"All right, all right," Faythe said. "I can't promise I won't ask you for an explanation later, though. And about the matter of forgiving, we'll talk more about that later."

"Uh-oh." Pammie looked at Deanna with sympathy. "Think some groveling is in order."

"Think so?" Deanna sighed, but nodded. "I can grovel. Haven't done it in a while. Can't remember when, actually. Still, if groveling is what it takes, grovel I will."

"Oh, please." Faythe had to smile despite everything. "Hilarious."

"Honestly. I don't want you to think I meant any of what I said." Deanna took Faythe's hand and rubbed her thumb over her knuckles.

"I see." Faythe's fingers tingled at the touch, and Deanna held on when she tried to let go. "Now, it's getting late, ladies, and I for one am very hungry." She glanced out the window. "Looks like it's raining pretty badly. I thought I'd call for takeout tonight. Why don't you two girls stay? Driving back to Grantville in this weather is hardly ideal when you're upset."

"You're asking us to stay?" Savannah looked baffled.

"Sure. We still have lots to talk about. It would be nice to just chat away about everyday stuff. Just to relax some."

"This sure hasn't been relaxing," Pammie said. "I'd love to pig out on Chinese food, though."

"Oh, me too," Deanna said, surprisingly. "Something about fried rice just—"

"Comfort food," Savannah added shyly. "I never had that type of food when I lived at home, but after I moved out, I happen to live just one block from a terrific hole-in-the-wall Chinese restaurant. They deliver too."

"So you recommend them?" Faythe grabbed her cell phone.

"I do. I even know their number by heart." Savannah recited the phone number to Faythe. "You can order their special for four people so we'll get to sample all of their stuff. I guarantee we'll be full and then some."

"Sounds good." Faythe called and placed their order. "Thirty to forty-five minutes. That's not bad when you consider how many dishes we get to try."

"Oh, look at that!" Savannah pointed out the window where rain had begun to fall, and the wind seemed set on ripping the last orange and red leaves from the maple trees. "That doesn't look good."

"Thinking of our food or about getting home?" Deanna asked.

"Both. When it starts like that, like out of nowhere, it's usually bad news." Savannah peered up at the sky.

"I have plenty of guest rooms, so don't worry about a thing. Anyone need to call anybody?" Faythe wiggled the cell phone at the two girls.

Savannah shook her head and pulled her hands into the sleeves of her sweatshirt. "Nobody's expecting me until lunchtime tomorrow, at work."

"I'm fine too. I'm driving back to college tomorrow, but I can wait until Sunday," Pammie said. "Anything we can help you with? What about garden stuff that might blow into the water or something?"

"You're an angel." Faythe slapped her forehead. "The swing and the patio furniture I dragged down to the shore."

"We'll get it." Savannah looked relieved to have something to focus on. She dragged Pammie with her to the hallway.

"You can stick the stuff in the garage." Faythe gave them a set of keys before they headed out the door.

"They'll get soaked." Faythe looked worriedly out the window. "If they hurt themselves trying to keep a few garden chairs safe—"

"They'll be fine. Look. There they are already." Deanna pointed out the window. They had linked arms and were doubling over against the wind as they staggered toward the house. Faythe met them at the door and at first thought Savannah was crying. Doubled over, she hung off Pammie's left arm.

"I knew it." Faythe rushed to help them. "What happened? Savannah?"

Savannah looked up, and now Faythe saw she was wiping away tears from laughter. "I'm sorry, Faythe. I didn't mean to scare you. I just couldn't take it anymore."

"What? What happened?" Faythe asked as she helped them get rid of their wet jackets.

"Pammie. She got tangled in the string. I mean the rope. And she was *cursing*, worse than I ever heard her do before."

"What string?" Deanna had joined them.

"She tried to save the hammock." Savannah started to laugh again. "She managed to untie it, and when she was rolling it into a ball, the wind turned. The hammock would be a good sail, by the way. It nearly blew off onto the lake with Pammie."

"She's exaggerating." Pammie looked amused.

"Am *not*." Savannah blew at an errant piece of hair that hung over her eyes.

Faythe had forgotten about the hammock and could envision Pammie's struggle to keep it under control. "Well, thanks for taking care of the furniture. I appreciate it." She walked over to where she'd written down the ETA of the Chinese food. "Twenty minutes until the food gets here. Enough time for us all to get a shower and clean up our act."

"Good idea, except we didn't bring a change of clothing."

"Other guests have left some clothes over the years. They're in the guest room dressers, and you're welcome to anything of mine," Faythe said.

"Or mine," Deanna added. "Pammie's probably more my size."

"Could be." Pammie sized Deanna up. "We're the same height, give or take an inch."

"I believe so. I'll show you the guest rooms."

Faythe was grateful not having to walk around on her sore foot any more than necessary. When Deanna returned, Faythe tried to mask her limp as she crossed the living room to her bedroom.

"You're in pain again." It was obviously hard to fool Deanna.

"Just a bit. No big deal." Her bruised heart ached worse than her foot.

"A hot shower or, better, a bath, would do you a world of good."

"Way ahead of you. On my way to the shower."

"May I join you?" Deanna spoke carefully, enunciating every syllable, but she obviously thought Faythe would reject her instantly.

"All right." Faythe didn't know where she found the courage not to recoil. "I could use someone to scrub my back."

"I volunteer." Deanna cupped Faythe's chin. "Am I forgiven?"

"Do you believe me? Do you believe *in* me?" Faythe countered with questions of her own. She doubted Deanna really understood how profoundly she'd hurt Faythe with her words.

"Yes. If I hadn't been so upset, I never would've reacted the way I did."

"And the next time you're upset?"

"I don't think I'll ever doubt you again. If I even hint at anything in that direction, please slap me over the head and remind me of today."

Faythe laced her fingers through Deanna's hair. "I'd never slap you. Anywhere. But I'd smack you verbally and make you listen to me. No matter what."

"Thank you."

"And before we hit the shower, I have one more question."

"Shoot." Deanna leaned down and brushed her lips across the tip of Faythe's nose.

"Are you ever going to tell me the whole truth about what's been going on here these last two years?"

Deanna didn't answer right away. "Yes. Not right away. One day."

"All right." Faythe took Deanna by the hand and led her to the master bathroom. "Now, how about some mutual back scrubbing?"

"Oh, Faythe," Deanna said, her voice trembling. She undressed both of them in record time and pulled Faythe into the shower stall, where warm water engulfed them. "Sweetheart, I'll scrub anything you want."

"Mmm. Good to know. *Very* good to know."

CHAPTER TWENTY-FOUR

I can't believe you tricked me into this. What are we? Fourteen?" Deanna scowled at Faythe.

"Think of it as therapeutic," Faythe said blithely. "And quite elaborate. Spin the bottle is one thing, truth or dare another, but a mix between the two—that's a game for big girls. And besides, we have no electricity, which means no TV, nothing, nada."

"That may be, but I refuse to stand on one leg and drink raw eggs or anything."

"Ew." Savannah made a disgusted face. "Is that what they did way back when?"

"What do you mean, way back when?" Deanna stopped scowling and looked offended instead. "I'm thirty-four. Not a fossil from the Jurassic period."

"Sorry." Savannah appeared anything but contrite. Instead her broad smile hinted at the fun-loving young woman she might become if she could sort out the issues of her life. *Mainly her mother.*

"And yes, it happened to me a few times," Deanna said. "Especially if the shy boys there didn't dare kiss any of the girls. Plenty of times I preferred to drink raw eggs, especially if the 'God's gift to girls' boys were present."

"Yeah, I remember being so relieved once," Faythe said, "when I was supposed to kiss the super-nerd instead of the guy who had girls swooning and falling over themselves. So the stud set me up, thinking I despised the nerd as much as he did, and said I should kiss him for two minutes straight."

"Two minutes. Wow." Pammie rested her chin in her palm where she sat on the floor next to the coffee table. "So, how did it work out?"

"Maybe I should save that answer for when you nail me with a 'truth' question?"

"Aw, come on." Pammie winked. "Don't hold out on us."

"Yeah, tell us," Deanna chimed in. "What happened to the poor nerd?"

"He and I ended up going to the prom together. We stayed in touch until a few years ago when he and his male partner moved to Mexico City."

"His partner. Oh, so the nerd's gay?" Pammie said. "You never said what kissing him was like, though."

"I never kiss and tell," Faythe said primly, winking at Deanna.

"So it was bad, huh?" Pammie didn't let up.

"I didn't say that. Hopefully, neither of you will ever meet him. He was sweet."

"Sweet?" Savannah and Pammie exclaimed in unison.

"Yes. It was a sweet kiss. He showed more sensitivity than any of the other guys ever would've."

"Okay, okay, we believe you. Now it's time to get this show on the road." Pammie rubbed her hands together, then took the empty wine bottle. She placed it on a circular tray they'd found in the kitchen and wiggled it back and forth while she assumed a contemplative expression. "Let's see if I still have my magic touch." She spun the bottle on the tray, and after a few wild revolutions, its neck pointed at Faythe. Deanna had to laugh at her dismayed look. Faythe obviously had pictured Deanna being on the hot seat.

"All right. Truth or dare, Faythe?" Pammie asked.

"Truth."

"When did you realize you're a lesbian?" Pammie wasn't taking any prisoners.

"College, my first year. Not only because of my spin-the-bottle experiences," Faythe said, "but because I had zero interest in discussing the opposite sex with my friends. I just couldn't appreciate what they found so attractive about boys and men. So, I'd say, at nineteen."

"Wow. That was almost too easy." Pammie looked a bit disappointed.

"My turn." Faythe grabbed the bottle and spun it. It stopped, pointing at Pammie. "Aha. Payback." Faythe had a devilish gleam in her eyes. "Truth or dare?"

"Hmm. Truth."

"When did *you* realize that you had feelings for Savannah?"

"Wha—oh." Pammie looked completely taken by surprise.

"Well?" Faythe prodded.

"Um. Well…" Pammie looked everywhere but directly at Savannah. "I haven't told her in so many words, you know. I mean, I've told her many times that I love her, but I haven't…I haven't said I'm *in* love with her." She looked shyly at Savannah. "Guess you know, though."

"I do." Savannah's voice was soft and came off as just as shy.

"It was three years ago," Pammie said, "six weeks after summer break. Savannah was sauntering down the hallway with her entourage, and the September sun filtered through the windows above the main doors. It was as if she was being bathed in gold." Pammie blushed. "She didn't even look my way, but one of her cronies gave me the evil eye. I gave her the finger."

Deanna guffawed. She could imagine that such an action shocked and appalled the girls that used to hang with Savannah.

"I didn't know. I never had any idea." Savannah looked suddenly sad. "Maybe if I had, I wouldn't have—"

"Shh." Pammie squeezed Savannah's hand. "It's okay. Besides, I had a crush on you, was possibly already in love then, even, but I didn't like you very much."

"Nothing much to like." Savannah said ironically. "I was a self-centered bitch riding on her parents' positions."

"Didn't I just hush you?" Pammie shook her head in mock dismay. "Now, where was I? Oh, right. I think I answered your question, Faythe. Three years ago, almost to the day, since she was standing in the sunlight. There's something magical about the light in Vermont this time of year."

"I totally agree," Faythe said, and glanced at Deanna. Something convoluted flickered over her face and Deanna tried to decipher it. It combined wonder and alarm, and Deanna wanted to wrap her arms around her, reassure her, even if she had no idea what might cause such feelings.

"So, my turn again. Here goes." Pammie forcefully spun the bottle, nearly sending it flying off the tray. "Whoops." The bottle eventually stopped, pointing at Deanna.

Deanna had already decided on her answer. "Dare."

"Of course." Pammie nodded enigmatically. "Let me see. Oh, I know. Show how you give your best neck rub."

"Neck rub." Deanna wanted to groan, but anything was better than the ongoing inquisition. "All right. Turn around, Faythe."

"I hoped you'd pick me." Pammie winked. "My shoulders are super sore."

"Take the hint, Savannah," Deanna said, deciding to stop being so uptight and take this silly game in stride. "Watch and learn." She moved in behind Faythe while rubbing her hands together to make sure they weren't cold. In fact, the prospect of touching Faythe made her instantly hot. Savannah rubbed her hands the same way, while scooting in behind Pammie. She frowned as she focused, clearly set on mimicking Deanna's movements.

"That's right. Do exactly what I do. Feel good, Faythe?"

"Mmm." Faythe sat with her eyes closed, her head lolling a bit as Deanna kneaded tense neck muscles. *Is she that stressed, despite being on leave? Guess that's because of me.* Deanna wanted to make up for everything she'd dragged Faythe into and tried to give her the best massage available in Grantville. Another moan, this time from Pammie, made Deanna chuckle.

Savannah was glancing repeatedly at her out of the corner of her eyes. Deanna would never have guessed Savannah had this sweet, caring side in her that could make someone as strong and honorable as Pammie fall in love—and stay in love—with her. Deanna tried to envision the almost neurotic girl who'd latched on to her, smothered her with attention, unable to take no for an answer, but it was impossible. Instead she saw this broken young woman, trying to make up for her actions by denying herself her own future, professionally and personally. Deanna slid her hands up and down Faythe's upper arms, applying enough pressure to smooth out the small knots in her biceps. Twin blissful moans and a quick glance at Savannah showed that she'd copied that move as well.

Feeling small horns sprout on her forehead, Deanna slid her fingers up to Faythe's collarbones, where she massaged just above and beneath them. She moved her fingertips in slow circles, making sure Savannah didn't miss the soft way she touched Faythe, who looked up at Deanna with a puzzled expression. Deanna motioned toward the young women with her chin, and Faythe blinked twice before she obviously caught on. Her smile showed her approval and she settled back against Deanna. "Mmm."

Deanna caressed, rather than massaged, her way down to Faythe's breasts. She wasn't about to touch her lover intimately in the presence of someone else, but Savannah and Pammie didn't know that. She brushed the sides of Faythe's breasts with her thumbs, over and over. Feeling Faythe tremble, Deanna's heart melted. Just how far had she fallen for Faythe? Far enough to feel mortally wounded only hours ago when she thought Faythe had betrayed her.

"Oh." Pammie sounded breathless and her cheeks had bright red spots.

"There. That's my best technique," Deanna said, relenting with an innocent look on her face. "What do you think, Pammie? Savannah followed my instructions to a T."

"I bet she did," Pammie said in a mock growl. "And you're pleased with yourself, aren't you?"

"No idea what you're talking about." Deanna pushed away from Faythe and noticed that she seemed to have problems breathing. "Inhale, exhale, darling," she whispered, and noticed her choice of endearment only when Faythe became still. Not about to acknowledge her slip, Deanna acted casual as she extended a hand to Faythe, stroking her back.

"I'm breathing," Faythe said, giving Deanna a stern look. "No thanks to you."

"Huh." Deanna couldn't stop a wide grin. "I take that as a compliment."

"You would." Faythe returned the smile.

"It's your turn, then," Savannah said. She looked slightly flustered as she handed the bottle to Deanna.

"Okay." Deanna spun the bottle and it pointed at Faythe, who groaned loudly.

"Truth or dare, Faythe?" Deanna waited expectantly. She was enjoying this silly game more than she'd thought possible.

"Eh...truth. No more pseudo-erotic displays, thank you very much."

Deanna laughed. "You might just regret that statement."

"Hardly."

"Let's see." Deanna meant to ask a silly question, but suddenly she thought of the last hours when they'd shared so much and formed something between a truce and friendship. "Where do you see yourself in five years?"

"What?" Faythe blinked twice. "Where…?" She lowered her gaze and fiddled with the hem of her shirt. "Oh, uh, I envision myself writing. A novelist, a freelancer…you know. Not TV, or at least not as much. I hope I'm still living in Manhattan. I love my condo."

Deanna went cold. She had asked the question hastily—too hastily, she admitted. Catching Faythe off guard was not a good idea, never was, Deanna admitted to herself. Despite her warm, upbeat manner, Faythe was intensely private, and Deanna was only now beginning to comprehend just how conflicted Faythe was about herself.

"So, back to the core of writing, pen on paper, fingers on keyboard. What do you want to write?" Deanna wanted to keep Faythe talking before she clammed up.

"That's another question, for another bottle spin."

"Ah, but this is a multipurpose kind of question."

"Oh, *really*." Sarcasm oozed from the single word.

"Yes."

Faythe glared at her for long seconds, then made a big production of rolling her eyes. "Very well, if you insist. I've always loved reading memoirs and autobiographies and interviewing someone interesting, but going much deeper than the time frame my morning show allowed. I've wished I could dedicate the whole show to a lot of my interviewees, or several shows, like a series. They had so much to tell, lived such interesting, amazing lives."

"You'd be great at it," Pammie said. "That's what I liked best about your show, when you interviewed your guests. Nothing annoyed me more than when you had to interrupt them and go to commercial."

"I know." Faythe made a wry face. "Me too."

"And in a book you'd tell the story of the person you're writing about, uninterrupted." Savannah nodded. "Who or what kind of person would you write about first?"

Suddenly they forgot about the game they'd been playing, and Deanna listened carefully as Faythe talked about her dreams. Faythe's voice changed when she outlined a new life, one where she was in charge of her own future, doing what she loved to do rather than what others expected.

"If I can't do something I like, with quality in mind rather than celebrity and popularity, then what's the use?" Faythe said wistfully. "I can't picture myself doing the morning show anymore."

"I never would've guessed that your job wasn't *the* dream job." Savannah leaned her head on Pammie's shoulder. Pammie kissed the top of her head. "I mean, working on TV and all."

"Yeah, I used to think so too. And I won't lie. Some aspects of it are fascinating. You're in a world that can be glamorous and magical. The hours are grueling, but I got so fed up with my colleagues who complained endlessly. For heaven's sake, they should've tried working nights at a nursing home, or early mornings as a garbage collector downtown!" Frowning, Faythe shook her head. "You'd think what we did was brain surgery the way they carried on. People need to take pride in what they do, but they have to keep a healthy perspective."

"I agree." Deanna wanted Faythe to know she understood. "Take Miranda's teachers and caregivers, for instance. They work tirelessly for these kids, to provide an education and a good life for them, while they're at the school. For some of the students this is their only quality interaction with other people. Their parents are ignorant, overwhelmed, or sometimes even fed up. So that's why some jobs, like mine, seem… well, I wouldn't say less important, but—"

"Because you'd be wrong." Faythe took Deanna's hands. "I figured this out for myself after working in the entertainment industry a few years. I was starting to beat myself down because it was so superficial. Then I was reading a really good mystery novel, which took me away to dark alleys in another era and made me forget about several things in my life that were bothering me. When I finished reading, I felt refreshed and rested in a way that a night's sleep couldn't match. I had recharged my batteries, so to speak, thanks to this book, and ultimately thanks to the author." Faythe's soft expression made Deanna lean forward to kiss her before she remembered they weren't alone. Faythe clearly understood and the same desire showed in her darkening eyes. "So, you illustrate these incredible books for kids and adults, and you take them on a journey to some magical place, or a scary place, or…well, anywhere you can imagine."

"And you provide much-needed relief from reality." Pammie nodded enthusiastically. "You make it possible for brain surgeons, or social workers, or soldiers, to relax a bit and find the strength to go on one more hour, one more day."

"Exactly." Faythe beamed. "That's exactly it. I'm not on leave because my job is unimportant or it's beneath me to work on a morning show. That's not it at all." She sounded almost surprised, as if this was a revelation to her as well. "I need to change paths for *me*, because I need to do what's right for my own sake."

"Glad you figured it out." Deanna kissed Faythe softly on the lips. "And you're right, of course. About a lot of things."

"Thanks." Faythe had never looked so inviting, and she seemed completely relaxed. "It's time to hit the sack. It's late."

"No more spinning bottles?" Pammie looked disappointed. "Maybe some other time?"

"Sure," Deanna said. "It was kind of fun."

"Fun and enlightening," Savannah said, and winked at Pammie, who looked suddenly flustered.

The candles had burned almost all the way down, and as they blew them out and stood to go to bed, Deanna detected traces of a new confidence in Savannah. She didn't take her eyes off Pammie, and perhaps being in the presence of Faythe and Deanna made her comfortable enough to let her feelings surface, at least momentarily. *If anyone had told me this morning that I'd feel protective about that kid, I'd have said they'd lost their last marble.* Deanna sighed. She still felt conflicts, but at least they'd resolved one matter. Knowing that Savannah hadn't intended to be malicious was a huge step.

"You okay?" Faythe asked.

"Of course."

"Ready for bed? I mean together?" Shifting from one foot to the other, Faythe looked completely vulnerable.

"Absolutely."

Faythe laughed, a relieved, breathless sound. "All right, then." She walked ahead of Deanna to the master bedroom. When she glanced over her shoulder, her eyes were glossy from withheld tears. Faythe obviously hadn't been sure Deanna would say yes.

CHAPTER TWENTY-FIVE

Faythe placed the last dirty plate in the dishwasher, added detergent, and started it, glad they had power again. She wasn't thinking about the chore, though, but the previous evening. She concentrated on the silly game they'd played, because if she lingered too much on the night of passion she'd shared with Deanna, she'd lose her focus.

Faythe shook her head at herself for having indulged in such adolescent behavior, but it had been fun. Revealing and fun, she corrected herself. Deanna's question had really made her think in order to verbalize her wishes and tentative plans for the future. Her emotions had been and she'd felt raw ever since, especially regarding Deanna. Faythe had sneaked out of bed before Deanna woke this morning, even if all she wanted was to kiss her lover awake. She was afraid of how quickly Deanna had come to mean so much to her. Too much.

Faythe set the coffee machine to make a triple espresso latte. She had known since college that she wasn't cut out to be in a long-term relationship. Her parents had demonstrated why this was not in the cards for her. The utter irony of their behavior after the divorce seemed to completely elude them. *Great gene pool. Either a fake or a hoax.* Faythe took the mug of coffee and grabbed a cashmere blanket from the couch on her way out the door and onto the deck.

The morning air was crisp and clear, mist hung over the lake like a layer of cotton candy. Faythe curled up on one of the deck chairs, wrapping the blanket around herself. She sipped her coffee slowly, inhaling the aroma. It rejuvenated her more than this, but it still tasted great. *I suppose I'm tired after last night.* Faythe's cheeks warmed. She had turned to Deanna several times during the night, needing to feel her body against her own, over and over. Deanna in turn seemed to have to exorcise a few demons of her own, the way she passionately and determinedly made love to Faythe. They didn't say much during the lovemaking, or afterward.

Instead Faythe had clung to Deanna, suddenly needy in a way totally alien to her. She hoped Deanna hadn't noticed just how desperate she felt during those moments. Deanna had simply held her and allowed Faythe to hug and nuzzle her as much as she wanted. And unless she was reading more into Deanna's response than was actually there, Deanna seemed to like it.

"Good morning. You're up early." The sound of Pammie's voice made Faythe nearly drop her mug. "Whoops. Sorry, didn't mean to scare you."

Faythe moved, about to rise, when Savannah, who stood next to Pammie, stopped her. "No, no. Don't get up. We're on our way to work."

"You'll need some breakfast."

"We're grabbing some at Dixon's." Pammie took Savannah's hand. "Our first date," she said with an exaggerated sigh.

"Goofball." Savannah bumped Pammie with her hip. "Anyway, we wanted to thank you for putting us up…and for putting up with us. Having us here nearly screwed things up for you and Deanna."

"True," Faythe said, smiling wryly. "And still, look at how many topics we covered yesterday. Communication, my friends, is what it's all about." *Ha. I should talk.* She managed to keep her friendly, easygoing smile intact. "When will we see either of you again?"

"Sure you want us to come back?" Pammie looked genuinely surprised. "I mean, we're kind of trouble, especially this one." She tugged at Savannah's braid, which earned her a haughty glare.

"Of course I do. Not only because we still need to resolve some things, but because we're becoming friends."

Pammie and Savannah looked speechless for a few moments. "Really? Wow." Pammie grinned. "I was thinking that yesterday when we played that game. I kind of forgot everything about age difference and stuff."

"So did I." Faythe returned the smile. "You have my cell phone number, so let's call each other in a few days, all right?"

"Sure thing. See you later." Pammie began to walk toward her car. Savannah turned to follow her, but suddenly wheeled around and hugged Faythe tight.

"Thank you," she murmured. "Thank you, thank you."

"Hey, kid, it's all right." Startled, Faythe held on to her. "You'll be okay. You'll be fine, even. You've taken the first steps, and that's always the hardest."

"If not for you—"

"If not for Pammie," Faythe corrected softly. "This was all her doing. Don't lose sight of her. She's a keeper."

"I won't. I promise." Savannah pulled back. "Say hi to Deanna for us. Sorry we missed her this morning." In fact, Savannah looked relieved. Perhaps it was a good thing Deanna was still asleep.

"I'll tell her."

The girls drove off and Faythe returned to her deck chair after making another mug of triple espresso. Sipping it, she enjoyed the way it warmed her belly. Nothing like a mug of coffee in the morning, she mused. Well, *almost*, she corrected herself with a chuckle, thinking of the hot embraces she'd shared with Deanna during the night. They didn't compare to anything else she'd ever experienced. Her former lovers, few and far between, had been nice, most of them, but that was it. Nobody could ever come close to Deanna. It wasn't just the physical aspect, either; it was the whole package.

Am I falling in love? Faythe's heart plunged, and she knew this was what she feared the most. In her experience, relationships had a best-before date, and after that date, they went sour or ceased to exist. Faythe had always made sure she never went past this date, never got involved with anyone on a deeper level. It hadn't been hard to stick to the policy before she met Deanna. Now she was trying to estimate how long she had before the best-before date occurred.

"You look like you're trying to solve something on a Nobel Prize level. What might that be?" A throaty voice startled Faythe out of her reverie and she almost lost her grip on her mug.

"Hey, watch it, darling," Deanna said, and caught the mug before it fell. "Sorry, didn't mean to scare you. Thought you heard me."

"I didn't." Faythe accepted the mug back and carefully placed it on the small table beside her. "Sleep well?"

"Like a baby. You? Been up long?"

"A while. Said good-bye to the girls. They're off to work. They said to say hi."

"Oh. I see." Deanna looked disappointed.

"They promised to come back to see us in a few days."

"Good." Deanna brightened. "I never thought I'd say this, but I really like them. Savannah sure isn't the devil in disguise that I thought she was."

"No, her mother, the queen bee, has obviously filled that part."

"She's a piece of—" Deanna bit off an apparent profanity and shrugged. "Poor Savannah. She's figuring her mother's actions out as we speak, which has to be worse than what happened to me."

"Not sure if it's worse, but bad enough," Faythe said. "Want some breakfast?"

"I'll just grab something and go back to work. I have some editing of Bunny Buttercup to do."

"You sure? I don't mind cooking. Pancakes?"

"Nah, that's sweet of you to offer, but I'll have some Cheerios. And some of that coffee." Deanna kissed Faythe quickly and walked back to the house.

"Want company?" Faythe regretted the words as soon as they were over her lips, certain she sounded clingy. Hoping Deanna hadn't heard her, she turned away from the house and stared at the water where the mist was leaving. She had work to do to, even if she wasn't under any pressure to keep a deadline. She should just pull out her laptop and not bother Deanna when she had stuff to do.

"Always," Deanna said, suddenly back at her side, startling her for the second time this morning. "You never need to ask that." She buried her face against Faythe's neck and inhaled deeply. "Mmm. Nice."

A gentle flame of happiness glowed in the center of Faythe's rib cage. It permeated her bloodstream and carried elation, and, she confessed, relief, throughout her system. "Two cereals and two coffees, one laptop and your illustrations. Think we can manage to work in the same room?"

"It's well worth a try, darling." Deanna's voice sank an octave. "If you don't behave, I have ways of punishing you that will be mutually satisfactory."

Internal snapshots of Deanna punishing her in delicious ways flickered through Faythe's mind and she shivered in anticipation. "That's not exactly a deterrent, you know," she murmured.

"No?" Deanna allowed Faythe to turn around in her arms. "Maybe it wasn't meant to be. Maybe I'd like you to occasionally be a bad girl." She winked.

"Oh, sweetheart," Faythe said, her voice a low purr, "you have no idea how bad I can be." She slid her hands up Deanna's chest. "You might just have to be very inventive when it comes to dealing with me."

Deanna threw her head back and laughed, a thoroughly happy sound. "Oh, Faythe, just when I think I have you pegged, you say stuff that completely throws me."

"So do you." Faythe kissed Deanna lightly on the lips. "So, cereal. I haven't had breakfast yet either."

"Okay, cereal it is."

"And coffee. I'm only on my second triple espresso and it's gone cold. Again."

"And my girl likes it hot, huh?" Deanna said innocently.

Faythe glanced quickly at her, knowing she'd see the familiar little devilish sparkles in Deanna's eyes. Suddenly she realized what Deanna had said. Surely it was a slip of her tongue, part of the teasing? She knew so well how Faythe felt about things and there was no reason for her to call Faythe "my girl."

❖

Deanna put the pencil down and rested her chin in her hand. She'd worked nonstop for four hours without realizing how had time passed. This was normal for her work flow, and she wasn't tired at all. She had stopped adding more of the mushroom houses in Bunny Buttercup's forest only because Faythe's cell phone had rung and pulled her out of her creative zone.

She wasn't deliberately listening in. Faythe was sitting over by the fireplace in a La-Z-Boy recliner with her laptop propped up on an elaborate tray-cushion with built-in cooling fans. Deanna had placed her desktop easel on the dining table over by the window.

"Hello?" Faythe answered the phone in a preoccupied tone

of voice. "Oh. Ben. Hi." Faythe sat up, pushing the tray to the side. She became completely rigidness and tugged at her low ponytail; in fact, kept yanking at it in sharp little jerks. "Yes, I have given it some thought. I said I would."

Deanna waited a few moments to see if Faythe would leave the room to talk in private, but when she didn't, Deanna decided she could use another cup of coffee. *If I drink any more of that stuff today, I'll be swinging between the maple trees by the evening.*

"I said I would *think* about it, Ben, not do as you ordered." Faythe grabbed a fistful of Deanna's flannel shirt as she passed, stopping her. "Listen. I don't know why you keep insisting that I continue to work in a field that isn't making me happy. What possible motive could you have?" Shadows filled Faythe's eyes, making them almost black. Deanna instinctively sat down on the love seat and pulled Faythe down onto her lap.

"Selfish?" Faythe swallowed. "You're calling me selfish, Ben?"

Furious, and not waiting to consider if she was doing the right thing, Deanna grabbed the cell phone and quickly found the button for the speaker phone.

"...all the years I stayed in a loveless marriage for you. You would think that would count for something, but here you go throwing your career away for a whim, without any concern for me, who put you through college." The baritone voice belonging to Faythe's father came through loud and clear. Faythe didn't try to retrieve the phone.

"We both know the trust fund Granny Hamilton set up for all her six grandchildren put me through college. Or didn't you think I was aware of that?" Faythe spoke calmly, but the way she trembled against Deanna spoke volumes of how much he upset her.

"That's just it! If she hadn't been so damn charmed by you brats, that money would've gone to me."

"And your two sisters," Faythe said. "Besides, you don't know that. Nanny Hamilton had the right to leave her money to anyone she saw fit. The fact that she loved her grandchildren so much was a godsend when I was a kid. We were never together as a family, except to go to church. I needed the consistency she provided. I know you and Mother have blocked it out, but you fought like cats and dogs when you thought nobody was listening."

A low hiss followed the momentary silence. "That's a lie. We put up a perfect front for you. A little gratitude wouldn't hurt. Like sticking to a career that's worth anything."

Faythe winced. "So, we're back to that again." She leaned her forehead against Deanna's temple for a moment, then continued. "Listen now, *Dad*. I'm not going to let my own father coerce me or persuade me to do anything I don't want to. I don't know why you want me to stay at the network, and frankly I don't care. I know what *I* want. I want to write, as a freelancer, as an employed reporter somewhere, I don't care. I want to write. This is my final word on the matter and I refuse to talk about this again with you—ever."

"I'm not through—"

"Yes. You are. We're both through. And if this is all you want or care to talk about, I suppose we're through, period." Faythe slammed her hand over her mouth and tears rose in her eyes.

"You'd choose writing a fucking book before your own flesh and blood?" Ben sounded stunned.

"You would choose to bully your own flesh and blood into doing something against her will?"

"Damn it, you're making me out to be a monster. Everything depends on you. Our goddamn future hangs in the balance, and then you—" Ben cut off his sentence and the line seemed dead.

"Ben? What the hell are you talking about?" Faythe sat up, frowning.

"You don't have a head for business. You wouldn't understand." He sounded bitter and tired. "Just make sure you keep your job. Don't quit."

Faythe slumped back against Deanna, who automatically held her close. It was as if all energy had left Faythe's body; she seemed even too tired to tremble.

"What did you do, Ben? Please tell me you didn't offer my connections on a plate as part of the deal—again?" This was clearly what Faythe suspected, and apparently it had happened before. "You promised."

"It was a ridiculous promise." Ben sounded defiant. "And this was nothing. Just a few introductions to some Hollywood people. You know how that impresses some of the Japanese businessmen."

"Who did you try to sell them this time? Angelina? Jessica Alba? No, don't tell me. Jennifer Aniston. Or, oh yes, Katie Holmes." Deanna hardly recognized Faythe's voice, so filled with sarcasm and hurt. "I'm not doing it, Ben. Just forget about it. Try basing your business deals on your product, rather than some Hollywood glamour factor."

"You condescending little—"

Deanna had had enough. She pressed a button on Faythe's cell and hung up before Ben Hamilton managed to call Faythe something unforgiveable. She quickly browsed the phone settings until she found the silence feature. Not even allowing the phone to vibrate, she tossed it away with a weird feeling of not wanting to touch the damn thing.

"Thanks," Faythe said tiredly. "I'm sorry you had to listen to that."

"Shh. I'm glad I'm here. You shouldn't have to deal with such bullshit." Deanna wanted to wrap Faythe up and shield her from her father's callous treatment. "He's done it before, I understand."

"Yes. A few times. Each time he promised not to pull that stunt again, and I'm probably more naïve than I thought, because last time, two years ago, I believed him. He brought another Japanese delegation to the studio unannounced, which nearly cost me my job that day. That's why I thought he wouldn't do it again. And obviously I was wrong." Faythe hid her face against Deanna's neck. "You see what great and reliable stock I come from."

"You're nothing like them."

"You thought so before." Faythe blinked repeatedly, but persistent tears threatened to dislodge from her eyelashes.

"No, never."

"Yes. You did. You called me a chip off the old block when you were upset. When you found Savannah and Pammie here, remember?"

"Oh, Faythe." Deanna froze as a fuzzy memory surfaced off all the hurtful things she'd said to alleviate her own pain *I can't believe of all the things I could have said, I managed to play into her biggest fear.* Faythe had done everything humanly possible to help Deanna and showed her more love and affection than anyone ever had. *And this is how I repaid her.* "I'm so sorry. I had blocked that out, and I wish I could take those words back because they're untrue, every single one of them."

"Don't worry. I forgave you." Faythe smiled wanly, and her rigid pose told Deanna her words weren't entirely true.

"I think you want to forgive me, but until I fully realize just how much that hurt you, you can't, can you?"

"I—I suppose."

"And I do. I know you so much better now, and I trust you. You've got more character in your pinky than both your parents put together. As I see it, your parents have only one redeeming quality."

"What?" Faythe wiped at her eyes.

"They managed, somehow, to raise a child who turned into the most wonderful woman imaginable. They must've done something right."

"Hmm." Faythe shook her head, her gaze softening along with her body. "Really. Well, I never looked at it that way."

"It's the truth." Deanna brushed her lips across Faythe's forehead.

"Thank you."

"So, just to be sure there are no misunderstandings, you're not a chip off the old block. You're nothing like them, and you've got more intelligence and heart than they ever will."

"Thank you," Faythe said again.

"You're welcome." Deanna nuzzled Faythe's temple, wanting to emphasize her words. "I don't care about your parents, other than I'm furious at your father for hurting you." Deanna tipped Faythe's head back and looked into her eyes. "I just want you to follow your heart and do what *you* want to do. Regardless of them." She kissed Faythe softly, her heart hammering in her ears. "And regardless of me."

CHAPTER TWENTY-SIX

Deanna placed her last illustration in her portfolio and closed it with strong rubber bands. She was pleased with the Bunny Buttercup illustrations, and particularly with the painting that would become the book cover. She'd painted it using acrylics, which was her first love when she became serious about her art. Remembering how her mother had cheered her on and supported her, going to every student exhibition and even buying a few pieces, was bittersweet. Where are those paintings now? Perhaps put away in the attic or placed in a seldom-used room in the big house Angela shared with Percy and his girls.

"I'm going into town," Faythe said, barely limping anymore as she crossed the floor toward Deanna. "Want to join me?"

"No, I—" Deanna answered automatically, always reluctant to go into Grantville. "Hell, why not? I'm done with the edits and need to buy packaging for my illustrations. I'm ready to send them off to the publisher, but I always like to make sure they're packaged properly before I overnight them."

"Ah, excellent. Maybe we could try that cute coffeehouse by the park? The quaint and super-Vermontish one." Faythe looked so excited. She seemed so unlike the trembling bundle from that morning, Deanna didn't have the heart to decline. *In for a penny...*

"All right, sounds fun," Deanna said. "They do have the best coffee in Grantville, present establishment excluded, of course."

"Of course. Nice save." Faythe blew Deanna a kiss. "I'll change into something casual chic and be right back."

"Casual chic." Did Deanna have anything in her closet anywhere near chic, whether casual or not? "See you in a minute," she called toward the bedroom, not waiting for an answer before she hurried to her cabin. She grabbed the key hidden in a crack in the wall next to the back door and entered. She hadn't been there more than a few times to pick up art supplies since Faythe sprained her ankle, and the air smelled a bit stale. Deanna left the door open, hoping to air the place out a bit while she rummaged through her minuscule closet.

"Not that one," she said to herself, tossing a too-worn denim shirt on the bed. "Too casual. Not enough chic." She pushed and tugged at her clothes, beginning to think she wouldn't find anything to match whatever Faythe decided on, when her eyes fell on a plastic bag covering a wire hanger in the back of the closet. "Oh, God. I forgot." Deanna carefully took the hanger and the plastic rustled softly as she pushed it up and off the clothes underneath. Slate gray slacks and an ivory shirt looked as newly cleaned as the day she'd collected them at the dry cleaner. This used to be her work outfit, when she hadn't been in her smock. Deanna hadn't worn it since she quit Grantville High. Part her of recoiled at wearing the garments, but she was being silly. She wanted to look good for Faythe, who'd never seen her in anything but jeans and shirts. *And naked.* Deanna laughed at herself for allowing lewd thoughts to interfere with getting ready.

She rinsed off quickly in the shower and tied her damp hair into a low bun at the nape of her neck, then stared at her reflection in the mirror. This was how she used to wear her hair. Quickly she turned away and got dressed, smoothing the slacks over her hips. They felt a size too big; she'd obviously lost weight the last few years.

She was about to grab her leather jacket when she heard the rattling of fingertips on the frame of the back door. Smiling, she hurried over. "So eager to be seen with me that you can't wait, huh, Faythe—" Deanna stopped on the threshold, staring at Faythe standing next to Gloria Mueller, who looked bemused.

"Hi. Well, I was on my way over and ran into Mrs. Mueller." Faythe seemed to signal something with her eyes, looking back and forth between Deanna and Gloria.

"Gloria." Deanna nodded curtly. "What are you doing here?" She didn't intend to even attempt any niceties.

"Well, it's been a while since we talked, and when I ran into your lovely family, not to mention Ms. Hamilton here, I thought it was about time we caught up."

"Not sure what you mean. As far as I know, we've never talked. You've screamed at the top of your lungs and lectured me, but I don't call that talking." The small hairs on the back of Deanna's neck stood at attention. Something was very weird about Gloria showing up so shortly after her daughter's departure.

"Now, now, let's not exaggerate." Gloria smiled falsely. "What will Ms. Hamilton think?"

"Oh, I have a pretty good idea about my opinion thus far," Faythe said blithely.

"You do?" Gloria looked surprised.

"I do." Faythe moved to stand closer to Deanna. "Somehow you don't seem to be exactly a friend of my neighbor, Mrs. Mueller. We were actually on our way out, and if there's nothing more—?"

"Oh, but there is," Gloria said hurriedly. "I need to address the matter with Deanna in private, though. It concerns her sister." She emphasized the last sentence and looked pointedly at Deanna, who suddenly, but not unexpectedly, felt deflated.

"Just make it quick," Deanna mumbled and held the door open for Gloria, who gave Faythe an impressed look before she stepped inside the cabin. "I'm sorry. I won't be long," Deanna told Faythe, who looked worriedly at her.

"Don't let that cow get to you," Faythe whispered. "I'll be out here. Just shout if you need me."

"Shh. It'll be all right." Deanna had to smile at the hostile glare in Faythe's eyes. She closed the door and folded her arms over her chest. "I'm not going to ask again. What do you want?"

"I want you to stay away from my daughter." Gloria's expression had altered completely. "You've heeded my warnings for the last two years, and you're going to do so now, because I won't hesitate to act on my information if you don't."

"What the hell?" Deanna tried to figure out how Gloria knew Savannah had contacted her. Just because Gloria suspected that Savannah had talked to her, did she know her daughter had spent the night at Faythe's house? "I never sought your daughter out." Deanna didn't want to lie, and so far she hadn't.

"Lara Stockton told me yesterday that they ran into you at the supermarket. You are not to talk to my daughter, whether in private or in public." Gloria took a step toward Deanna, her hands clasped and a small muscle twitching next to her mouth.

Deanna refused to be intimidated. She'd never been afraid of Gloria Mueller, or any of her cronies at the school board, but she knew how strong their influence was in this small town. Deanna suspected Gloria had instigated her title as Grantville's First Lady and desperately clung to it even though her husband was no longer the town's mayor. "Not one step closer, Gloria." Deanna held up a hand, palm toward her. "I haven't sought your daughter out, nor do I intend to. I have no power over whom I run into in public. Grantville is a small place."

"If you value spending time with your sister, you will make sure you're at a safe distance." Gloria sneered. "Savannah's reputation is only just beginning to repair itself, and I will *not* have you destroy the gains she's made."

Deanna didn't know whether to laugh or cry. *The woman's clearly delusional.* Still, the threat was real enough. If Gloria wanted to interfere with Deanna's rights to visit Miranda and her school, she could. And Gloria wouldn't think twice about doing so, if she thought it served her purpose.

"Well?" Gloria tapped her foot.

"Nothing's changed. I hear you." Deanna spoke through clenched teeth. "You have me by the throat."

"If I didn't have to put my own poor daughter first, I would've made sure you weren't allowed anywhere near that school, or any other school for that matter." Gloria clutched her purse.

"You mean, you put yourself and your precious reputation as self-proclaimed royalty in this godforsaken town first." Deanna had never spoken to Gloria in such a way before. "You could have acted a dozen different ways, if you'd had only Savannah's best interest at heart. I may be forced to do as you say, but let's be honest, Gloria. You're only looking out for number one, and I'm obviously not talking about your daughter."

"Don't you dare talk to me like that. You're an immoral bitch who—"

"Who what, Mrs. Mueller?" Faythe seemed to materialize just inside the door. "I could hear the yelling all the way out to the deck."

"This doesn't concern you, Ms. Hamilton." Gloria had obvious trouble regaining her composure. "Deanna and I have old issues that we're trying to work out, and…well, I suppose it might sound worse than it is."

"It sounded like you called her an 'immoral bitch,' actually," Faythe said coolly. "Sounds bad enough if you ask me. How would you improve on that if you wanted to make it actually sound worse? Well, I suppose you could call her a *fucking* immoral bitch." Faythe tilted her head and looked pensively at Deanna. "Wouldn't you agree?"

"That does sound worse," Deanna said weakly. She tried to signal Faythe wordlessly not to antagonize Gloria any further, but it was probably too late.

"Eh, Ms. Hamilton. May I call you Faythe?" Gloria actually squirmed, which was something Deanna had never seen or thought possible.

"You can call me anything you want, as long as 'immoral bitch' isn't part of it."

"Well, eh, ha ha, I see. Of course not." Gloria coughed. "Deanna and I go back quite a few years, and we haven't always seen eye to eye."

"Who can blame Deanna for being mad at you, shocked even, when you're not doing more to set the record straight?" Faythe looked genuinely concerned, as if she really was trying to figure out Gloria's dilemma. "I'm sure you've racked your brain endlessly about how to get the point across without causing your daughter any unnecessary harm." She patted Gloria's arm. "Enough to give a poor mother sleepless nights, isn't it?"

"Yes, it sure is," Gloria said, and nodded eagerly. "A mother does what she has to, to protect her offspring. It's the law of nature."

"Sure is," Faythe echoed. She paused, glancing between them. "It's when the nature of *things* is on a collision course with the law of *man* that things can get hairy."

"Exact—what?" Gloria staggered sideways, only a fraction of an inch, but it was obvious to Deanna, and she knew from Faythe's pleased look that she'd seen it too. Deanna had given up trying to discreetly signal Faythe; instead she took the more direct approach.

"Gloria has invisible ways to help people see things her way. No matter what the law is, you could say." Deanna hoped Faythe would see beyond the jest in her voice.

"But you see, that's where I come in. I know you're the top hyena in this town, Gloria, with all the rest of the hyena-wannabes nearly falling over themselves to be on your good side. I suspect they're a bit afraid too. They don't want to become your next target." Faythe wasn't speaking tongue-in-cheek anymore, and Deanna could only watch what she feared was a complete train wreck right before her eyes.

"I never!" Gloria spat, her eyes actually bulging.

"Well, Grantville may be your playing field of choice, your home ballpark, Gloria," Faythe continued, undaunted. "However, Grantville, as lovely as it is, is a small speck on the map of America. Where I reside, Manhattan, New York, the network's studios, we reach and influence millions on national television. As you may know, we cover all sorts of stories, and this vendetta, based on lies and emotional extortion, would really tug at the American heartstrings. And if you think I'm joking, think again. No matter what you've got up your cashmere sleeves, it's not enough."

Gloria's jaw had slacked, but now she slammed her mouth shut. Deanna had listened to Faythe's fiery speech with a sinking heart, knowing she had to stop her before she made Gloria cause irreparable damage.

"Faythe," Deanna said, her voice husky and barely audible. "Faythe, it's not necessary. Gloria and I…understand each other."

"Deanna?" Faythe frowned. "She's hurt you for years by spreading these damn lies. You can't let that—"

"Faythe. Please." Deanna wondered if she could stop this new woman standing in front of her. This was the professional Faythe intertwined with the loyal, caring Faythe. "I've got this. I really do."

"I'm glad you're not going to allow this woman to meddle." Gloria spoke in a low snarl. "She may be from the big city, but that doesn't mean anything in this town. You know what you did to Savannah was wrong. I see the way this big-city woman looks at you. It's wrong. Morally wrong, and wrong in the eyes of God—"

"Enough." Gloria's self-righteousness made Deanna's blood boil. No way would she stand idly by while Savannah's mother poured her poison over Faythe. Deanna stepped closer, towering over the other woman, and for the first time, Deanna raised her voice at Gloria. "You've made my life a living hell for the last two years, but I'll be damned if you're going to insult Faythe under my roof, just because she cares enough to defend me. And don't you *dare* drag religion into this. You started attending church when your husband ran for office, but you don't do that as much anymore, do you? You're nothing but a hypocrite," Deanna thundered.

"Think of what you're saying. Pick your words very carefully, Deanna," Gloria hissed, sounding not half as triumphant as she did only moments earlier.

"You're fond of making threats," Faythe said. "And you're holding some sort of Damocles sword above Deanna's head." She leaned her hip against the dresser inside the door, folding her arms over her chest. "The only real power you possess these days is your position on several private school boards." Faythe blinked. "Oh."

Gloria went off on another tirade, but Deanna could only stare at Faythe and watch her connect the dots. "Faythe."

"Tell me, Gloria," Faythe said, pale now. "How do you sleep at night?"

"Don't." Deanna pleaded now. No matter how they cornered Gloria, no matter how wrong Gloria's actions were, all that mattered at the end of the day was Miranda's well-being. "Don't, Faythe. I can't risk it."

"I don't understand. She's blackmailing you into compliance and silence." Faythe was clearly still trying to wrap her brain around everything.

"It doesn't matter." Deanna raised her voice when Faythe didn't understand. "Don't you see? It doesn't matter. *I* don't matter." She gestured emphatically, then sagged against the wall. "Miranda's innocent, and she's the only one who does."

CHAPTER TWENTY-SEVEN

Faythe wanted to reach across the table and shake some sense into Deanna. After they got rid of Gloria Mueller or, rather, watched her run between the maples to her car and drive off in a cloud of fallen leaves, Faythe suggested they keep their date and go to the coffeehouse as intended. Deanna hadn't said a word on the road into Grantville and only uttered a few while ordering her coffee and turkey sandwich. Faythe tried several light topics, but now frustration was making her angry, despite her best intentions to remain calm and understanding.

"Come on," Faythe said, and sighed impatiently. "Are you so mad at me that you can't even think of any insults?"

Deanna looked up from her coffee mug in apparent confusion. "What? No. No, no, I'm not mad. Not at you, at least."

"Then talk to me." Faythe scooted closer, leaning her elbows on the table. "Please, don't shut me out. Even yelling at me beats the silent treatment."

"I'm sorry." Deanna looked stricken. Had she gone so deep into her old habit of internalizing that she hadn't noticed how she simply switched off? "Guess I'm not very good company."

"That's not it. Not at all." Faythe took Deanna's hand and squeezed it gently. "I'm not talking about being entertained. I want to help you, be part of the solution to this mess. Gloria will cause even more trouble from now on unless we do something while she's trying to regroup." Faythe had managed to rattle Savannah's mother and now was the perfect time to act.

Deanna winced, but didn't pull her hand free. "Why can't you understand that I can't risk Miranda's well-being?" Emanating pain and bewilderment, Deanna looked so vulnerable that Faythe wanted to wrap her arms around her and never let go.

"In your life, Miranda is the only constant, and she comes first. That's great and how it's supposed to be. Irene Costa was clear that you're the main reason Miranda's doing so well. But do you really think that Miranda will benefit from having an increasingly stressed-out, blackmailed sister who is filled with anxiety and constantly looking over her shoulder? That's bound to come back to bite you. And her."

"I can't see any way out of it that doesn't risk everything we've accomplished." Torment gave Deanna's voice a strangled, husky tone. "Miranda takes two steps forward and one step back at the best of times. More often than not, she takes two forward and three back."

"I know. And what exactly is Gloria Mueller threatening if you don't comply?"

"Not here." Deanna looked around the room. Faythe couldn't see anyone paying them any special interest, but nodded.

"Okay. Let's go over to the park. It's a gorgeous day and we can take more coffee."

"All right." Deanna looked ready to bolt to avoid the conversation, but followed Faythe as she ordered two more cups of latte to go.

The day was cool, and their breath created small misty clouds as they warmed their hands around the paper cups. "How about there?" Faythe pointed at a park bench by an ancient-looking oak tree. "That's out of earshot."

"Why not? Not many people around."

Faythe sat down on the bench and patted the spot next to her. Deanna hesitated only briefly, but her body language showed how uncomfortable she was. *She looks afraid.* Faythe wanted to convey her encouragement and support, but a public display right now would be the last thing Deanna wanted. "Okay, tell me what Gloria Mueller's up to."

"When Savannah told us her mother had read her diary and knew the truth about what she'd done, or, rather, what I hadn't done, I realized that Gloria knew she and her family would lose face. That all makes sense now. I never could figure out why she was so vindictive, when all her friends and allies were on her side anyway." Deanna pulled her left leg up and hugged it against her.

"You can't underestimate her influence. She's on several school boards in this town—the public one, as well as private schools. Gloria can be persuasive and charm the pants off anyone when she wants to. That's why she's such a successful fund-raiser, among other things. When she told me she'd make sure I never set foot in Miranda's school again, I believed her. She was going to pull all the strings she needed to make that happen, if I didn't willingly leave my position at Grantville High. I wanted to fight, Faythe," Deanna said throatily, the coffee mug shaking in her hands. "I wanted to take that damn school and its board to court and make them try to prove their allegations, but I couldn't. If they had cut me off from Miranda, she'd lose so much of what she's learned."

"Your mother—"

"Is not my strongest supporter, as you could tell at the outing? She thinks I hate her, and I know she's disappointed in me."

Faythe wasn't ready to believe what Deanna said, but said, "Go on."

"When I tried to bluff Gloria, saying that I'd talk to my parents, she showed just how far she would go to keep her position in this damn town." Deanna drew a deep, trembling breath. "She told me she'd talk to Miranda directly and tell her I'd never visit her again because I was tired of her. That from now on, I had new friends and she wasn't good enough, especially since her stepsisters were normal and more fun to be with. Well, you get the picture."

"Damn her to hell." Faythe could hardly believe her ears and suspected she was as pale as Deanna was. "She'd take her own petty vengeance out on your autistic, defenseless sister for something her own daughter did?"

"Yup." Deanna exhaled audibly. "I can't risk her doing anything to Miranda. I just can't."

"There must be a way around this. You can't let her hold this over your head until Miranda graduates. That's several years from now!" Faythe was furious, angrier than she'd been in a long time. "We have to do something."

"There's no *we* in this mess," Deanna said sadly. "There's only me and what I need to do to keep Miranda from paying the price for something she knows nothing about. It doesn't matter that it's unfair. Miranda can't get caught in the crossfire. It would take only Gloria minutes to destroy what it's taken years to build."

"Oh, we won't risk anything." Faythe's mind raced with different approaches to their problem. "We have to figure out a way to get Miranda out of her way and make Gloria harmless in the process."

"I've tried to think of something, but haven't come up with anything that will work. Maybe I'm blind because I've lived with this for so long, but it seems undoable."

"Sweetie." Faythe took Deanna's hand. "It's not undoable. Not when we pool our resources. I know what we need to do first."

"What?" Deanna held on tight to Faythe's hand, which she took as a sign of trust. Hopefully Deanna knew she wasn't alone in this anymore.

"We need to talk to your mother and tell her everything."

"No, I—"

"Stop, listen to me." Faythe shook her head at Deanna's gut reaction. "This is a matter of emergency damage control. You need to bury any hatchets when it comes to your family. You want to put Miranda first, right? Well, your family needs to do so too, if it's going to happen."

Deanna stared at her with eyes so icy blue, Faythe began to think she'd refuse. Eventually, Deanna's expression mellowed. "For Miranda," she said quietly.

"And for you." Faythe squeezed Deanna's hand. "You matter just as much as your sister, you know. You deserve to be free from this."

"Thank you." Sipping her coffee, Deanna didn't take her eyes off Faythe, who wondered what Deanna was thinking. The pensive expression on her face was undecipherable.

"Okay, time to go back to the house and brainstorm," Faythe said, "and start making phone calls."

"God." Deanna freed her hand and tugged at Faythe's low ponytail. "I wonder if Gloria could ever guess what she's in for."

❖

"Mrs. Bodell? Angela? This is Faythe Hamilton. We met at your daughter Miranda's school. Both Miranda and Deanna are okay, but we have a bit of a situation here and we need your help. To be blunt, both your daughters need you badly."

Faythe started the ball rolling after she spent several hours taking notes and double-checking facts over the Internet. Deanna knew a lot about focusing, about getting into the zone so far that she didn't notice if she was hungry or thirsty, and admired Faythe both as she did her research and talked to Angela.

"So you were driving this way tomorrow anyway? Perfect. Have you ever been to Deanna's cabin? No?" After providing clear directions she said, "Hers is the eighth house on your left and mine is the ninth. That's where we'll be."

Nervous, Deanna closed her eyes. She had come out to her mother when she was twenty-two, and her mother handled it well. Angela was always supportive and caring, always putting her girls first. Did her mother realize she was sleeping with Faythe? Angela probably would have difficulty imagining the wholesome TV personality Faythe Hamilton, beautiful and feminine, as a lesbian attracted to her daughter. As open-minded as her mother used to be, she was also a woman of her generation who would have stereotypical ideas of what a lesbian looked and acted like.

"Good. Good. Excellent." Faythe beamed and made a thumbs-up toward Deanna. "Around noon will be perfect. I can't say how much this means to Deanna and Miranda. And to me, since I care deeply about De—about both of them." Faythe colored faintly and cleared her throat. "I know you've been out of touch with Deanna for a long time, but, trust me, that's at an end." She was quiet for a moment while Angela talked. "Yes. I definitely think you should bring Percy. This is a family matter, and if the girls didn't have school, they should be here too, in my opinion. Yes. All right. See you tomorrow." Faythe disconnected her cell phone and took a deep breath. "Whew. That wasn't as hard as I thought it'd be."

"How did she sound?" Deanna felt a bit silly that she hadn't made the call, but to do so, after all these years, even if they'd met only recently at the outing, seemed impossible.

"Surprised at first, probably because it was me calling, and then decisive and excited. Confused, since I didn't give any details, naturally." Faith pushed her hair out of her face. "She said she loves her daughters and she'll give you whatever you need."

"Wow." Deanna clasped her fingers and tugged at them. "That's generous. I thought she'd say no."

"That's your insecurity talking, which is understandable, but Angela's not like that madwoman Gloria. Of course your mother loves you and Miranda, and tomorrow should prove that once and for all."

"I hope so. I'm probably just as much to blame for our estrangement. I could have been more approachable. For Miranda's sake."

"For your sake too. And for your Mom's." Faythe disentangled Deanna's fingers with gentle hands. She raised one hand to her lips and kissed Deanna's fingertips, one after another. Deanna shivered at the soft caress and could feel the caress of Faythe's tongue against them. She moaned quietly as she cupped the back of Faythe's neck with her free hand.

"I want this to end. I do. I want to be whole again. I want my life back. Not necessarily that job, but I don't want to be shackled by false rumors, by being emotionally blackmailed—"

"And you won't," Faythe said hotly. She placed Deanna's hand against her chin and only then did Deanna realize Faythe was crying. Her cheek was damp and new tears were forming in the corners of her eyes. "You won't have to put up with any of that anymore. I won't allow it. I've seen what it does to you, and I can't watch it go on any longer. I just can't. You mean too much to me." Faythe's expression altered from anguish to wide-eyed realization. "You mean the world to me," she whispered.

Deanna trembled and wrapped her arms tight around Faythe. "What?"

"You." Faythe spoke into Deanna's shoulder. "Heaven help me, I tried to tell you I'm not good at any of this. I mean relationship stuff."

"I know you did. You were wrong, you know."

"That's just it. I *don't* know." Faythe rubbed her cheek against Deanna. "All I know is that I care more about what happens to you than what happens to me."

"And for the first time since this nightmare began, I feel that enough is enough." Deanna tipped Faythe's head back. She kissed her damp cheeks gently and then her soft, parted lips. "Because of you."

"These feelings are completely new to me." Faythe looked like she was ready to bolt, but her body pressed impossibly closer. "You know that, right?"

"They're just as new to me, Faythe." Deanna couldn't get enough of Faythe's nearness. "I'm in uncharted waters."

"Scared?"

"Yes. Mostly about losing you." Deanna held her breath. What if Faythe didn't understand just how hard it was for Deanna to be open and honest about how she felt? Especially since she constantly expected Faythe to withdraw and remind her about her attitude toward steady relationships.

"Oh, sweet Jesus, baby." The words left Faythe's lips in a gush. "I don't want to lose you either. Ever." She tugged Deanna even closer, pressing her lips against hers. Deanna returned the kiss hungrily. She had no idea what tomorrow might bring. They might crash and burn, making a bad situation even worse, but right now she was where she belonged. Faythe's hot tongue explored her mouth, and Deanna sensed a new, more intense feeling behind their caresses.

"I want you. I want you so badly, darling," Deanna said against Faythe's lips.

"Yes. Oh, yes." Faythe's hands pushed Deanna's shirt up, spreading greedy fingers over her stomach. "Any way you want, for as long as you want."

Deanna knew Faythe wasn't talking about a life perspective, but her foolish heart still jumped in her chest. "Bed, then?" Deanna walked toward their bedroom, stopping intermittently to kiss Faythe again. Perhaps, if the deities granted her more time, Deanna would be able to convince Faythe that she was capable of forever.

CHAPTER TWENTY-EIGHT

Pammie nearly fell over the threshold when Faythe opened the door. "Hi, there. You okay? We got here as soon as Nana found someone to cover for her at the animal shelter."

"For goodness' sake, breathe, kiddo." Faythe shook her head at the battle-ready Pammie and pulled both girls in for a group hug. "So good to see you. You look great." It was true. Pammie was vibrating with life as always, but she also was positively glowing for another reason, Faythe suspected. Savannah was less exuberant, but her pallor from last time was now a healthy glow, and she had a small smile on her lips that didn't look like it would go away anytime soon.

"So do you." Savannah returned the hug, then wrapped her arm around Pammie's waist. The open display of affection spoke volumes and Faythe sensed that these two were about to figure out things in general, and between them in particular.

"Deanna, the girls are here!" Faythe called out.

"Oh, great. Coffee, ladies? Tea?"

"Coffee for me, please." Pammie grinned and bounced out into the kitchen. "I'll help."

Savannah and Faythe looked at each other under raised eyebrows. "Coffee will do that to you." Faythe shook her head. "I think Deanna's had four mugs of double-espresso lattes today. That's normal for me, but not for her."

"She's nervous. Who can blame her?" Savannah said softly. "I'll have some tea."

"How do you feel about today?" Faythe walked to the living room with Savannah in tow.

"I'm okay. I've been working toward this moment ever since we left here last time. It was the only way this could happen, really, so I figured I'd better get ready for it." Savannah looked serious, but also calm and prepared. "I'm not looking forward to what Mother will say, especially not what she'll say to Deanna, but this has to stop."

"You're a brave girl. I loathed you once for what you put Deanna through, but you're doing everything possible to help her now, which is what really matters." Faythe sat down on the biggest of the couches and patted the seat next to her. "Despite your mother's best intentions, you're a good person."

"Thanks." Savannah blushed faintly. "I worried about becoming completely estranged from my mother for putting her on the spot like this, but I can't see any other way. And we actually can't get much more estranged than we are. I rarely see her or talk to her."

"And your father?"

"Is a man of his generation. Doesn't want to know, doesn't want to get involved, and is content to let Mother run the show." Savannah sighed. "I was never Daddy's girl. He didn't have time when he was running for office and realizing his political ambitions, except when he needed to display his happy home, complete with his stunning wife and well-brought-up daughter."

"Ah, the joys of politics. Seen enough of what goes on behind the scenes there to never want that type of a career."

"As a matter of fact, I might run for office one day," Savannah said. "Who knows, I might become the first lesbian president of the United States."

"Hear, hear," Deanna said, entering the living room with a tray loaded with six steaming mugs next to the large plate of assorted sandwiches.

"They're here, I take it?" Faythe asked, checking Deanna's expression carefully as she placed the tray on the coffee table.

"Yup. I'll go greet them, all right? Be right back." She walked toward the back door, and Faythe debated if she should go with her. *She would've asked me if she needed me.* Faythe put a damper on her protectiveness and remained on the couch.

It only took Deanna a minute to bring her mother and Percy in to join them. "Mom, Percy, you remember Faythe? And these are our friends Pammie and Savannah. Pammie, Savannah, this is my mother, Angela, and her…my stepfather, Percy."

After shaking hands with everybody, Angela sat next to Faythe, and Percy chose one of the armchairs. Gazing around the room, he looked impressed. "What a great place you have here, Ms. Hamilton," he said, clearly set on keeping a polite tone.

"Faythe, please. And it's not mine, exactly, it's my aunt's. She's in Florida this time of year."

"Please, have some coffee. It's fresh from Faythe's aunt's state-of-the-art espresso machine." Deanna gestured at the table, her smile a little too wide.

"Thanks, honey. Sandwiches look lovely." Angela sipped from her mug and nodded approvingly. "This is good coffee."

"Why don't we get right to the point, instead of tiptoeing around each other in this rather uncomfortable way?" Faythe said.

"All right." Deanna drew one leg up underneath her as she sat down in the other armchair. "I suppose I should start."

"I admit I was startled yesterday," Angela said. "But as long as you and Miranda are all right, we can figure things out." She glanced at her husband. "Right, Percy?"

"Of course." Faythe couldn't quite figure out Percy's tone of voice, but he seemed serious.

"All right, then." Deanna exchanged a quick glance with Faythe before she continued. "You remember the woman you met at the picnic, Gloria Mueller?"

"Yes."

"She's been blackmailing me for the last two years." Deanna's complexion turned grayish and she pressed against the backrest of the chair.

"What?" Angela jerked, nearly spilling her coffee. "She's after money? You're successful, but not rich. Or are you?" Angela looked confused.

"No, Mom, I'm not rich by any standard. I do okay, but that's it. And no, Gloria Mueller is not after money. She's quite well off."

"My mother wants to keep her position as the leading lady of

Grantville, the spider of the web, the queen bee. Whatever you call it, she'll do anything to maintain her position of power." Savannah looked as pale as Deanna now, scooting closer to Pammie.

"Your mother? You're Gloria Mueller's daughter?" Angela spoke slowly. "And this woman is under the impression that Deanna stands between her and her position in Grantville? Who the hell is this megalomaniac?"

Faythe smiled inwardly at Angela's astute word choice. "Why don't we give you the short, fact-filled version?" she suggested, then told Angela and Percy what Savannah had done two years ago, and what had transpired the last few weeks. Angela and Percy listened without interrupting, but Angela's eyes kept darkening.

"And what is she threatening to do, exactly, that keeps Deanna from taking her to court?" Percy asked when Faythe quieted.

"She knows that Mom and I haven't been on speaking terms for years, and she also knows how important Miranda is to me."

"She always was everything to you, from the day she was born," Angela said softly.

"Yes." Deanna pushed trembling fingers through her hair. Faythe couldn't remain on the couch any longer. She moved and sat down on the armrest of Deanna's chair, placing her hand on her shoulder in a clear gesture of support. "Anyway, she knows this about me, and she thinks it wouldn't be hard to convince you two to see things her way."

"How dare she—?"

"Until last week, wouldn't you have believed her? Or at least listened to what she had to say?" Deanna spoke quietly, and the pain in her voice made Faythe squeeze her shoulder gently.

"I...I suppose." Angela sobbed once. "Go on."

"So, what if I had taken her to court, called Savannah a liar in public, and raised holy hell like I wanted to?"

"I'm so sorry..." Savannah had apparently had enough and burst into tears. "It's all my fault. No matter what, it's all my fault."

"Oh, sweetie." Pammie threw her arms around Savannah and held her tight. "Come here." Her fiery eyes darted between them, daring anyone in the room to say anything accusingly to Savannah.

"Child, you're a hundred times more honorable than your mother," Angela said. "That woman lacks basic human decency as far as I can tell, but you don't. You did something that was very wrong, but you've come forward and dealt with it. And you're here, helping to save my daughters from any further harm." Angela turned to Deanna. "So, what else does Gloria threaten to do?"

"She knows I'm helpless when it comes to Miranda and said if I cause any trouble whatsoever, she would have me banned from visiting Miranda. You know what that would do to her. She said she would also make sure Miranda knew I was evil and did horrible things to young girls, and that she wasn't safe with me and couldn't see me again." Deanna tipped her head back against Faythe and closed her eyes briefly. She squeezed Faythe's thigh through her jeans before she continued.

"She relied on the fact that you and I weren't talking. But that's not the only reason Faythe managed to convince me to invite you." Deanna looked up at Faythe again, as if debating how to go on. She rose and stepped over to her mother, where she knelt next to her and took Angela's hands. "I was so hurt that you chose Percy over Miranda and me. I was furious that you sent Miranda away after we had been a family, our little trio against the world, for seven years. I felt you replaced us with Percy's two perfect girls, and that you didn't want us anymore."

"Nothing could be further from the truth."

"I know that now. I mean, intellectually I realize that. I've seen how Miranda has thrived at the school, learned skills I never thought possible. It was the right decision to give her that opportunity." Deanna rubbed her thumbs over her mother's hands. "And my feeling of being replaced won't go away easily."

"Neither will the pain you caused when you gave me that ultimatum. You opted out of our life, Deanna. One day you called me every name in the book, and the next you were gone and I didn't even know where you were for months."

"We can't deny that we've caused a lot of pain. We can't erase it and pretend it never happened."

"I suppose. But maybe we can learn to live with it eventually?" Angela's hopeful tone was heartbreaking, and Faythe wondered what was going through Deanna's mind.

"I'm willing to try." Deanna spoke abruptly, but kept her physical connection with her mother. "Now, our main concern is Miranda. We can't allow Gloria access to her. You have full custody of her, Mom."

"Perhaps now is the best time to talk to Deanna about our plans, honey?" Percy said, and everyone looked at him.

"Plans?" Deanna snapped her head back toward her mother.

"Percy's right. Come here. Sit next to me." Angela patted the couch cushion. "Trista and Laney want to attend a private school in Manhattan, and they both have made such good grades that they've received full scholarships. Percy's office is opening a new branch in New York, which they want him to head up." Angela looked almost afraid when she tried to smile despite trembling lips. "I want to move Miranda to another facility, very much like this one, but with actual college classes available for young people at her level."

"Move her?" Deanna looked shell-shocked. "When did you know about this?"

"About the girls applying, I've known for quite some time. But about the scholarships and Percy's job? Three days."

"Ah." Deanna stood and walked over to the window. "Guess that's the answer. All you have to do is move Miranda out of Gloria's reach and—"

"No, no. That's not the answer to everything. This woman has caused you harm. She will *not* get away with it." Angela was fuming. "If we're going to have a chance to function as a family, all six of us, we must show solidarity with every single family member and not allow anyone to sacrifice herself."

"Okay." Deanna looked at Faythe, her eyes black with stormy emotions. "Okay, Mom."

"We're here to plot and plan, I suppose." Percy produced a small PDA phone. "Planning is what I do. I have a flow sheet that, when properly applied, will keep us from forgetting any angles and minimize the risk of making a mistake."

Faythe had to pinch her thigh hard so she wouldn't giggle. Suddenly Pammie and Samantha were sitting on the armrests on either side of Percy as he drew up the basic plan, and their interest in his tech toy seemed to charm him.

Faythe moved to Angela's other side, cupping Deanna's cheek briefly. Angela gazed warmly at them. "While they're doing the planning, why don't you two tell me what your relationship is exactly?" She sounded genuinely interested. "Are you a couple?"

"Mom!"

"Well, I have years of questions to ask. So, are you?" Angela looked quite hopeful at the thought.

"Not exactly—" Deanna began.

"Yes. Yes, we are a couple." Faythe heard herself speak, but couldn't fathom her own words. This was probably the scariest, most spontaneous thing she'd ever done. Deanna's eyes darkened even more, yet a new light went on as soon as Faythe spoke. No matter how their plan to deal with Gloria turned out, Faythe vowed she would not be responsible for snuffing out that light.

CHAPTER TWENTY-NINE

Miranda was dressed in black jeans and a light blue T-shirt adorned with a flowery pattern she had created herself during art class, using potatoes as stamps. Deanna's heart was ready to explode with all the overflowing love she felt for her sister. It had taken Deanna more than half an hour to convince Miranda that packing a suitcase with her most beloved possessions and a few changes of clothes was part of what Miranda labeled "surprise fun," a term they always used when it was necessary to break Miranda's routines. Miranda was always suspicious when it came to surprises, and today had not been any different. Now Deanna snapped the suitcase closed, and with an arm around her, she guided her out of the room she'd lived in for nearly ten years, except for summer breaks and holidays.

Outside, Irene Costa was waiting to say good-bye, clearly struggling not to cry and upset Miranda. Faythe stood next to her, according to their plan, carefully recorded into Percy's flow sheet four days ago. She had informed Irene of every sordid detail while Deanna helped Miranda.

"Deanna," Irene said, her voice choked. "I never liked her, but I had no idea. I wish you'd told me. I could have kept her away from Miranda."

"You couldn't work twenty-four/seven, Irene." Deanna shook her head sadly. "There would always have been the risk that she would sneak into Miranda's room and scare the living daylights out of her. Your duty was toward Miranda, and you've been great. Absolutely fantastic. Miranda's done so well here, and you're very much the reason for that."

"I'm going to miss her." Irene's voice broke and she drew a deep breath. "Here she is now." She smiled brightly at Miranda, who left her room behind Deanna, carrying her beloved pink roller bag. "Got everything, honey?"

"Yes. My bag." Miranda patted the handle lovingly.

"Your pink bag. Goes so well with your outfit, Miranda." Irene looked like she wanted to hug Miranda and not let go, but instead she merely kissed her forehead. "Have fun and let's talk on the phone, all right?"

"Yes. All right." Miranda nodded. "Chat."

"Exactly. We'll chat." Irene stood and waved as they walked down the corridor.

Faythe helped Miranda stow her bag into the trunk of Deanna's car, and it warmed Deanna's heart to see how readily Miranda seemed to accept Faythe's presence. Faythe, in turn, behaved as if she'd been around Miranda all her life, mindful of her personal space, which was larger than most people's.

"Where do you want to sit, Miranda?" Faythe asked. "Backseat or up front?"

Miranda halted and looked confused. "We have to buckle up," she said uncertainly.

"Miranda always sits in the back. The front seat is probably a little too daunting for her." Deanna pointed at the passenger door to the right. "Take your seat, young lady."

Miranda opened the door and climbed in. She buckled up meticulously and draped her pink scarf across her handbag. This was her routine every time she rode in a car, and Deanna knew it provided comfort and a sense of security.

They drove off, heading for Faythe's house where the others were waiting. Deanna worried how Miranda would respond to the fact that her mother was there as part of the surprise, as well as Savannah and Pammie.

"Are you all right, baby?" Faythe asked quietly, briefly touching Deanna's thigh. "You're gripping that steering wheel so tight, I may have to pry you off when we get to the house."

"Oh, right." Deanna loosened her grip. "Yeah, I'm okay. Just a bit nervous."

"No wonder. But we'll be fine. Miranda will be fine too, and so will your folks. I was impressed with how your mother took charge and also how incredibly organized Percy is. That flow sheet on his phone was something."

Deanna had to laugh. "That's Percy for you. Before we got crosswise with each other, we had some interesting conversations and…well, I suppose if things hadn't happened the way they did, I wouldn't have found him half bad."

"It's not too late to get to know each other." Faythe suddenly looked wistful. "I wonder if I'll ever get on the right foot with my father again. I mean, my mother I can deal with. She's a bit shallow, but since I know that, I can factor it into everything she says." She sighed. "My father, though, is a whole different ballgame. I don't think he cares about me as a person. I'm an asset. He'll use my 'fame' in a heartbeat to gain advantages, which really sucks. I only want him to see me as his daughter, someone he loves, regardless. Talk about Utopia." Faythe looked out the passenger window, drumming her fingertips on the armrest.

"We all want to be validated by our parents." Deanna wanted to smooth away the wrinkles that marred Faythe's forehead. "You're not asking for anything that ought to be too much for them to figure out. If they can't bring themselves to see you for the amazing woman that you are, then it's not your fault and they don't deserve you."

"Thanks, baby. I know. I mean, intellectually I know that."

"And in your heart?"

"In my heart, I just want my dad to say he's proud of me, that he believes in me. But I may have to face the fact that it's not going to happen." Faythe looked composed, but her voice was hollow in a way that infuriated Deanna. She had a second chance to patch things up with Angela, and now Faythe was the one with a long list of unsolved family issues.

"No matter what, you know I'm in your corner, right?" Deanna took Faythe's hand, keeping the other firmly on the wheel and her eyes focused on the road. "You're the most amazing person I've ever met, all categories. You've made all the difference in my life."

"Deanna—"

"You have. You know how depressed and resigned I was. I didn't see any end to any of this, and you just didn't give up. As infuriated as I was occasionally, you didn't stop. And it looks like I'll have my life back soon. I never anticipated that. Frankly, I had given up."

"You were suffering from post-traumatic stress disorder, if you ask me," Faythe said in a low voice, glancing over her shoulder. "Wow, she's asleep already. What have we been driving for, five minutes?"

Deanna checked her rearview mirror and saw Miranda's head resting against the neck support. "Oh, she does that. I think she finds the outside world so stressful, she simply conks out." Turning on to the road leading to the lake, she mulled over Faythe's words. "PTSD? Really?"

"Obviously, I'm no psychiatrist, but your reactions are completely understandable from that point of view." Squeezing Deanna's hand, Faythe raised it to her lips and kissed it gently. "It's about to end, though, baby."

"I know. It's just…I have this dreadful feeling that this will blow up in my face and become even worse for everybody." Deanna checked the rearview mirror again. Miranda was still asleep, her pink lips slightly parted. It wasn't often she saw Miranda this relaxed while she was awake, if ever, and Deanna had to force herself to return her attention to the road ahead.

"If it does, and I don't think it will, you'll have your family behind you. And the girls. And me." Faythe winked. "It will be interesting to see what Pammie and Savannah managed to do with the *Grantville Times*. Was it Pammie's aunt who was the chief editor, or was it Savannah's?"

"Fortunately for us, it was Pammie's. Her father's youngest sister, I believe."

"Ah. Yes, I remember. Lucky. If it had been a relative of Savannah's, they would most likely have been under Gloria's spell."

"Under her thumb, you mean?"

"That too." Faythe wrinkled her nose, looking cuter than she'd ever want to know. "Pammie said that she let Savannah do all the writing, since this has to come from her, in her own words. If anyone else meddled in it, it could be a long, interesting time in court for the *Grantville Times*."

"Still could be, I suppose." Deanna shuddered at the thought.

"Hardly, if Savannah has written it the right way."

"Well, you're the media expert here, and I trust your judgment. Here we are." Deanna turned off the road and onto the driveway leading up to their houses. She stopped next to Pammie's little Toyota, which was parked behind Percy and Angela's Chrysler 300.

The door flew open just as Deanna engaged the parking brake and turned off the ignition. Two whirlwinds moved toward the car and Deanna barely recognized her two stepsisters. "Something's wrong," she muttered, glancing nervously at the backseat. Miranda was still asleep.

"What? What's the matter?" Faythe looked alarmed.

"They're smiling. The bra— The kids. They're smiling." It was true. Trista and Laney were rapidly approaching, looking excited.

"So they are." Faythe seemed to catch on quickly. "I'll go while you wake Miranda."

"Thanks." As Deanna circled the car and opened the passenger door, she glanced over her shoulder, worried about what might be going on. Were the two teenyboppers there to gloat, or what? This didn't look good.

❖

"Hi Trista, Laney," Faythe said, stopping in front of the two excited girls. "Hold it just a second, okay? Miranda's asleep in the backseat, and you know how easy it is to spook her. If she sees the two of you hovering, no matter how happy you are to see her, she might get scared and freak out."

"Oh," Laney said, and the corners of her mouth turned down. She wasn't pleased that anyone would keep her waiting. "We just wanted to talk to Deanna really quick."

"Well, you'll have time for that. I suppose you came with Angela and Percy after all. I mean, it's Wednesday, a regular school day." Faythe put one arm around each girl's shoulders and moved them toward the house. "I'm so glad you came to support your stepsisters," she said, playing devil's advocate.

"Eh, well, yeah. We wanted to know what was going on. Angela and Dad have been so secretive. Mysterious, even." Trista smirked. "So we nagged them into letting us come. We also wanted another chance to hang with you and hear about all the celebrities you meet and stuff. We sure got everyone's attention at school when we told them we met you."

Faythe exhaled slowly, suppressing an exasperated groan. She could just imagine being the topic among the girls at the girls' school. "Great," she murmured. "So, will you promise me not to crowd Miranda? If you give her some space and a little time, you'll be surprised how brilliant she is."

"Brilliant? Her?" Trista glanced over her shoulder. "She's retarded."

"That's such a dreary word, Trista." Faythe wanted to pinch the ignorant girl. "Miranda has autism, and I'm sure Angela and Percy have told you what that means. "

"Yeah, I suppose. I...I didn't listen very well. I guess I should've."

"Yes." Faythe didn't want to put Trista on the defensive. "But you know what, if you have any questions and you don't feel like talking to a family member, you can always ask me. I've worked with autistic experts on my show, and actually, quite a few celebrities have kids or siblings with autism." She knew she was being manipulative now, playing on what she knew impressed the sisters, but it was true. Awareness of autism had peaked during the last decade, and getting a celebrity to put a face to a disease or a condition generated more focus, and thus more money for research. And the interest of two shallow teenagers, who were being teenagers.

"You're very cool. And nice." Laney looked appreciatively at Faythe as they entered the house. "Just wait and see what's in the paper today. You know, that local paper. That bitch is going to flip."

Faythe surmised that the bitch Laney was talking about was Gloria Mueller. "I'll guess I'll hear all about it in a sec."

"We've read some of it. Pammie and Savannah brought the papers over, and, wow, Savannah's gorgeous, isn't she? I can't believe she was never homecoming queen." Trista managed to look starstruck and affronted at the same time. "That's what I plan to be."

"Huh. You might just have some competition in Manhattan," Laney said scornfully. "You may be all that in the stupid, tiny town we live in now, but in New York, thousands of girls are prettier than you."

"You don't know anything about *anything*!" With a furious sob, Trista ran into the house in front of them and disappeared into one of the guest rooms, slamming the door behind her.

"Wow. Sure feels like home," Percy said from the living-room couch. "Laney, what's up with Trista?"

"Same old. Egomaniac with a hurt ego."

"Laney." Angela came out of the kitchen, carrying a tray. "You know how Trista is. Why set her off?"

"Because it's fun?" Laney pouted, but walked over to the guest room and knocked on the door. "Hey, Trista. Come on. I was only messing with you."

"Piss off."

"If I do that, will you come out? You wanted to see the look on Deanna's face, remember, when she read the *Grantville Times*."

Faythe frowned at Laney's choice of words, but then Trista stuck her head out, wiping her wet cheeks. "Yeah, I did. Out of my way, *sister*. I really want to see what she thinks of Savannah's text. That Mueller woman will get what she deserves now after what she did to Deanna."

So it was Gloria they were gloating over, not Deanna. Faythe sighed in relief and turned to Angela, who was setting the dining table. Percy had gone out into the kitchen where Faythe could hear Pammie's and Savannah's voices.

"Let me help you," Faythe said, and began to fold the napkins Angela had found. "What are we having?" She pointed at a wrought-iron pot sitting in the middle of the table.

"I thought a nice autumn casserole might be a good idea. Miranda likes it because of all the colors."

"Sounds terrific." Faythe glanced over at the door, where there was still no sign of Miranda and Deanna. "Wonder what's keeping them?"

"Don't worry. It usually takes quite a while to get Miranda out of a car. Once she decides to come in, she'll be fine."

"I'm worried that being around strangers in a strange house will be too much for her."

"We'll just have to keep an eye on her. If she starts to get agitated, I'll bring out one of her coloring books with flowers. That usually gets her attention and she can relax again." Angela smoothed down the table cloth at her end of the table. "There. Rather pretty, if I may say so myself."

"Sure is." Faythe hesitated for a moment. "Angela, can I ask you something personal?"

"Fire away." Angela circled the table and leaned against it, her head tilted as she gazed up at Faythe.

"When Deanna was so distraught and gave you that ultimatum, you had to choose between sending Miranda off to a special-needs school and then never seeing Deanna again…" Faythe took a deep breath. "Did you ever think it's not worth it, to lose Deanna this way?" Afraid that she had stepped into a minefield with both feet, Faythe briefly touched Angela's shoulder. "I'm not judging you at all, it was an impossible ultimatum."

"Yes, it was. I had to choose what was best for my youngest daughter, at the expense of my oldest child." Angela trembled and Faythe placed her arm around her shoulder, surprised when Deanna's mother leaned readily against her. "Deanna was fierce. She looked at me with such hurt and contempt, so sure I was exchanging a 'flawed set of kids' for the perfect girls that Percy brought into the equation. I tried to explain, but I had painted myself into a corner and no matter what I said, I only made things worse."

"And sending Miranda to Tremayne School and Foundation was the right thing to do."

"Yes, it was. But the timing was lousy." Angela shook her head. "I had a new husband and a new set of stepdaughters who were completely spoiled by their father. I mean, I could understand why, since he'd been alone with them for five years, but to Deanna… Well, how could she have interpreted my actions any other way? I should've waited. Miranda wouldn't have been worse off if I had waited a year and let the idea sink in more."

"I'm glad to hear you say that, Mom." Deanna's voice startled Faythe, and Angela jumped. She stood just inside the doorway to the living room, holding Miranda's hand. Miranda in turn clasped her bag and scarf to her chest, looking around curiously.

"Sweetheart, we can't let any more time go by and not be a family." Angela let go of Faythe and walked up to her girls. She cupped Miranda's cheek and the girl flinched, but then allowed the caress. Repeating the touch with Deanna, Angela spoke softly. "I love you.

More than anything, I love the two of you. I let pride and hurt feelings get between us and the really important things in life."

"So did I," Deanna said huskily. "I was so angry, for so long. And the last few years, I was lonelier than I've ever been." Her eyes lifted over Angela's head. "Until Faythe came along." Deanna smiled gently. "That's when things began to change."

"Thank goodness for that." Angela stepped back and motioned toward the table. "Let's get everybody out from the kitchen and eat some."

"I want to read the *Grantville Times* first," Deanna said. "I'm dying of curiosity."

"You may not like it," Savannah said from behind them. She exited the kitchen, followed by Pammie and Percy. "It's very blunt and honest."

"Facts are facts." Deanna passed Miranda's hand over to Angela and headed over to the coffee table, where she gave a copy of the local weekly newspaper to Faythe. Faythe began to look for Savannah's contribution with trembling fingers.

"I told Lara and Brandy the truth, everything, before the newspaper came out." Savannah slumped a little. "Considering that I shocked the hell out of them, and that Lara called me traitor for not leveling with them, they took it pretty well."

"Did they understand, though? What your mother's put you and Deanna through?"

"Yeah, eventually. I think." Savannah gestured toward the paper. "Read now.

"So, Pammie's aunt is the chief editor, eh?" Deanna asked Savannah and began turning the pages.

"Yeah, and she was floored when she saw my text. She didn't think twice about running it, so at least that's reassuring," Savannah said bleakly.

Faythe turned the page, and there it was for everyone to read.

CHAPTER THIRTY

"Oh, sweet Jesus," Deanna heard Faythe say, and she nearly echoed the stunned words.

Savannah had written a long piece, a two-page spread, about what really happened two years ago. She'd chosen to use a short-story format, but clearly stated in the disclaimer above that the people were real, and the names were real. "This is like interviewing myself," she wrote before the story began. Deanna read along and realized immediately that Savannah hadn't spared herself for a moment. She wrote about her childhood and adolescence, and the feelings she'd harbored, which all led up to what happened when she was eighteen. Her mother's part in the whole mess was obvious, and Deanna couldn't even picture the meltdown the woman had to be having by now.

Deanna finished reading, captivated by the text, even if she knew most things about it beforehand.

"You're a talented writer, Savannah," Faythe said, and looked up from the paper. "You should pursue this. I know you love animals and feel you need to repent, but you could do that and more with your writing."

"Really?" Savannah looked stunned. "I just sat down at my computer and started typing, and the words came pouring out. You know, through my fingers and onto the keyboard. Maybe it's because of the topic, because it has brewed in me for so long. I might not be so good at writing other stuff."

"I think you would be," Deanna said.

"You okay with what I wrote?" Savannah asked quietly, pushing a strand of her long black hair behind her ear.

"Yeah. And you told the absolute truth. I can't believe you were able to go inside my head the way you did and describe how all this affected me. That's both disconcerting and rather fantastic."

"I promise I won't write about you ever again." Savannah's lips trembled. "Honest."

"Good." Deanna pursed her lips. "Now, you took the wind out of your mother's sails with this piece, but you may also have burned your bridges to her, and to your father."

"Guess it's time to find out." Savannah pulled the cell phone out of her back pocket and flipped it open. "I turned it off this morning," she confessed. "No time like the present, I suppose." She pressed a button and the opening tune rang out, a song by Christina Aguilera. It was quiet for a few seconds, and then one beep after another echoed throughout the room.

"Oh, boy!" Pammie leaned over Savannah's shoulder and read the display. "Tons of messages and missed calls. How many from Mommy Dearest?"

"Pammie." Faythe shook her head at the phrase, but Savannah didn't seem to mind.

"Wait. Oh. At least thirty, I think. No. Forty-three. And more than fifty text messages." She handed the phone over to Pammie. "You do the honors."

"Sure." Pammie's fingers flew over the keys. "What's the PIN for your voice mail, sweetie?"

"Five, four, five, three."

"All righty, then, let's see." Pammie entered the number and soon the unmistakable voice of Gloria Mueller filled the room.

"Savannah! What have you done? What were you thinking? Where are you? I want you here this instant. We have to figure out what to do, to fix this. We need to fix this! Call me and come home immediately. I'm home all day. I can't show my face anywhere after this!"

The next message was similar, but each time Gloria talked into Savannah's voice mail, she sounded increasingly desperate. Deanna knew how it felt when your world was crumbling around you, and right now, Gloria Mueller's little empire was about to turn into ruins.

Deanna lost track of how many messages they'd listened to, probably about twelve or fifteen, when Gloria suddenly began a new one, sounding completely different. This time her voice was a low growl, hate-filled and acidic.

"That evil woman got to you, didn't she? That woman and her celebrity mistress. They probably convinced you that it's okay to screw your mother over and live the happy gay life. You listen to me, Savannah. You listen to your mother when I tell you that you've ruined all our lives. My life, your father's, and your own. You're probably smart not to come home. If I were you, I'd stay away from me and from Grantville from now on. I've sacrificed everything for you and—"

In the sudden silence, Deanna realized Pammie had disconnected the voice mail. Savannah was white as death and trembling all over.

"Sweetie, I've got you." Pammie wrapped her arms around Savannah and tugged her close. "You need to lie down. Can we borrow the guest room we used last time?"

"Sure. Let us know if you need anything. We can bring you some of the casserole." Faythe looked worriedly at the sobbing Savannah as Pammie guided her away. "Jesus, she's going to pay a high price."

"She'll gain more than she realizes now," Angela said. "Her mother will be mad, and perhaps she'll stay mad, but a lot of people will respect Savannah for setting the record straight and preventing her mother from committing another crime."

"Yeah, let's hope so," Deanna said. "Why don't we eat something and relax for a bit. I don't want to hear any more of that woman ranting anyway."

"Me either." Faythe squeezed Deanna's arm and looked up at her with stormy eyes. "You think she'll come over here and cause problems?"

"No, I don't think so." Deanna sat down and folded a napkin over her lap. "I honestly don't think she'll dare leave the house."

"Hope you're right." Faythe glanced up and frowned. "Laney, Trista, you okay over there?"

Deanna's stepsisters sat on the couch, quiet and pale. "Yeah. Just not so hungry yet."

"What you heard bothered you, didn't it?" Faythe asked gently. "You hadn't counted on Savannah's mother being so vicious."

"We guessed she was a bitch, but on the phone she sounded like evil." Laney fiddled with the hem of her shirt. "Didn't think people talked that way to their kids. Not really."

Deanna knew this rude awakening for the girls was a lesson also. Not everybody was fortunate to have an Angela or a Percy in their lives. "Come on, girls. Mom's casserole's too good to waste."

Trista hauled Laney up from the couch and they joined the others at the table. And as her family started to eat and talk about everyday things, Deanna began to relax. Her mother teased her husband mercilessly when he spilled some gravy on his paisley tie. Trista and Laney finally lost some of their paleness and began their usual chatter, asking Faythe about the celebrities she'd come across. Percy then made his daughters groan by telling baby stories from their first few years. Faythe made everybody laugh when she told how she took the old rowboat out and Deanna saved her.

Miranda sat at the far end of the table, next to her mother. She kept touching Angela's black hair, rolling a short curl around her index finger over and over. Angela reminded her to eat every now and then, and she became entirely absorbed by the colorful meal. Eventually Savannah and Pammie joined them. Savannah looked better and Pammie had a determined expression on her face.

Deanna met Angela's eyes over the table, and suddenly she swore she could read her mother's thoughts. *This is what having a family is like. You cry, you tease, you fight, you reconcile. You're together.* Something cold and barren in Deanna's chest dislodged. Faythe's arrival in her life had loosened it, and now it broke off and began to melt.

The loneliness she'd carried like an icicle through her heart the last two years was gone. Instead of bleeding out, like she'd feared she would if she let anyone close again, happiness filled her to the brim. She took Faythe's hand under the table and wanted to tell her what had just happened and how she felt about her, but knew she had to wait until they were alone.

❖

Faythe stood on the patio, resting her forearms on the railing. The lake was mirror calm and the moon reflected its pale light in the water. She and Deanna had just waved good-bye to the Bodells. Pammie and Savannah had retired to their room, where they planned to spend the next few days before they left for New York. Savannah was going to stay with Pammie at the small apartment she shared with a friend while she got her life in order.

How many times had Faythe stood by the patio railing like this since she arrived in Grantville, inhaling the fresh, crisp air, with a lot on her mind? This was where she'd seen Deanna the first time, a lonely figure standing on the deck of her cabin. She'd slammed her fists into the railing, a gesture born from a frustration that Faythe couldn't comprehend back then. Deanna walked up and wrapped her arms around Faythe.

"You're far away."

"No, not really. Actually, I was just thinking."

"Yes?"

"I keep thinking we need to talk, you know, really talk, but something always comes up. Your stuff or mine."

"This time my whole family came up."

"And that was a good—no, a great thing." Faythe turned within Deanna's embrace. "It's just that—and this is going to sound totally selfish—but the closer you're getting to your family, the farther away I'm becoming from mine. I'm not begrudging you this new chance, you know that, right?"

"I know." Deanna held Faythe close, stroking her back. "And I wish I could do something for you the same way you did for me."

"Don't think that's possible, babe." Faythe tried to smile encouragingly, but her lips felt rigid and she could only manage to grimace. "You have a great set of people in your family, even the girls, when push comes to shove. My folks, well, they're not going to change anytime soon, I fear."

"I know you feel abandoned."

"How do you know that?" Faythe was surprised at how astutely Deanna read her.

"Because that's how I'd feel, how I have for quite some time. Now that things are different for me, it's not hard to spot the same feeling in you. Just know this, darling, you're not alone."

"I know. I know I'm not." Faythe quickly wiped away a tear. "And I also know that nothing has changed in my life, when it comes to my parents. They've acted this way for more than ten years, and before that, they were only putting on a show to keep up appearances."

"You're the one who's changed." Deanna kissed Faythe's temple softly. "You're the one who sees things differently, because you've taken a step, several steps, actually, in the right direction."

"Is it the right direction when this new path leads me away from my family?"

"Yes, because you have to listen to your own heart, what you want, and you can't keep fulfilling everybody else's idea of what they think you should do."

"I suppose." Faythe buried her face into Deanna's neck. "You're right. Of course you're right. There might come a day when my parents are willing to accept that I'm in charge of my own life. I might be cynical, but I have a feeling that this'll only happen if I become a bestselling author. You know, something they could brag about."

"You're worth bragging about no matter what."

Faythe chuckled despite her solemn mood. "I am, huh?"

"Yes."

"Glad you think so." Faythe leaned her head against Deanna's shoulder. "I guess only time will tell if they'll come around. I don't think I'll ever stop dreaming of it."

"Like you said the other day. We never stop hoping to be loved and validated by our parents." Deanna's voice was filled with tenderness.

"Yeah, I know. I'm not going to hold my breath waiting for it, though. I need to move on with my life and that brings me to the other thing I was thinking of. Us." Faythe tipped her head back and studied Deanna's strong features. "We've come so far, in such a short time, really, and maybe that's why it feels to me that it's been longer than it has."

"Where are you going with this?" A hitch in Deanna's voice told Faythe she needed to be clearer and faster.

"You mean everything to me, Deanna." She ran her hands up Deanna's chest and around her neck. Pulling her down, she kissed her thoroughly, exploring the sweet softness that was Deanna's mouth until they were both oxygen deprived. "I know you've wondered if I would ever be ready to commit. And I've certainly asked myself that question a million times."

"And?"

"I'm still scared. I don't have any frame of reference when it comes to relationships. I mean of the lasting kind."

"So?" Deanna nibbled at Faythe's neck, kissing here and there in a way that nearly made Faythe's knees collapse.

"So, if you want to risk hooking up with a girl who's a total newbie at this, I have something important to tell you."

"I'll risk it." Deanna raised her head. "What do you want to tell me?"

"Deanna." Faythe clasped her hands behind Deanna's neck to keep them from trembling and to help support her trembling legs. "I love you. I love you and I want to be with you. Live with you. Wherever you want."

"Faythe!" Deanna nearly lifted Faythe off the ground when she hugged her close. "Damn it, Faythe. I love you too. I love you so much. I have from the moment I saw you."

"You did, you know. *See* me, I mean," Faythe said, looking into Deanna's eyes. "When you drew my portrait, I realized that somebody really saw me, the essence of me, for the first time." She coughed against the silly tears that ran down her cheeks and into her mouth. "I can't believe you love me back. I really can't believe it."

"Neither can I, but I'll take your word for it." Deanna kissed Faythe again, this time with a slow passion that made it impossible to stay erect. Faythe collapsed against Deanna, who caught her and eased her onto a deck chair where someone, it had to be Deanna, had placed soft pillows and a large fleece blanket. On a small side table two crystal glasses sat next to a bottle of wine.

"I thought we could stay out here for a while and be cozy."

"What a great idea." Faythe let go of Deanna only long enough for them to arrange themselves in a comfortable position of tangled arms and legs. Deanna tucked the blanket around them and poured some wine. As she handed Faythe a glass she looked stunning in the moonlight, the most beautiful sight Faythe had ever seen.

"To Miranda and to Savannah, who showed such courage today, each in her own way." Deanna raised her glass.

"To your family, who showed what they're made of when push comes to shove."

"To Pammie, who set the ball rolling."

Faythe pondered the next toast. "To us."

"You're so right." Deanna clinked her glass against Deanna's. "To us."

They sipped their wine and, after that, they had no need for any more words, merely a strong need for each other. Then, as the moon traveled over the velvet black sky, they soothed their passion temporarily; and cocooned in sheets and blankets with Deanna, Faythe felt happier and more loved than ever before.

EPILOGUE

New York City, New York

"Pammie!" Slender arms wrapped around Pammie as she stepped inside the door to their minuscule apartment. "I got the job!" Savannah said and hugged her fiercely. "At the local animal shelter. We can keep the apartment!"

Pammie whooped and swung Savannah around. "You're kidding!"

"No, I'm serious. They're not going to pay me a fortune, but enough for half the rent and to help with the groceries and stuff."

"Now we can plan for your application to Columbia. We can sit down and...what?" Pammie travelled from exhilaration to fear in a nanosecond.

"I want that. I really do. But I'm afraid of asking for too much." Savannah closed her eyes and a small tear ran down her cheek. "I'm so happy with you, but I don't deserve it. I stirred up all of Grantville a month ago and then just left my parents to deal with the mess."

"Hey, sweetie. Come here. You need to hear a few truths. Listen up." Pammie took Savannah's hand and led her to the small couch in their one-room apartment. Savannah curled up against her, their habit after living together for a month after Pammie's roommate left unexpectedly. "You say you left your parents to deal with things. True. But it was their situation to deal with. Well, your mother's, anyway. You started this mess, and you've atoned for it and apologized to the person you hurt. Your mother, on the other hand, deliberately acted in a criminal way when she blackmailed Deanna to cover up the truth. Writing your story in the paper, which was a very smart way to tell everyone the truth, if I may say so myself—"

"It was your smart idea." Savannah kissed Pammie's shoulder. "Very efficient. Very scary."

"Don't interrupt, I'm on a roll. Where was I? Oh, yeah, when you pulled the plug on her scheme, you saved little Miranda from being another pawn in her game to get you married to a rich, prominent young man. You couldn't have lived with yourself, knowing she'd gone after a defenseless autistic kid. It would have killed your lovely spirit forever."

"You're right." Savannah shuddered. "And she would have." She said the last part with such sorrow, Pammie squeezed Savannah tight.

"You're not her. You've proven that a thousand times over. You're nothing like her."

"I suppose. After that phone call from Dad when he said she's telling everybody she has no daughter after my betrayal—"

"Stop, stop. *Her* betrayal."

"I think he agrees with her. Or he doesn't dare not to, after following her lead for so many years." Savannah looked stricken. "She always said she got him elected, and it's probably true."

"I'm not so sure you're right. In time, your dad may bring about a reconciliation, even if that seems impossible right now."

"Oh, Pammie. Thank you. Thanks. I needed some reassurance."

"I'll reassure you every day if that's what it takes to keep you with me." Pammie looked down at Samantha. She was so ethereally beautiful. They were living together, and sleeping together, but Pammie hadn't dared take that last step into full intimacy yet. They had kissed and cuddled, and occasionally touched each other's breasts through their clothes. Pammie longed to see Savannah's naked body and touch every single inch of her.

"I never want to leave you. I love you, Pammie. Surely you know that." Drawing patterns on Pammie's jeans-clad thigh, Savannah ignited a fast-burning fire.

"God knows I love you too, Savannah. I've loved you for a long time."

"I know. And I'm grateful you haven't given up on me."

"How could I? You've spoiled me for everyone else."

"I have?" Savannah's eyes twinkled and she snuggled closer again, looking up at Pammie. "So does that mean you find me attractive?"

"Attractive? Are you kidding me? You're the most beautif—" Pammie started, stunned that Savannah might think differently. Then she saw the twinkle multiply and turn into a full-blown glitter. "Oh, you brat!" She towered over Savannah and kissed her as a mock punishment, a kiss that quickly turned scorching hot. Savannah tugged at her, and suddenly her hands were underneath Pammie's clothes, searching, caressing.

"I love you, and I want us to be more. Be together. For real." Savannah's eyes darted back and forth between Pammie's. "You want me, right?"

"Do I ever." Pammie held Savannah's face between her hands and kissed her face all over before seizing on her mouth again. "Why don't we do our magic and turn this lumpy couch into a lumpy bed, and I'll show you just how much I love you."

Savannah was up on her feet before Pammie could finish her sentence, already pulling at the cushions.

❖

"Mmm, nice, very nice." Faythe leaned back against Deanna where they sat in her hot tub on the semi-glassed-in balcony of her Manhattan penthouse apartment. It was early November and cold for the season, but they were chin-deep in hot water, overlooking the many lights of the houses surrounding them. Deanna had been sure she wouldn't like living in the city, but the view from Faythe's balcony was spectacular. The whole neighborhood had a small-town feel to it, which surprised her. People were, generally speaking, nice, and it was such a welcome change to live a bit anonymously in a big city, after being the talk of the town for years.

"Glad you remembered to turn off the outdoor lights this time. Didn't like imagining any telescope-lens-equipped paparazzi aiming their cameras at us from the rooftops," Deanna said drily.

"Well, live and learn." Faythe waved her hand in the air. "Yikes, too cold." She hastily dipped it under the water again. "Brrr…how we're ever going to get out of here, I don't know. Can't remember it being this cold last time."

"Could be because we were busy running from the paparazzi on the opposite rooftop."

"Could be."

"So what was your big news, darling?" Deanna massaged Faythe's shoulders.

"They want me to write a book about the drama that took place in Grantville."

"Oh." Deanna didn't know how to react at first.

"I won't unless you say it's okay, and the same goes for Savannah and your mother. I told the publisher that." Faythe scooted around and rubbed her cheek against Deanna's shoulder. "I have plenty of other offers, so you have to be completely honest with me. If you say you'd rather I don't, then I'll move on to plan B. You're far more important to me than any book deal."

"So, they want you to write about it as nonfiction?"

"I can choose whichever format. If I want to do it as a novel, they're still interested."

"Wow. You're the latest thing, then. Who would've guessed that a career change could generate such interest?"

"It might be that I'm together with the main character in the story that's doing the generating. Seriously, Deanna, as far as interest goes, as long as you are interested in me, I don't care much about the rest. I do like the idea of writing for a living, though."

"I understand." Deanna pondered being the source of Faythe's big break in the writing industry. "And I'm thinking, if you don't write our story, it may be passed down to somebody else, someone who wasn't there and who doesn't care about the people involved. If Mom and Savannah say it's okay, it's fine by me."

"Thank you. I'll ask Savannah and Mom ASAP." Faythe lowered herself farther into the hot water. It was endearing to hear her refer to Angela as "Mom." "Ready to brave the elements, as in the November wind fifteen floors up on Manhattan?" Faythe asked, wrinkling her nose.

"Ugh. Guess I don't have much of a choice unless I want to turn into a very cold prune. Here goes." Deanna slipped out of the tub and wrapped her robe around her naked body faster than she'd thought was humanly possible. "Here. I'll hold this up, just in case."

"Yeah, can't be too careful. Some sicko with binoculars could be across the street. That's the downside of all these tall buildings." Faythe stood and Deanna flung the robe around her.

"And I'm not about to share your naked body with anyone. Not even seagulls."

Faythe laughed, and her fit of giggles made Deanna burst out laughing too. "You're just such a goofball, baby. And that's actually a flattering assumption."

"Goofball. Now that's a compliment a girl can only dream of, usually." Deanna padded over to the door and held it open for Faythe, only too happy to get inside. They went through the now-so-familiar ritual in the bathroom, then went to bed, Faythe reading for half an hour while Deanna drew yet another picture of her.

"How many drawings of me do you have by now?" Faythe asked.

"Um, I'm not sure. I've lost count. Maybe a hundred or so." Deanna felt her cheeks warm a little. "You don't mind, do you?"

"Not one bit." Faythe wiggled her eyebrows. "Let's just be glad the roles aren't reversed."

"What do you mean?"

"Well, I do a mean stick figure, but that's it." Deanna listened to Faythe's laughter and knew she would never grow tired of hearing it. Faythe in turn had commented several times how much she enjoyed seeing Deanna smile so often these days.

"I'm so glad you'll be in the audience with your family Saturday. I've never spoken to such a large crowd before, and I want to do a good job of raising money for kids like Miranda." Faythe put her book down, and Deanna did the same with her sketchbook. "I just couldn't bring myself to ask my parents. There might come a day when I can, but right now, they'd both be there for all the wrong reasons."

"I'm sorry, darling." Deanna knew Ben and Cornelia wouldn't mind basking in their daughter's fame, when it was so obvious that all Faythe needed from them was their approval and love.

"Don't feel sorry for me. You'll be there, that's all that matters."

"And Pammie and Savannah."

"Oh, God, yes. I thought they were going to choke me with their hugs when I handed over their tickets."

"And Miranda will watch it on TV." Deanna thought of how she had surprised them all by settling in at her school much quicker than anyone would've thought. "She'll have her nose pressed against the screen. I know her."

Faythe's eyes glittered. "She's such a wonderful girl. I love her to bits."

"Seeing you interact with her makes me love you even more."

"You're wonderful too," Faythe said huskily.

Deanna reached for Faythe, humming against her neck. To hug Faythe and feel her hands all over her was as natural as breathing, but infinitely more exciting. Allowing Faythe to take charge, Deanna just lay back and enjoyed how her lover's caresses and appreciative murmurs mixed with her own moans and whimpers. Her body was ready to accept Faythe's most intimate touch, and when it came, Deanna knew this was all about love.

About the Author

Gun Brooke, a Lambda Literary Award finalist, Alice B. Medalist, and three-time Golden Crown Literary Award–winning author, lives with her family on the west coast of Sweden. Writing her books in a small cottage in her Viking-era village, she makes good use of all the characters she collects on her bianuual travels to the U.S. Gun loves creating 3D art, especially portraits, as well as Web site graphics. She also enjoys spending time with her little grandson, her dogs, and watching science fiction TV shows and movies. Gun is currently working on yet another romance and also another science fiction novel in the Supreme Constellations series.

Books Available From Bold Strokes Books

Late in the Season by Felice Picano. Set on Fire Island, this is the story of an unlikely pair of friends—a gay composer in his late thirties and an eighteen-year-old schoolgirl. (978-1-60282-082-1)

Punishment with Kisses by Diane Anderson-Minshall. Will Megan find the answers she seeks about her sister Ashley's murder or will her growing relationship with one of Ash's exes blind her to the real truth? (978-1-60282-081-4)

September Canvas by Gun Brooke. When Deanna Moore meets TV personality Faythe she is reluctantly attracted to her, but will Faythe side with the people spreading rumors about Deanna? (978-1-60282-080-7)

No Leavin' Love by Larkin Rose. Beautiful, successful Mercedes Miller thinks she can resume her affair with ranch foreman Sydney Campbell, but the rules have changed. (978-1-60282-079-1)

Between the Lines by Bobbi Marolt. When romance writer Gail Prescott meets actress Tannen Albright, she develops feelings that she usually only experiences through her characters. (978-1-60282-078-4)

Blue Skies by Ali Vali. Commander Berkley Levine leads an elite group of pilots on missions ordered by her ex-lover Captain Aidan Sullivan and everything is on the line—including love. (978-1-60282-077-7)

The Lure by Felice Picano. When Noel Cummings is recruited by the police to go undercover to find a killer, his life will never be the same. (978-1-60282-076-0)

Death of a Dying Man by J.M. Redmann. Mickey Knight, Private Eye and partner of Dr. Cordelia James, doesn't need a drop-dead gorgeous assistant—not until nature steps in. (978-1-60282-075-3)

Justice for All by Radclyffe. Dell Mitchell goes undercover to expose a human traffic ring and ends up in the middle of an even deadlier conspiracy. (978-1-60282-074-6)

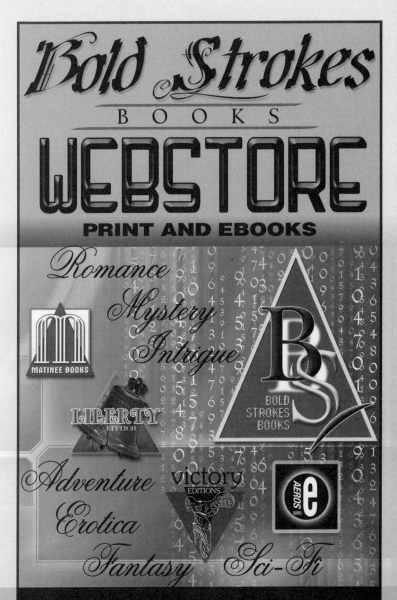